# THE CASE OF THE

# AUSTRALIAN ATLASES

## and other Sherlock Holmes

## adventures

**Paul Metcalfe**

Hardcover ISBN 978-1-80424-715-0
Paperback ISBN 978-1-80424-716-7
ePub ISBN 978-1-80424-717-4
PDF ISBN 978-1-80424-718-1

Published by MX Publishing
335 Princess Park Manor, Royal Drive,
London, N11 3GX
www.mxpublishing.co.uk

Cover design by Awan

Dedicated to Lisa, who believed in me.

# Contents

The Case of the Australian Atlases   6

The Derringley Towers Mystery   36

The Curious Death of Amos Amberdale   66

The Case of the Nervous Neighbour   91

A Cry for Justice   118

The Questionable Existence of
Mrs. Carberry's Companion   145

The Adventure of the Benevolent Thief   175

The Case of the Stolen Alma-Tademas   202

# FOREWORD

First and foremost, I must thank Sir Arthur for providing the world with the characters of the world's first consulting detective and his trusty companion and biographer. Writing words for the mouths of such literary figures as Sherlock Holmes and Doctor Watson is truly an honour.

Apart from the inspiration and background furnished by the original stories, I must also acknowledge the following research materials: The New Annotated Sherlock Holmes, edited by Leslie S. Klinger; Sally Mitchell's Daily Life in Victorian England; and Crime and Punishment in Victorian London by Ross Gilfillan. For geographical information I found the Ordnance Survey Illustrated Atlas of Victorian & Edwardian Britain very useful; and of course I don't know how any writer does without Peter Mark Roget's most excellent thesaurus. I am also much obliged to Tony Hughes-D'Aeth for his book about the Picturesque Atlas, Paper Nation, and to Bonnie MacBird and Laurie R. King for setting the standard (and replying to my emails!).

My gratitude must go those who read the first draft of my first story and provided much feedback and encouragement: my daughters Pia and Persey, and Robyn, Christina, Jodie, Tam, Rebecca and Mel.

Thanks also to Steve at MX Publishing, David Marcum and my editor Rich Ryan. And finally, the biggest thank you and much love to my own partner in crime, Lisa, for continually saying 'you should do it.'

# THE CASE OF THE AUSTRALIAN ATLASES

It was a crisp mid-December morning of 1888, and I was breakfasting on my own. Holmes had gone out in the late afternoon of the previous day, working on a case. I had offered to accompany him, but he had informed me it was likely to be a long, cold night and stealthy surveillance was the object of the outing, so for these reasons it was best that he operated alone. As he had not come down to breakfast, I assumed his night had been a late one and he had not yet arisen. I was thus a little surprised when halfway through my kippers, I heard his brisk footsteps coming up the stairs, and moments later he appeared in the doorway, dressed as a common loafer, unshaven and looking not a little dishevelled.

"Morning Watson," he said cheerfully. "I've ordered some more kippers from Mrs. Hudson on the way in – pour me a coffee, there's a good fellow. I trust you didn't lose too much money at cards last night?"

"No indeed, I think I finished about four pounds to the good, so –" I stopped. "I'm sure it's obvious, but please explain how you know that I played cards last night. And please, don't say that it's elementary."

He chuckled.

"Very well. I knew by observing the fact that your shoes are drying in front of the fire, and by knowing your habits old friend."

"Go on, I am still in the dark."

"Then let me enlighten you. Yesterday as I was leaving, you intimated that you would be dining at your club. I am aware that when you do this, you generally browse one or two periodicals whilst enjoying an after-dinner cigar and brandy, and

6

then you make your way home by ten o'clock. Now as I was out all last night, I know that it started snowing quite heavily just before midnight. Indeed, upon my return to Baker Street just now, I noticed there is still some few inches of snow on parts of the pavement. Your shoes must have got wet in the snow as you traversed the distance from the cab to our door; if you had arrived home before midnight, before it snowed, they would not have got wet. On the few times in the past you have stayed at your club that late, it has always been to play cards, and, I'm sorry to say, to lose. Hence my deduction that you lost at cards last night, but I am overjoyed to hear that I am wrong and you have come away a winner on this occasion."

"Yes, the cards fell in my favour for once. Now will you allow me to make some deductions of my own?"

Holmes smiled. "Certainly, dear chap."

"Last night, you solved the mystery of the dowager duchess and the missing silver reliquary, and the culprit was Johnson, the footman."

Mrs. Hudson chose that moment to enter with Holmes's breakfast, frowning at his disreputable attire.

"Thank you, Mrs. Hudson" said Holmes. "I shall change quickly before I sit down to partake of your delightful repast. Now Watson, you are entirely correct in your deductions. Pray tell, what led you to them?"

"Yesterday before you left, you said that your night's work would prove which one of the two suspects was in fact responsible – the footman, Johnson, or Fletcher, Her Ladyship's groom. You stated that if it were the former, you would have to spend the night watching from up a tree, and if the latter your night would be spent hidden in the stable. You do not appear to have any straw lodged in your clothing, but you do have some bark adhering to your right shin and a leaf in your left trouser turnup. Thus, you have spent the night up a tree. You also ordered breakfast, and had a pleasant demeanor upon your arrival. Usually when a case is unsolved, you are irritable, and fret and smoke rather than eat, so I deduce that the case is therefore solved and Johnson is guilty. It is elementary!" I said triumphantly.

"Bravo Watson! I shall have to watch myself, or people with their problems will start beating a path to your door, not mine." He spoke jestingly, but I could sense he was pleased that I had applied his methods to good effect.

An hour later, Holmes had changed, shaved and eaten, and was sitting staring into the fire, smoke rising lazily from his pipe. I was perusing *The Times*, when I suddenly became aware of footsteps ascending the stairs.

"Do come in, Inspector," Holmes said, raising his voice slightly, and Lestrade entered, though I could hardly identify him, so swaddled in coats and scarves against the cold was he.

"Come warm yourself dear fellow," Holmes continued. "Watson – it is somewhat early in the day, but a sustaining brandy would not go amiss, I feel."

Lestrade nodded gratefully and sank into the chair closest to the cheerful blaze. I pressed a glass into his hand, and he took a large swallow before speaking.

"Thank you, Doctor. Now I am fit to speak, I have a case that I would like your opinion on, Mr. Holmes. It's murder, plain enough, a man's head crushed by a heavy blow, but there's an oddity in what was stolen, and I know you like all that is odd in matters of crime."

Holmes and I both leaned forward, expectantly.

"What is the odd thing?" I asked.

Lestrade unearthed his pipe from his coat pocket, filled and lit it before answering. Holmes's brow furrowed at this delay.

"Have either of you heard of a publication titled the *Picturesque Atlas of Australasia?*"

We both shook our heads.

"What about it?" Holmes said shortly.

"It is a recent publication in three large volumes," Lestrade went on, reading from his notebook. "The murdered man, John Henry Colton, was a career soldier who spent most of his time in the Army serving in Australia. He retired at the rank of major some five years ago and settled down here in London, but he retained an interest in Australia and owned a small library of books about the country, including the atlas I have named. But why, gentlemen, would someone break into his house last night, murder him and then steal only one of the volumes of this atlas, when all three were there for the taking?"

"Curious indeed," I observed.

"Nothing else was taken, just one volume of a three volume set?" interjected Holmes.

"That seems to be the case, and I would be obliged if you would accompany me to the scene of crime in Hampstead and take a look. I cannot find a single clue to the murderer."

"Indeed!" said Holmes, "surely it is not as bad as that. I have never known a murderer yet who did not leave some indication, even of the slightest and most trivial nature, as to their identity. But we shall see, for I am intrigued."

"I anticipated you would be, and have a growler waiting," stated Lestrade, rising from his chair.

Five minutes later we were on our way to Hampstead. Holmes remained silent, puffing at his pipe, while Lestrade and I talked on several inconsequential subjects. The weather was cold but clear, and snow still lay on the ground, thinly in some places but a foot deep in others. As we arrived and stepped out, Holmes asked, "What is the nature of Major Colton's establishment? Are there staff?"

9

"There is a housekeeper, who also cooks and cleans," replied Lestrade, "Mrs. McAndrew by name. There is also a lad who comes in occasionally to help with the garden."

The house itself was a comfortably-sized villa, set back from the road with a well-kept garden. The path to the front door was trodden slush, and I knew Holmes would not find any footprints of use there. Obviously the path had been used by Mrs. McAndrew to raise the alarm, a constable or two had arrived, and Lestrade had then been summoned and left to fetch us. Perhaps the small lawn and garden would yield some traces I thought.

We entered the hallway and saw a constable on guard at a doorway ahead. "Alright Jenkins, that will be all. See if Mrs. McAndrew will provide you with a cup of tea," said Lestrade. The constable nodded and disappeared further into the house. "This is the study, gentlemen, and the body awaits within." He opened the door for us, and Holmes stepped forward, saying "I beg you will wait here while I complete my examination. The less disturbance to the scene, the better my chances of finding any relevant data."

Holmes stood in the doorway for a time, his eyes sweeping the room, especially the carpeted floor. He then stepped into the room, keeping to one side. Lestrade and I stood and watched as he approached the body carefully, the legs of which I could see projecting from behind a large mahogany desk in front of the window. He knelt beside the body for some minutes, then stood and examined the windowsill with his powerful lens. He then opened the window and looked out, then slowly traversed the room, measured some apparent marks in the thick carpet with his tape, ending up at a table near the door upon which were piled some papers and envelopes, several stacks of books and two large books which I suspected must be the remaining two volumes of the atlas.

"I have finished," he said, "you may enter."

"What have you learned?" asked Lestrade. "I should be grateful if you would share any indications as to the murderer."

"I would first like to see Mrs. McAndrew. Could you arrange it please, while I take a look around the house." And with that he bustled out of the study.

Ten minutes later, Lestrade and I were sitting at the kitchen table enjoying the tea and scones Mrs. McAndrew had provided, when Holmes joined us, coming in through the back door.

"Ah, Mrs. McAndrew I presume," he said, "pray seat yourself, I have a few questions for you if feel able."

"Certainly, sir, the inspector said you would. If I can help you clear up this terrible business, I will."

Mrs. McAndrew was a tall thin woman, her brown hair greying at the temples. I hope I did not do her a disservice when I estimated her to be in her mid-fifties. She sat at the table facing Holmes and Lestrade, looking quite composed.

"Can I pour you a tea, Mr. Holmes?" she asked.

"No, thank you. Now, what can you tell us about the events of last night?

"Very little I'm afraid, sir. I made the Major his supper and he dined about seven as usual. He then went to his study, while I washed up and tidied the kitchen. I then sat in here mending a pillowslip. I usually retire early, so at 9:30 I went to the study to ask the Major if he needed anything before I went upstairs. He was seated at his desk writing, smoking a cigar. He didn't want anything, so I said goodnight. I didn't hear anything in the night. I awoke at six, and it was only when I took him his usual tea in his bedroom at quarter past the hour that I discovered he wasn't there. Thinking he had arisen early for some reason, I went through the house looking for him. It was then I found him, in the study."

A tear crept down her cheek as she continued. "He was cold, so I knew he was dead. I was going to walk down to the police station, but just as I got to the gate, the baker's van arrived with our delivery, so I asked him to fetch the police, as he would be quicker. He agreed to do so, so I went back inside, locked the study and waited in the kitchen until a sergeant and a constable arrived about fifteen minutes later. He was a kind man, Major Colton, a pleasure to work for. I can't imagine why anyone would want to hurt him."

"Thank you, that is a very clear statement. Had he appeared nervous, or acted out of the ordinary lately?" Holmes asked.

"No, not at all. He lived quietly, had no friends outside his club, where he dined two or three times a week. He went out for occasional walks."

"Of which club was he a member?"

"It was the United Services Club, Pall Mall."

"What can you tell me about the Australian atlas on the study table? The third volume is missing."

"Yes, I pointed that out to the inspector. He hadn't had it long. He had served in Australia for years, and liked to read about the country. It is very strange that only the third volume has been taken. I don't think there is anything else missing."

"It wasn't a valuable book?"

"Not really. It was sold by subscription in monthly parts, which you could then have bound as your taste decreed and your budget allowed. I believe it has taken about two years to complete, and the third part has not long been back from the binders."

"Do you know which binder the Major employed?"

"Yes, it was Pritchards."

Holmes was silent for a moment. "Thank you Mrs. McAndrew, that will be all for now. It's possible I may have more questions later, depending where my inquiries lead."

She nodded, arose and left.

"What do think Holmes?" I ventured.

"Her story is corroborated by the cigar stub in the ashtray, and a letter on the desk to his bank concerning an investment. His bed has been slept in, so he obviously retired sometime after 9:30 when Mrs. McAndrew last saw him, having finished the cigar and the letter. And then at some point before midnight he was disturbed by a noise, and came downstairs to investigate.

"And then what happened?" asked Lestrade. "I'm inclined to think the stolen atlas is a blind of some sort, taken in haste to give the impression of an attempted theft which got out of hand, and to disguise the real reason for the murder. Surely nobody would want to steal just one of a three volume set. Would you not agree?"

Holmes snorted. "There are several smaller, lighter and more valuable items in the study than a folio size atlas Lestrade, if a blind were the intent. No, the theft of the atlas was the reason for gaining entry – the murder was unintended, and forced upon the thief because of their discovery by Major Colton."

Lestrade looked a little nettled. "Is there anything else, any other theories you have?"

"The muderer is a right-handed person of about six feet, so probably a man – not many women are that tall. He picked the back door lock to gain entry, and made his way to the study. He was standing at the table, possibly with the missing volume of the atlas in hand, when he was surprised by the entry of Major Colton. The Major was then struck on the left temple with a cylindrical blunt instrument of approximately one and half inches diameter. This did not kill him however, though no doubt he was stunned. The assailant then made for the window, which he had probably opened immediately on entering the room so as to facilitate a quick escape should it become necessary. The Major followed him around the desk, and after a short struggle was felled by another blow, striking the back of his head on the desk as he fell. This was, I believe, the fatal injury. The footsteps visible on the carpet, the blood trail from the table to the window, the blood and hair on the corner of the desk, and the bruising on the Major's head are all conclusive. The murderer then escaped through the window in some haste, removing some of the paint from the sill with his boots as he did so. This all happened before midnight, as the snow on the path outside the window is pristine, and as Watson and I know, it started to snow around midnight." He looked at me with a slight smile as he said these last words.

"Well, if you're convinced the atlas is the key to this, and it's not valuable in itself, then perhaps there was something inside it that had some value to someone – a letter perhaps," suggested Lestrade. "As it was newly arrived from the binders, I think I shall start there – Pritchards, Mrs. McAndrew said."

"A good idea with some possible merit," said Holmes. "I have another lead I shall follow first, however. With your permission of course."

Lestrade knew Holmes too well, and needed his help too much to deny him. "Certainly, Holmes, investigate as you see fit. You'll let me know how you get on?"

"Of course. Let's go Watson."

We left Lestrade writing in his notebook and went outside to the street. "Where to now Holmes? What is this lead you wish to investigate?" I asked, hailing a passing hansom.

"United Services Club, my good man," Holmes instructed the cabbie, answering my question, and we climbed aboard. "If I am right about the atlas being the intended object of the raid on Major Colton's house," he continued as we set off, "then the murderer must have known Colton owned it. Therefore, I believe the killer was probably known to the Major. Colton led a quiet life we have heard, with his only social circle at his club. So perhaps we can learn something there, from those who knew him. I must admit however, I am still puzzled why only one volume was stolen."

"They are large and heavy books, and so a little unwieldy if one wanted to steal all three volumes" I offered.

"True, Watson. Yet I feel certain if we knew why only the third volume was taken, it would lead us to the solution of this mystery." He knitted his brows and gazed out at the passing street life, remaining silent until we pulled up outside the United Services Club.

A half-crown ensured the cabbie would wait for us, and we then entered the imposing edifice. Holmes asked to speak to the manager. We were ushered into his office, where an impeccably dressed middle-aged man came around the desk, proffering his hand. "I'm Mr. Godfrey Radcliffe, manager of the club. A pleasure to meet you Mr. Holmes, I have read of some of your cases in the newspapers. How can I help you?"

"We are here on a serious matter, sir." Holmes replied, "Major John Colton, one of your members, was murdered at his home last night, and we are here to learn what we may about his background, his habits and his friends."

Radcliffe's face immediately fell, and he seated himself behind his desk, looking very distressed. "That is most – I mean, what a terrible thing to happen," he eventually got out. "How can I help?"

"How long had the Major been a member here?"

"Let me see. He applied and was accepted about four years ago, when he returned to this country from Australia. You are aware, no doubt, that club membership is limited to men of the rank of major, naval commander or higher, so he was eligible."

"How would you describe him? What sort of man was he?"

"I won't say he was a popular man; he was rather reserved, but convivial enough with the other members. He was on speaking terms with most of them, and friendly with several, especially those who had spent time in Australia. He was always more respectful than others with myself and the other staff, I think due to spending a long time away from this country and its, shall we say, conventional class attitudes?"

"Can you name any members with whom he particularly associated?"

"He dined with and played at billiards or cards most often with General Sir Grenville Fortescue, Colonel Arthur Barrington, and Major George Elkington. They had all spent time in the Australian colonies, the general had even been the governor of one of them for a time."

"Are any of these gentlemen here now?"

"I know the General is holidaying at his Scottish estate at present. I will check if the others are here lunching." He left the room, but returned after a minute. "Sorry Mr. Holmes, but the Colonel and Major are not here at this moment."

"Very well," said Holmes, "may I have their addresses, and the General's as well? I will need to speak to them."

"That would be a little irregular, but under the circumstances, I will provide that information." He consulted a ledger and wrote the addresses on a slip of paper, which he handed to Holmes. "I hope this will help you in your search for Major Colton's killer." he said in a low voice. "What a tragedy!"

As we left the club, my stomach reminded me that it was past my usual luncheon hour. "Holmes, what are your plans now? Will you visit Colton's friends immediately?"

He chuckled. "I will, Watson, as I am not hungry. I have a different task for you though, after you have satisfied your inner man. I want you to go to the British Museum Library and discover all you can about the *Picturesque Atlas of Australasia*. Is there anything about it that may bear on this mystery I wonder?"

"I shall certainly find out all I can," I replied.

"Capital, Watson! We shall meet at Baker Street this evening and compare notes."

After consuming a steak and kidney pie and an ale at a local public house, I went to the library to fulfil Holmes's request for information about the atlas, and thence arrived back at Baker Street a little after the early winter sunset. I was thawing myself out in front of a crackling fire and drinking tea when Holmes returned, accompanied by Lestrade.

"Lestrade was knocking on our door just as I arrived, Watson. Scotches all around I think, then we shall see if we can throw some light on this problem with the results of our combined researches."

After we were settled comfortably with our drinks and pipes, Holmes started. "Inspector, do tell us what progress you have made."

"Very little on my own account, but I did find something out by accident I am sure will interest and perhaps even astonish you."

"Indeed! Do go on."

"I first went to Pritchards bindery as I told you I would. There I learned nothing of use. They had bound Colton's first two volumes as they were completed, and when the third volume arrived they bound it in the same manner – red morocco, gilded title, et cetera. There was nothing out of the ordinary in the process, nor did anything unusual happen whilst the book was in their possession. So I went back to the Yard. And now here's the interesting part. I was taking tea with a colleague, Inspector Greenjohn, who deals with major burglaries, and telling him about this case; just to pass the time you understand. When I mentioned the atlas, he stopped me and said 'The Picturesque Atlas of Australasia you say? How curious. Six days ago, an army officer went on a trip to the north of England for two days and nights. He allowed his servants, a housekeeper and valet, the two days off to visit family, and so his house was empty. When the valet returned just before his master's arrival home, he discovered the house had been burgled, quite thoroughly. The items taken were some small paintings and bronzes, a selection of silver, some rare books and about one hundred pounds in notes. But I remember, on the list of stolen items provided by the owner was a three volume *Picturesque Atlas of Australasia.*'"

Holmes raised his eyebrows. "Remarkable! Volumes of the same atlas stolen from two places within a week. That cannot be a coincidence. But all three volumes were taken on the first occasion, and only one on the second. I shall have to speak to this burgled army officer – who is he?"

"His name is Colonel Barrington, who –"

"Not Colonel Arthur Barrington, of Knightsbridge?"

"The same, but how did you know?"

"This is even more extraordinary, eh Watson? Two copies of the same atlas stolen in a week, from two friends who belong to same club?" The game is definitely afoot!'"

Holmes quickly gave Lestrade the results of our visit to the United Services Club. "I then went to visit the friends of Major Colton. Firstly, Colonel Barrington. He was not home, and his rather surly valet declined to tell me where he was. When I said it was concerning an important matter and asked him where I might find the Colonel, he became rather quite rude – rather more rude than one would expect of a servant tasked with meeting his master's visitors at the door. I left my card and said I would call again tomorrow. I then visited Major George Elkington, who was actually born in the Victorian colony, and spent his first two decades in Australia. He then came to the land of his parents and joined the army, serving in the Indian Mutiny and the Second Afghan War. He retired six years ago, and is, I think, what he appears to be – a widowed, retired army officer who is active in his church and collects antique swords. Had I known about the theft of the Colonel Barrington's atlas then, I would have asked him if he owned a copy himself."

"As you say Mr. Holmes, this is no coincidence. This atlas is at the heart of the burglaries and the murder, but where do we go from here?"

"A penetrating question, Inspector. But let us hear from Watson before we decide any plan of action. What did you learn at the library today?"

I consulted my notes. "The atlas was published by an Australian company formed for the purpose, and obtainable by subscription for either five shillings per monthly part or ten guineas in total payment. It is a beautiful publication; I have seen the library's copy. The illustrations are numerous and all hand-engraved. There are perhaps not as many maps as you might consider a work calling itself an atlas should have, but all the Australian colonies, New Zealand, New Guinea and some of the Pacific islands are represented. But there are also many essays on the history, geography, geology, native peoples, and the flora and fauna of these regions, and descriptions of places of unique beauty and interest. It is a publishing tour-de-force in all respects, I am assured by Askwith, the librarian with whom I spoke. However, I was unable to determine if any of this information helps our enquiry."

"It does not appear to I agree, Watson, but we are none the worse for having complete information concerning the object of these two thefts. Thank you. Lestrade, I assume you would like to participate in an interview of Colonel Barrington tomorrow, so would you prefer to meet us there or will you collect Watson and I on your way?"

Lestrade stood up. "I'll come for you; shall we say ten?"

"Excellent. I must cogitate for a time now, so goodnight."

As Lestrade's footsteps diminished down the stairs, I said,

"This case presents some extraordinary features Holmes."

"It is a pretty puzzle Watson, I grant you. But I have little data as yet. We must hope the circumstances of the theft at Colonel Barrington's will provide us with more."

\*\*\*\*\*\*\*\*\*\*

The next morning, Lestrade drew up in a carriage just before the hour we had agreed, and we set off to Knightsbridge under a leaden sky that promised rain later. Upon our arrival, Holmes rapped on the door with his stick. A young man dressed in black, with a truculent expression, answered. "It's Mr. Holmes again, isn't it?"

"And Inspector Lestrade of Scotland Yard," said the inspector, showing his warrant card.

He bowed stiffly. "This way gentlemen please. If you'll wait here in the hall, I'll let the Colonel know you are here."

He said this in an almost insolent fashion, with a faint accent on the word "gentleman" which implied he thought we were not worthy of the honorific. Holmes was right I thought to myself – he does not possess anything like the necessary civility for a good servant.

Two minutes later, a tall dark-haired man in his forties with a strong masterful face came down the stairs.

"In here please, gentlemen," he said in a rich baritone, showing us into a room that obviously fulfilled the functions of library and study. After we had introduced ourselves and were all seated, he continued. "You are here investigating the murder of Major Colton, an acquaintance and fellow club member. I learned of his death at the club last evening. It's a terrible thing. How may I assist you?"

Holmes looked at Lestrade, who nodded for Holmes to lead the questioning.

"How long had you known the Major? You met at the

club?"

"I have been a member there for more than six years, and I met him there shortly after he joined. We discovered we had a common interest in Australia, both of us having served there."

"When were you there, and in what capacity?"

He looked at Holmes for a moment. "I was there for five years in the 1870s, as a liaison officer between the British Army and the government of the colony of New South Wales."

"I see. Can you tell us anything which might help us? Had Major Colton confided anything to you which indicated he was in any financial difficulties, or trouble of any kind?"

"No, nothing at all. He had been his usual self. We played cards and billiards at the club, we talked of current events, cricket, and army life as well as our time in Australia. He had been stationed in Victoria for many years."

"Now Colonel, I understand that several days ago while this house was empty, you were robbed of several items of substantial value, and some one hundred pounds in notes? Is this correct?"

"Well, yes, but how does this relate to Colton's murder?"

"Because there is a common thread. The Major was also robbed, but he surprised the thief and so we believe he was killed so the thief could make good his escape. The only item stolen was the third volume of the Major's copy of the *Picturesque Atlas of Australasia*, all three volumes of which you reported stolen during the burglary which occurred here."

The Colonel looked taken aback by this information. "How remarkable," he said.

"So you see why this intrigues us. You and Colton are both members of the same club, are well-acquainted with each other, you both served in Australia and now have had the same book taken from your possession. How did you come to own the atlas?

"For the same reason as Colton – we both had an interest in the country, but I also collect books, usually on the subject of militaria. Several more valuable books than the atlas were stolen, as well as some silver and artworks. Are you of the opinion then, that the same person committed both burglaries and the murder?"

"I have not made up my mind on that, but it is certainly possible. It is obvious the two events must be connected. Who knew that this house would be empty for the two days during which the theft occurred?"

"I told the club I would not be in during that period, and I suppose the baker and greengrocer were told by my housekeeper to hold their deliveries."

"Thank you, Colonel. Have you any questions, Inspector? No? Then we will bid you good day sir, but I would like if I may to have a few words with your housekeeper?"

"Certainly. Mrs. Abercrombie will be in the kitchen no doubt," said the Colonel, showing us back into the hall and leaving us. Lestrade and I waited there until Holmes returned from the rear of the house – was it my imagination or did I detect a gleam in his eyes?

"What now Holmes?" asked Lestrade, as we stood on the pavement outside the colonel's house. "Was there anything in the Colonel's statement which helps us?"

"Perhaps one or two things, Inspector, but I must investigate further before I may pronounce on their value to the case. What will you do now?"

"Well, it occurred to me that if there is someone going around stealing copies of this atlas, perhaps they have done so on more than the two occasions we know about. I thought I would check the burglary records with Inspector Greenjohn and see if this has happened before."

"Very well. I shall pursue other lines of enquiry."

After Lestrade had left in the carriage which brought us, Holmes said "What did you think of the good Colonel, Watson?"

"A sound enough chap. Perhaps he showed less emotion about the death of Colton than one might expect, but possibly they were only acquainted, and not the best of friends."

"He said one thing which interested me, and so did Mrs. Abercrombie. To elucidate some details of the colonel's greengrocer's family, and his term of service in Australia I will need to travel alone to a particularly vile alley near the docks, and Pall Mall."

"Are you sure you won't need me Holmes? I said dubiously. "Vile alleys are not generally safe."

"Your presence would only complicate matters. But thank you, Watson, I will be careful."

"And Pall Mall? You intend to visit the club again?"

"I intend to visit a club Watson, but not the United Services Club. I will see you back at Baker Street this afternoon." And with that he hailed a passing hansom and left me. I hailed the next one, and spent the journey back to our domicile trying to think how the Colonel's time in the Antipodes and his greengrocer's family connected to the mystery, without coming to any conclusions.

The rain arrived after lunch, a steady drizzle which started to ease as evening drew in. I was enjoying tea and crumpets when Mrs. Hudson knocked and entered, bearing an envelope on a tray.

"A telegram for Mr. Holmes, Doctor."

"Thank you, Mrs. Hudson." I looked at the envelope and was wondering if I should open it when Holmes strode in.

"Were your enquiries successful Holmes? I asked eagerly.

"Yes quite – but what's this? A telegram has arrived."

"Yes, just moments ago."

Holmes quickly opened the envelope and read the enclosure. "This case grows more and more fascinating Watson. A third theft of this atlas has occurred!" He threw me the telegram, and I read :

*Another atlas stolen. Come at once!*

*Lestrade*

There was an address in the fashionable Belgravia district appended.

"A third atlas stolen! This is incredible. Surely it is the work of a madman!"

"No, Watson, there is method and intelligence behind these thefts. Let us make haste to Belgravia!"

We raced in a hansom to the address given, which turned out to be a large Georgian house in its own grounds. An elderly butler showed us into the library, where we found Lestrade pacing up and down in front of the fire. "Ah, Holmes, here you are. And Doctor Watson of course. Perhaps there is now hope of solving this mystery which I confess has me completely baffled."

Holmes smiled. "I have a theory, Lestrade, which will be confirmed or destroyed by two facts with which you can now furnish me. Firstly, did the theft of the atlas from this house take place today, or at some time in the recent past, perhaps several days ago?"

"How did you guess, Holmes! Yes, the owner has been away for two weeks. The theft was only noticed today upon the owner's return, but could have happened anytime while he was absent."

"You know I never guess," said Holmes sternly. "And secondly, were only two volumes of the atlas stolen, the first and second?"

Lestrade looked as if Holmes had suddenly appeared in a

puff of smoke bearing horns and a pointed tail. "Again you are correct, though how you could know is beyond my imagination," he stammered.

"And the owner of this house is General Sir Grenville Fortescue, member of the United Services Club, acquaintance of Major Colton, and who returned today from his Highland sojourn?"

"Indeed, sir," said a voice behind us. "This house is mine, and I have just come back from Scotland. But what do my club and Major Colton have to do with this burglary?"

We turned to see a tall man obviously in his sixties but still with a fine physique, and with the air of one used to command.

"Sir Grenville, this is the detective, Mr. Sherlock Holmes, who is assisting me with this enquiry. And his companion, Doctor Watson," said Lestrade.

"I have heard of you Mr. Holmes," said the General, "but surely your powers and attention are wasted on a commonplace theft such as I have suffered?"

"You compliment me, Sir Grenville," said Holmes, "but this burglary is only one in a series in which the very same atlas that was stolen from you was taken from others, and a murder has been committed in the course of one of them. Your friend and fellow club member Major Colton was killed trying to prevent the theft of his *Picturesque Atlas*, and we are endeavouring to ascertain why."

"Colton killed? How tragic. He was a good fellow, and I enjoyed his company. If I can help bring his killer to book, then I am at your disposal, gentlemen. Please be seated, and ask of me what you will."

"Thank you, General. Please tell us about how you came to own your *Picturesque Atlas*, and how you discovered it was missing."

"Certainly. Some years ago I was given the governorship

of the South Australian colony. I spent five years in the position, and I grew to like the country. There are a lot of British people there of course, but there is a growing proportion of the citizenry who have been born and raised there for several generations in the century since it was established as part the British Empire. These Australians are a tough, hard-working and industrious breed in the main, and more inclined to treat a man based on his deeds and behaviour, rather than his position in society or his accidental birth into a noble family. I found this attitude refreshing, and I was somewhat saddened when my tenure as governor was over.

"I still retain an affection for the country and its people, so when some two or three years ago I learnt of the proposed publication of the atlas, I subscribed immediately, as did Major Colton and Colonel Barrington when I told them about it one evening at the club. You are aware that it was published in monthly parts, and that it is only recently the final part was published?"

"Yes, we knew that," replied Holmes. "I suspect that the reason only the first and second volumes of your atlas were stolen is because the third volume was at your binder?"

"True, Mr. Holmes. I sent it to them before I left for Scotland. No doubt it will be returned to me shortly. The other two volumes were on that desk there when I left, so I noticed they were missing as soon as I entered the library. Then I discovered the window had been forced, so I sent for the police. Nothing else appears to be missing."

"The servants heard nothing?" Holmes asked as he crossed to the window and examined the broken latch.

"Nothing. There were only three left here in my absence; the remainder accompanied my wife and me to Scotland. None of them has been in here in the last two weeks, save the maid to dust yesterday, and she did not notice the broken latch. She would not know what books were supposed to be here or if any were missing."

"Thank you, General, you have been most helpful. I think the solution to this mystery is within our grasp now. A few details to discover, and a trap to be set – then we shall with any luck have our thief and murderer."

"That is indeed gratifying. I wish you well gentlemen," said the old soldier, and he escorted us to the door.

As we left the general's house, Lestrade gave voice to my exact thoughts.

"You say you have almost solved this puzzle Holmes – would you care to share the name of the guilty party, and on what evidence you assert their guilt?"

"Not at this juncture Lestrade, as I do not yet have all the facts, only theories. And as you well know, theories will not convict anyone in a court. Would you please take Watson back to the no doubt delicious supper Mrs. Hudson has prepared – I must seek brother Mycroft's aid immediately to organise the trap of which I spoke." And with that he left us, striding swiftly down the general's driveway.

Holmes returned to Baker Street as the clock struck ten. "You wish to see the conclusion of this case, Watson?"

"Of course. I have followed it with great interest but little understanding so far. You have solved it then?"

"I believe so, but the evidence we need will not be available until tomorrow morning, if my plans come to fruition. Be ready by six, and we shall try to apprehend our atlas thief, murderer and if I'm right, a threat to the security of the Empire."

"I see. So there is more to all this than the atlases. And the security of the Empire is where Mycroft comes into the picture."

"Exactly, Watson. Now let us get what slumber we may before our early rising will hopefully catch us our worm."

\*\*\*\*\*\*\*\*\*\*

A hansom was waiting as we slipped out of the front door the next morning into a frosty half-light. We had dressed appropriately however, and we were on our way the instant we climbed aboard. After a short journey the hansom stopped, in front of a post box and a laneway servicing the rear of a row of houses. We alighted from the hansom, which immediately rumbled off. Holmes grabbed my arm and pulled me into the lane, where I saw a muffled figure awaiting. "Lestrade!" I said, "You are joining us in the hunt then."

"Yes, Doctor," he said through chattering teeth, "though let's hope it is not a wild goose chase."

"Your constables are in place, Lestrade?" asked Holmes in a low voice.

"Yes Mr. Holmes, as you directed. Two at the other postbox, two at this end of the street, and two watching the rear of the house."

"Good. We shouldn't have too long to wait."

It was only about fifteen minutes later that Holmes tensed. "He's coming!"

There were several pedestrians on both sides of the street, including some coming toward us. One of them slowed as he reached the postbox, and as he reached inside his coat and pulled out an envelope, Holmes and Lestrade ran out, Lestrade grabbing the man by the wrist of the hand holding the envelope, and Holmes grabbing the other arm. I hurried up in time to hear Lestrade say "I am Inspector Lestrade of Scotland Yard, and I have reason to believe that this letter contains information injurious to the British national interest." Holmes plucked the letter from the man's hand and then pulled down the scarf half-muffling the features of their captive, to reveal the scowling face of Colonel Barrington's valet. "I have nothing to say," he spat out. Two constables then ran up, one them handcuffing the

28

struggling manservant. "Take him away," Lestrade ordered.

Holmes meanwhile had opened the envelope, and studied its enclosure briefly. "It is as I expected. We must now arrest his master."

Lestrade collected the two other constables on watch in the street, sending one of them to alert the others watching the rear of Barrington's house. We then approached the front and knocked. A plump, middle-aged woman answered the door. "Mrs. Abercrombie, nice to see you again," said Holmes genially, "is the Colonel at home?"

"Yes sir, he's in the study. I'll let –"

"That won't be necessary, we'll just show ourselves in, we know the way," said Holmes, pushing past the confused housekeeper. Lestrade, the constable and I followed. Holmes opened the door to the study and we all trooped in. Barrington rose up from behind the desk. "What is the meaning of this?" he snarled. "You can't just –"

"Yes we can, sir," said Lestrade evenly. "We have your valet and the letter he was about to post for you. I'm arresting you for the murder of Major John Colton. Other charges may follow."

The colonel's eyes narrowed and he half-crouched as he looked at the four of us. Obviously deciding that forcing his way past us was impossible, he stood up straight. "Beaten am I?" he said harshly. "Your doing, Holmes, I take it? It was the atlases that gave me away I suppose, but I had to have them."

"I'd like to think I contributed materially to your demise, Colonel. And yes it was the atlases. The third theft, of Major Colton's atlas, intrigued me. The first theft, of your atlases, put me on the track, and the second theft, when we became aware of it, confirmed it. Lestrade, after you have secured your prisoner in a cell, won't you join us for breakfast? I will then be happy to clear up any points which still mystify you."

"There are also one or two points I don't quite understand," I said drily.

Holmes laughed. "Indeed Watson, then let us go home and ask Mrs. Hudson for one of her best efforts at a breakfast, and then I shall enlighten you both as to how I solved the case of the Australian atlases!"

\*\*\*\*\*\*\*\*\*\*

"So as you rightly remarked at the time, Watson," said Holmes, "the first theft we heard about, of a single volume of a three-volume set, was curious. All three volumes were there for the taking, and there were also other more valuable and more easily transportable items available, if theft for monetary gain was the intention. You remember I said at the time that this indicated that the atlas, and only the atlas, was the object of the theft. But I was still puzzled then as to why only the one volume was stolen."

He spoke between puffs of his pipe, the debris of our hearty breakfast on the table between us. Lestrade took a sip of coffee. "Why did you let me waste my time going to the binders, while you went to Colton's club?" he asked.

"It wasn't like that, Inspector. I did think that there was more to be learned at the club, but there was a chance that some clue might be found at Pritchards, so I was happy to let you follow that lead. No stone unturned. The United Services Club provided the names of Colton's closest associates and the fact that they had all at some point in their lives been in Australia. Since the stolen atlas concerned Australia, there was a connection there, if somewhat tenuous. I then visited Colonel Barrington, who was not home. His valet did not impress me, but it is not a crime to be rude. An interview with Major Elkington did not raise my suspicions, but then Lestrade brought us the news that Barrington had also had his copy of the atlas stolen some days previous to the burglary at Major Colton's.

These happenings were too coincidental to be unrelated, but I still had too little data to form a theory. When we did interview Colonel Barrington the next day, two things gave me pause."

"You mentioned his greengrocer's family and his service in Australia, as I recall."

"Correct, Watson. He stated that he had been a liaison officer between the army and the New South Wales colonial government. In my experience, army officers who 'liaise' between the army and other agencies are very often in a particular branch of the army."

"Intelligence!" I cried. "That's why you said you were going to another club in Pall Mall. You meant the Diogenes Club, to ask Mycroft if Barrington had been an intelligence officer."

"Correct again, Watson. Mycroft confirmed that Barrington was not only an intelligence officer, but that he had worked on several top-secret matters lately. His record was exemplary, however. But I had also found out from Mrs. Abercrombie that she had indeed told the baker and greengrocer to halt their deliveries for two days, and that the household supplier of fruit and vegetables was none other than Benjamin Fuller, a grocery establishment of excellent repute in the district."

"The name sounds familiar," I frowned.

"It should, Watson. Some weeks ago, Inspector Bradstreet asked me to find out anything I could about the newly formed and well-organised gang of house-breakers he had come across. You remember I set some of the Irregulars on to the task? They reported to us that one of the gang members was Albert Fuller, eldest son of Benjamin Fuller and employee in his father's grocery business. So it was entirely possible that Albert had learned through his father that Barrington's house would be empty for two days. He supplied this information to his gang, who saw an opportunity to purloin most of the valuables from the house at some leisure. They did so, stealing Barrington's *Picturesque Atlas* along with other books, silver, artworks and cash. I confirmed this by looking through several windows of a warehouse near the docks, the headquarters of Fuller's gang and discovered by one of the Irregulars a few days ago. There I saw the proceeds of several robberies, and Bradstreet will be cleaning up that little rat's nest today.

However, Fuller's gang being responsible for the burglary at Barrington's meant that they would not have known about Colton's atlas. This inferred that instead of one person stealing two atlases from different owners, which was strange enough, there must have been two different thieves stealing the two atlases, an even stranger proposition. Who else would have wanted Colton's atlas, and only the third volume at that? I deduced it was someone who had just had their copy stolen, someone who knew Colton possessed the atlas, and someone who had already replaced the first and second volumes. So my suspicion rested on Barrington."

"So that's how you knew only the first two volumes had been stolen from Sir Grenville, and that they had been taken prior to theft at Colton's!" exclaimed Lestrade.

"Yes. He knew the General owned the atlas, and he knew he, his wife and the majority of his servants were in Scotland. He decided to steal the General's copy, not realising that only two volumes were in the house, the third being at the binders. That is why he broke into Colton's a few nights later and took only the third volume he needed to complete the set. He didn't reckon on being interrupted however, with the result we know."

"But why Holmes? Why the obsession with replacing his stolen atlas?"

"The answer to that Watson, lies in the letter we took from Barrington's valet. His name is Jacob Whistler by the way, a convicted thief and general ne'er-do-well before finding employ with Barrington. After the theft of Sir Grenville's atlas confirmed for me that Barrington was our man, I had to flush him out and catch him red-handed. I went back to Mycroft and he arranged that Barrington should be sent for by his commanding officer immediately, and advised of a significant change in the details of the latest secret government operation with which he has been involved. The change was fictional of course, but we wanted to see if he would try to pass on the information to anyone. Lestrade, you have the letter?"

Lestrade took a sheet from his jacket pocket and handed it to me. It read :

V175C1207    V188C140  V3645C215    V2421C2161
V1230C257    V2402C212  V3615C189    V2279C29

"A code obviously," I said. Can you read it?"

"Yes, Watson, I knew how to break the code from seeing the letter when I took it from Whistler's possession. But Lestrade has done the actual work. He found the stolen atlases in Barrington's study, and by the using key to the cipher which I gave him, he has worked out the message before joining us. You see Watson, each string of characters has a V and a C in it. When I realised the V is always followed by the numeral one, two or three, and that the C is always followed by the numeral one or two -"

"Volume and column," I interrupted. The atlas has three volumes and each page has two columns of text. The other numbers must be the page number and word number. Holmes, is this not a similar code to the one we came across in the Birlstone case earlier this year?"

"Yes Watson. If you recall, an associate of Professor Moriarty named Porlock sent us the cipher but then did not tell us the book to be used to solve it. We had to use pure reason to obtain the solution, which turned out to be *Whitaker's Almanac*. In this case, the first word in the message is word 207 in column one on page 75 of the first volume. Barrington had to have a copy of the atlas in order to send and receive coded messages from his contact, hence his panic to replace it when his was stolen. It is a foolproof code which cannot be interpreted unless one knows the book you are using. Barrington had suggested to his contact they use the atlas, as it was not a common book and he had it to hand. Obviously the contact has a copy as well. But as it was published by subscription, and therefore not available in bookshops for purchase, he was compelled to steal it."

I turned to Lestrade. "And what is Barrington's message then?" I asked.

He handed me another sheet which read :

IMPORTANT CHANGE TO STUART PLAN. TWO THOUSAND POUNDS.

"The amount named is the price of his treachery," said Holmes. "If this information were genuine, and the contact had paid the sum, Barrington would have betrayed the secret and his country. Who knows what secrets he has already betrayed? The Stuart Plan, whatever it may be, will now have to be changed or cancelled in case it has already been divulged by Barrington. I realised that Barrington would wish to inform his contact as soon as possible of his newly-acquired knowledge concerning the plan, hence our early morning surveillance of the nearest postbox to Barrington's residence. There was another postbox slightly farther away in the opposite direction, and two constables were assigned to watch it for Barrington, or more likely Whistler, who was well aware of his master's true occupation as a freelance agent and seller of his country's secrets."

"What of Barrington's contact?" I questioned. "Could he

not be found through the address on the letter?"

"It is addressed to a large hotel in Paris, to be kept until called for. Mycroft will work with the French authorities and see what can be done. Are there any other points on which either of you are unclear?"

Lestrade stood up. "No, Mr. Holmes, you explained it all beautifully. You make it sound so obvious after the fact, but I have no problem admitting it was too deep for me. I thank you for your assistance in this case, and your country owes you a debt of gratitude."

I knew that Holmes disliked praise of any sort, and was indifferent to official recognition; the solving of the problem was its own reward for him. But he was gracious enough to reply.

"You are welcome to any credit, Lestrade. After all, you yourself did apprehend Whistler and his villainous master. As for our country – well, I should not expect any reward for doing my duty as an Englishman."

# THE DERRINGLEY TOWERS MYSTERY

Holmes and I were engaged one evening in a discussion concerning Landsteiner's recent discovery of the differing blood groups in humans, and its application to the solving of crime. Holmes maintained that it was not only important medically but for law enforcement as well.

"As far as we know," he said, "though the science is new, fingerprints are unique to each human being, so they are a great help in the solution of crimes. Imagine, however, if there were no fingerprints found at the scene of a murder, because the perpetrator was lucky, or wore gloves. But if the blood of the criminal were found, perhaps under the nails of the victim who had scratched the assailant during the attack, then determining the blood group of that assailant would help narrow the list of suspects.

"Yes, I see that," I replied. "But that would entail taking blood from every suspect and determining their blood group. Obviously, some of the suspects will prove to be innocent, and they may object to being treated in this manner. There are also those who have a fear of syringes. Can we then force people to give a blood sample, even in the cause of justice?"

"Under current law? Probably not, Watson. Though laws can be changed of course, it is a balance between bringing criminals to justice with more rapidity and certainty, and the private rights of the citizen. Though if I were innocent of some crime, I would be happy to have blood taken to prove it. I am not averse to the needle, as we both know."

I was about to answer when the telephone rang. As I was closest, I answered its summons.

"Gregson here, Doctor. May I speak with Mr. Holmes?"

"Certainly," I replied. "Holmes, it's Inspector Gregson for

you."

Holmes got up and I handed him the telephone.

"Gregson, how are you? What can I do for you?" he said cordially.

There was a pause, and Holmes scribbled something on the notepad kept near the telephone.

"Very well, Inspector, you may expect us shortly." he said, hanging up.

"A case," I suggested. "Gregson is at a loss, then?"

"On the contrary Watson, Gregson has solved the case, but he is unwilling to accept his solution and its possible repercussions. He wishes me to verify his work before arresting the fourteen-year-old son of Lord Derringley for murder!"

\*\*\*\*\*\*\*\*\*\*

We had rattled along in a hansom for some minutes before I had regained my composure enough to speak.

"Fourteen – and the son of a peer. It sounds impossible."

"It is not unheard of, Watson. There was a lad aged fourteen convicted of manslaughter a few years ago in Liverpool. In '92 I believe, a boy of thirteen was found guilty of killing his uncle in Italy, though there were extenuating circumstances in that case. Neither was the son of a nobleman, however. In this case, we have no data as yet, so I will not form any theories until we do."

A short drive brought us to the address given to Holmes by Gregson. Derringley Towers was a large mansion in the Gothic revival style, with a much-ornamented tower at each end giving the building its name. It was situated in quite extensive grounds, with a formal garden in front and what appeared to be a small copse at the rear. Inspector Gregson was pacing up and down outside the front door as we pulled up.

"Evening Mr. Holmes, Doctor. Thank you for coming so

promptly. It's a bad business, and if I follow where the evidence leads, it will be worse business still. Come inside, and let me give you a few details before we go into the library and see the body."

We entered the house and Gregson led us into a morning room off the hall. We sat down, and Gregson looked at his notebook.

"Lord Henry Derringley is 41, scion of a well-respected and long-established family line. His first wife, Jane, died giving birth to their son Arthur, who is now seventeen. His Lordship has remarried, and his second wife Constance has borne him two children, Charles who is fourteen, and Charlotte aged eight. The marriage appears to be a happy one; at least, the servants I have spoken to say they have never seen them engage in anything but the mildest of disagreements.

"The children have impressed me as polite and considerate, and display nothing of those attitudes that sometimes manifest themselves when children want for nothing their entire lives. Though they are all naturally in shock, as are their parents. The rest of the household consists of the usual staff of a house like this; a butler, housekeeper, cook, governess, and a number of footmen, maids, gardeners and grooms. Some twenty servants in all.

"Now, to the events of this evening. Charles states he was sitting in the library, reading. He had the window open for air, as it was a lovely summer evening. Just after eight o'clock, he says a man came in through the open window, saw him and pulled a knife from his pocket. He then pointed the knife at him, holding his finger to his lips. At this point, there was a knock on the door and Carter, one of the footmen came in. Carter immediately ran towards the intruder and there was a short struggle. The intruder managed to get Carter in a headlock from behind with his left hand, and pulling Carter's head back and up, he slit his throat with the knife. Carter was facing Charles at this time, and the boy was sprayed in blood from the severed artery.

"The murderer then dropped his knife and escaped back through the window. Charles yelled for help. The butler, Marston, was in the hall when he heard the boy shout, and he says he arrived in the library within thirty seconds of hearing it. From the doorway, he saw Carter on the floor dead, and Charles standing nearby, blood all over him. Hearing footsteps in the hall behind him, he turned and saw one of the housemaids approaching. Not wanting her to see the body, he told her to fetch His Lordship immediately, and she ran off to do so."

Gregson paused, and looked at Holmes.

"I won't tell you what I have discovered in the library; I will let you form your own opinion from your own observations. Then we can see if our conclusions agree."

"That is what I would also prefer," said Holmes, rising. "Lead on, Inspector."

Gregson led us out into the hall, then down a corridor with several doors, outside one of which a constable stood guard. Gregson stopped outside this door, pausing with his hand on the doorknob.

"The body is as it fell, gentlemen, but I will have to have it removed soon," he remarked, opening the door and bidding us enter.

Holmes nodded, and we entered the library. It was a large room, appointed in a manner usual for a house of this size. There was a fireplace with two sofas facing each other in front of it to our left, and a low table between the sofas. A large mahogany desk and a magnificent floor globe dominated the space to our right, and there were three windows in the wall facing us. Bookshelves lined most of the remaining walls, except for a second door in the corner behind the desk. The body of the unfortunate footman lay face-up before us, in the centre of the room, a small knife lying beside him. A large pool of blood had formed around his head.

I stood to one side out of the way, with my notebook in my hand, while Holmes commenced one of those thorough examinations of a crime scene that he excelled in. Gregson waited beside me, and I knew from previous experience he was happy to watch and perhaps learn something of the techniques of the acknowledged master of detection.

Holmes approached the body and inspected it closely with his powerful lens, especially the throat wound. He then measured the body with his tape, and felt in all the pockets. He picked up the knife by the blade using a handkerchief and looked at both sides of the handle. Moving around the room, he went first to the open window, looking at the lock, the sill and then peering outside at the ground. He then checked in turn the other windows, the desk, the sofas and the table between them. He examined the myriad splashes of blood which were evident on the carpeted floor, the sofas and the table, and picked up a book laying on the table and flipped through it. He then turned to Gregson with a grim expression on his face.

"When you telephoned you said the evidence pointed to the boy Charles having murdered the footman," he said. "Why do you think so?"

"For several reasons," Gregson replied. "I can find no evidence that there was ever an intruder in this room. You looked out the window; surely anyone entering through it would have left footprints in the flowerbed below the window, or broken the stems of some of the plants. If he did not do so on his way in because he was exercising some care and trying to make no noise, surely he would not employ the same care in his scramble to escape after killing the footman, with the alarm raised and speed of the essence? And what of his motives for entering in the first place?

"If he were a thief, why choose a time in the early evening

when the lights were on and there were obviously people still about? In my experience, thieves wait until the early hours and the household is asleep. When this alleged intruder reached the window, he must have seen the boy sitting on the sofa reading, so if plunder was his object he was particularly brazen to still enter the room. And if theft was not his reason for entry, then what was? Did he want to murder Charles, or perhaps kidnap him? And then there is the book."

"Ah, you noticed that then," said Holmes.

I must have looked mystified, as Holmes continued. "Please explain for the benefit of Watson's notes the importance of the book, or rather the bookmark within it."

Gregson smiled. "Certainly Mr. Holmes. Doctor, imagine you are a fourteen-year-old boy sitting there reading. A stranger climbs in the window and menaces you with a knife. Are you not terrified? A great many children would drop the book, perhaps on the floor or on the sofa beside you. A few might conceivably throw the book down on the table. But it would take considerable *sangfroid* to ensure you do not lose your place and insert your bookmark before putting the book on the table, do you not think?"

"Yes, that would be a remarkable thing to do, for a child under threat with a knife," I agreed.

"And I concur with your other remarks, Inspector," said Holmes. "It may just be possible to jump the distance from the lawn to the window, leaving no footprints, but it seems an unlikely effort to make. It also seems unlikely a thief or even someone bent on murder or kidnapping would embark on such a quest at that time of night, with the family and servants about. And there is one further thing – Watson, would you examine the wound please, and tell us what you note about the angle of the cut?"

I knelt beside the body and looked closely at the terrible

gash in the footman's throat. It stretched not quite from ear to ear, but it was deep.

"The angle of the cut is unusual," I observed. "I have seen other cases of throats being cut from behind, and the cut is generally parallel to the ground as the blade is drawn across."

"Exactly," Holmes replied. "This man Carter was approximately five feet and eight inches tall in life. Charles stated that the alleged intruder had placed him in a headlock from behind with one arm and then slashed his throat. Assuming the intruder was about the same height, then the wound would most likely be close to horizontal. In fact, the cut is somewhere between thirty and forty degrees to the horizontal, lower at the front. The inference is that the wound was inflicted from in front, not from behind, by a much shorter person who reached upward with an angled blade. How tall is Charles, Inspector?"

"He is slightly built, and I would say a bit less than five feet tall," said Gregson slowly.

"So we are left with the conclusion that the intruder did not exist, and the consequent inference that Charles fabricated him to cover the fact that he himself murdered Carter."

There was silence as we all digested this revelation.

"We must be absolutely sure of our facts before we arrest a fourteen year-old, especially one in such a position in society," commented Gregson.

"We should *always* be sure of our facts, Inspector," replied Holmes. "The suspect's position in society is immaterial. When we seek justice, it is of no importance to me that the suspect is a beggar or a king. However, we have not finished our investigation. We need to interview all members of the household, and the servants. Have you summoned a fingerprint specialist to check the knife?"

"I did so just before I called you. They should be on their way."

"Very good. Can we use the morning room for the interviews?"

"Certainly, that is where I spoke to some of the servants earlier. Save a few words with Charles immediately on my arrival to obtain the basic facts, I have not interviewed the family as yet; I wished you to be here for that. You'll want to start with Charles I assume?"

"I'd prefer to start with the governess if you don't mind, Inspector," said Holmes.

"The governess! But she was in her room at the time, and heard and saw nothing," exclaimed Gregson.

"That may be so, but governesses often have more contact with the children than the parents, and more importantly are willing to divulge their honest opinions of them. I find parents generally like to think the best of their offspring, and are also sometimes over-protective of them. We will gain some useful insight into Charles's character from the governess, I'll wager, and that may be of importance in solving this mystery."

"Very well, if you say so. I'll go fetch her."

He left the library, and we made our way back to the morning room. He joined us a few minutes later, accompanied by a pale young woman he introduced as Miss Victoria Jones.

"I've made arrangements to have the body removed, and also to have some tea brought in," he said.

"Excellent, Inspector!" said Holmes. "Now Miss Jones, please be seated. Inspector Gregson has already told us that you were in your room and have no direct information about the events of last night. However, I have a few other questions if I may."

"Certainly, Mr. Holmes," she said in a quiet, refined voice.

"How long have you worked for Lord Derringley?"

"Nearly six years."

"What can you tell us about the children in your care, their characters, their behaviour, their relations with each other and with their parents?"

"Is it proper for me to say Mr. Holmes? What do the children have to do with a burglar killing poor Mr. Carter?"

"Your loyalty and discretion does you credit, Miss Jones, but I assure you any information you can give me will help us in the solution of this crime, which may not be as straightforward as it first appeared."

She thought for a moment, then obviously came to a decision.

"Very well, I will tell you what I know. Arthur, the eldest, is a quiet, studious, thoughtful young man. There is no vice in him. He is to read history at Oxford next year, and I believe he will do well there. Charles is also intelligent and studious, but is more confident than Arthur. If he has a fault, it is that he likes to get his own way. If there is one piece of cake on a plate, or a single apple in the bowl, he will take it for himself regardless of the other children's desires. He does not like to share.

"Lord and Lady Derringley are aware of this aspect of his nature, but although His Lordship will admonish him on occasion, his mother appears unwilling to take any action. Charlotte is a delightful child, generally well-behaved and playful. She is her mother's favourite, but being the only daughter, this is not uncommon. I think Charlotte is aware of this, and uses it to her advantage sometimes, but she is only eight, and again this is not unusual behaviour."

"Is there any tension, any animosity between Arthur and the other two children due to Arthur having a different mother, now deceased?" Holmes asked.

"I have not discerned any," said Miss Jones. "The boys used to tease each other and come to blows occasionally when they were younger, as brothers will. But they fought over toys and other trifles, not because Arthur has different parentage. Charles would always come off best in those encounters. There is three years difference between them, but Arthur is small for his age, and they have always been of similar size."

At this point there was a knock, and a maid brought in a tea tray. I poured tea for everyone while Holmes continued.

"Can you think of anything unusual, anything out of the ordinary, that has happened in the lives of the children recently?"

Miss Jones hesitated for a moment.

"I came across Arthur crying last week. He said he was worried about going to Oxford. Not only would he miss his family, he thought he might be bullied due to his size. I tried to comfort him. And Charlotte has been upset the last three days because her cat has gone missing. He has gone wandering for two or three days at a time before, so I expect he will return soon."

"I'm sure he will," I said.

"Inspector, do you have any questions for Miss Jones?" Holmes asked.

"No, that will be all. Thank you, Miss Jones. Would you have Charles come down to see us please?"

"I will, though I imagine His Lordship would like to be present at any interview of his son."

"Perfectly understandable and reasonable," replied Gregson.

As Miss Jones rose to leave, there came a knock and the butler entered.

"Inspector, there is a Scotland Yard fingerprint officer here to see you," he announced.

"Thank you, Marston," acknowledged Gregson.

Turning to Holmes and me, he said "Won't be long, I'll just instruct him on where to check for prints."

When the inspector had left, I put a question to Holmes.

"Did you learn anything of importance from Miss Jones?"

Holmes took a sip of his tea before answering.

"I am not yet sure why, and I need to think further about it, but it seems to me significant that Lady Derringley will not try to inhibit or repress Charles's dislike of sharing," he said thoughtfully.

My face must have given away my lack of understanding.

Holmes smiled and said "Let me explain. In my many encounters with the criminal class over the years, I have come to believe that certain types share similar characteristics and ways of thinking. I don't mean what we call a criminal's *modus operandi;* that is their way of committing their crimes, their method. No, I am referring to the way they behave and think, their mental perspective or psychology.

"As you are well-read Watson, you will know that the work of an obscure Moravian monk named Mendel forty years ago, has over the last two years been confirmed by various other scientists working in Germany, France, England and the United States. Mendel discovered that plants inherit physical traits from the parent plants, and that the inheritability of traits can be assigned mathematical probabilities. Of course, farmers have known for centuries about breeding animals for a particular trait, but now we have a scientific basis for the phenomenon. I have not performed any rigorous research yet, but my experience tells me that there are some psychological and behavioural traits which may be inherited, just as physical characteristics are. I don't mean to say that a criminal father is bound to have criminal children; there is also the fact that we are all to some degree products of our upbringing and parenting. But I am considering writing a monograph on the subject of the psychology of criminality, and to what extent it depends upon these inherited factors from the parents, childhood experiences, upbringing or perhaps other influences."

"That would be a fascinating –"

I was interrupted by the entrance of Inspector Gregson, followed by three people whom I assumed were Lord and Lady Derringley, and Charles. We rose from our seats, and I was proved right as the inspector introduced them.

His Lordship was a man of average height and build, with dark hair and a small moustache. He was quietly but expensively dressed. His wife was also dark-haired, petite, but had, I thought, a rather haughty expression. Their son, Charles, as Gregson had told us, was a slightly built youth; like his mother he too had a somewhat condescending air, but he nodded politely as the inspector mentioned our names. I noticed he had a small bruise on his left cheekbone.

"Inspector Gregson tells me you are assisting him in this enquiry, Mr. Holmes," said Lord Derringley. "I am not sure why this would be necessary, as it seems a simple matter to me. Carter lost his life protecting my son from someone who entered my house intent on some devilry. You should be out there looking for this person."

"The police are always happy to have the benefit of Mr. Holmes's wisdom in important or difficult cases, Your Lordship," said Gregson, looking slightly uncomfortable. "Let us all be seated, and perhaps we can clear this matter up quickly."

"I hope so, Inspector, as we are all upset at this disturbance. My son is also very young to have endured such a frightening incident, and needs rest."

"Yes sir, we appreciate this is a difficult time for all of you," said Gregson. "Now then, Charles, would you please tell us what occurred in the library this evening?"

The boy looked at his mother who sat next to him. She smiled reassuringly and took his hand. Charles then started to speak in a composed, even tone.

47

"I was in the library, sitting on the sofa facing the windows, reading a novel. I had opened one of the windows when I entered, as it was a warm night. Suddenly, a man climbed in the window. He saw me of course, and pulled a knife from his pocket. He pointed the knife at me and put his finger to his lips for silence. He started to walk around the other sofa towards me, when I heard a knock on the door and Carter came in. He at once saw the man with the knife, and rushed towards him. They struggled together for a short time, but eventually the man got Carter in a headlock from behind, then he – then he – he killed him.

"There was blood everywhere. I had a lot on my chest and face. I think the man then realized what he had done, as he dropped the knife, backed away and then quickly climbed back out of the window. I called out for help, and after a short time; less than a minute I would say, Marston came in. He turned around and told someone I couldn't see to fetch my father. He then put his jacket around me and started to escort me upstairs. We met my father in the hall; Marston spoke to him, but I was in a daze by then and didn't really hear them. I remember my father continued on, and Marston took me to my room, where my mother joined me a few minutes later."

"Very good, Charles. Can you describe this man?" asked Gregson.

"He was of average height, a well-built, strong-looking fellow. He did not have a full beard, but it was obvious he had not shaved in several days. He had longish black hair, and wore dark trousers, a light brown shirt, a dark jacket and brown leather gloves. All his clothes had seen better days, he was quite scruffy, and looked like any common working man you see in the street."

"Thank you. Mr. Holmes, do you have any questions for Charles?"

"Just a few, Inspector. Charles, what did you do with the

book you were reading, after the man climbed in the window?"

"I – I'm not sure sir. I might have dropped it, I guess. I was feeling quite scared."

"Of course you were, very natural in the circumstances. So in all the time the intruder was in the room, you were seated on the sofa? You never moved?"

"No sir. When the man had left, I got up, called for help, and went over to Carter to see if he was alive. Though I didn't really think he would be."

"My last question – how did you come by that bruise on your cheek?"

Charles raised his hand and touched the bruise.

"It's nothing to do with what happened tonight. I was in the garden this afternoon, and tripped over a tree root. My face hit the ground. My own fault entirely," he said with a half-smile.

"I see," said Holmes. "Now then Inspector –"

"I do wish to say, sir," interrupted Charles, "that Mr. Carter was exceedingly brave, and perhaps he saved my life. Not every servant would have acted as he did. I'm very grateful."

Holmes nodded understandingly.

"Inspector, if I may?" he asked.

"Certainly, Mr. Holmes."

"Your Lordship, could you tell us what you know of the events of this evening? Where were you when the alarm was raised?"

"I was in the drawing room with Arthur. We were talking of Oxford and the time I spent studying literature there, when Sally burst in and said that Marston needed me urgently in the library. I told Arthur to remain where he was, and was heading to the library when I saw Marston with his arm around Charles leading him to the staircase. Charles had Marston's jacket on, but I could see that there was blood on Charles. Marston told me

Carter was dead, assured me that Charles was not hurt, and that he would take him to his room. He told me that the police would be required. When I saw the situation in the library, I immediately locked the library door and telephoned the police. The inspector here arrived within perhaps twenty minutes."

"That is correct Mr. Holmes," confirmed Gregson. "I arrived here at eight-thirty."

Holmes turned to Lady Derringley.

"Your Ladyship, please tell us what happened from your perspective."

"I can add little, Mr. Holmes. I was upstairs in my bedroom and knew nothing of what happened until my husband came in and told me that Carter had been killed, Charles had witnessed the murder and was now in his room. He asked me to tend to him while he looked after things downstairs and waited for the police. I rushed to Charles's room and found Charles in a state of shock. Marston was there, and had given Charles a little brandy in water. I said he could leave and I stayed with Charles, washing the blood off his face and helping him change his clothes. By the time the inspector came in to talk to him, he had recovered somewhat and was able to tell him what happened."

"Where are the clothes Charles was wearing?" asked Holmes.

"I have them Mr. Holmes," replied Gregson. "When I talked to Charles in his room, they were in a pile on the floor. I wrapped them in brown paper and secured them as possible evidence."

"I'll need to see them. And Marston, and the maid – Sally was it? Meanwhile," he said as he rose, "I think we can leave Lord and Lady Derringley and Master Charles in peace. Thank you very much for your time, sir, madam."

Lord Derringley nodded, and escorted his family from the room.

"What do you think, Holmes?" asked Gregson anxiously."

"I think...that I have never heard three witness statements that agree and corroborate each other so perfectly. It is almost like they were..."

"Rehearsed?" I finished.

"A bold statement, Watson. But what was most interesting was not so much what Charles had to say, but the way he said it. Did you notice anything unusual Inspector?"

"Well, Mr. Holmes, now that you mention it, I did. I have taken a great number of witness statements in my time, but his was one of the calmest, clearest and detailed I have heard. It was almost like he was just reciting poetry, or reading a list of groceries."

"Exactly," replied Holmes, with some force. "He did not strike me as your average fourteen-year-old boy who has just been scared to death, threatened with violence, and covered in blood from seeing a man's throat being cut in front of him. He noticed a number of important details about the alleged intruder, but the only thing he was unsure of was what he did with his book."

"So are we agreed there is sufficient evidence to arrest him for the murder?" queried Gregson.

"Not just yet, Inspector. I am not absolutely certain that Charles killed Carter, though the circumstantial evidence is black against him. We also have no apparent motive for him to do so. I am certain there was never an intruder, so he is lying about that. I am also certain we have not determined the whole story just yet, and that information is being withheld from us. Let us hear what Marston and the maid, Sally, have to say."

Gregson left and returned a few minutes later with Marston and the maid. Marston's story added nothing to what we already knew – he had been walking through the hall, heard the call for help and rushed to the library. He sent Sally to fetch His

Lordship, whilst he gave Charles his jacket to cover the blood and walked him to his room. He met Lord Derringley on the way and advised him that Carter was lying dead in the library, he believed Charles had witnessed the murder but was not hurt, and that the police needed to be summoned. He had stayed with Charles in his room and given him brandy. Lady Derringley had then arrived a few minutes later and taken over.

The maid said she had heard someone call for help, and ran towards the library. She had seen Marston enter, then come back out a moment later and he had instructed her to fetch His Lordship immediately. She knew he was in the drawing room, so ran there to deliver the message. She concluded by saying Mr. Carter had been such a nice man, always kind and helpful.

"In what way?" asked Holmes.

"Well only this afternoon, I had to change the curtains in Master Charles's bedroom sir. He was walking by and saw I was struggling to get the new ones up, so he came in and offered to help. It wasn't his job really."

Her brow furrowed and she looked a little distraught as she said this, and this prompted Holmes to inquire as to the reason.

"Well sir, saying about the curtains reminded me – while he was helping me with them, I dropped one of the curtain rings and it fell behind a chest of drawers. He crouched down and reached behind the drawers to get it, and then he swore. It really surprised me, sir, I never saw Mr. Carter get angry or say a cross word with anyone before. I couldn't see exactly what he was doing with his back to me, but I think he put something in his pocket, muttering something under his breath. He apologised to me for swearing, and then we got on with the curtains."

"Do you have any impression at all as to what he might have said?" asked Holmes intently.

"Well sir, I am not very sure, but as you ask it sounded like he said several words I couldn't catch and then the word 'stopped' at the end."

"That's most helpful," said Holmes. "You and Marston may go about your duties now. Thank you both."

The servants stood up, Marston bowing and Sally giving a curtsey before exiting the room.

"Was it helpful?" questioned Gregson.

"I am beginning to form a theory," Holmes replied. "But let us examine the clothes Charles was wearing and see if any fingerprints have been found, and where."

"I shall fetch the clothes and meet you in the library," offered Gregson.

"Very good, Inspector."

We parted in the hall, Gregson disappearing towards the back of the house while we made our way to the library. The same constable was still on duty at the door, and he touched his helmet respectfully as we entered. The body had gone, and the fingerprint officer was just packing up his case. We introduced ourselves, discovering his name was Sergeant Jackson. Inspector Gregson then joined us, carrying a brown paper parcel tied up with string.

"Ah, Jackson," he said. "How did you get on?"

"I've checked everywhere you asked sir, and photographed the results. The window frame has several prints on it, some quite small. These would be most likely from a woman, or the lad. They are all on the frame in the place you would expect them to be if they had opened the window from inside. There are no prints the other way around, where you'd find them from someone climbing in the window."

"And the knife?" asked Gregson.

"The knife has no prints whatsoever I'm afraid," said the sergeant. "Is there any member of the household you wish me to take prints from, for comparison purposes?"

"That won't be necessary. Thank you, sergeant, you may go now" said Gregson, turning to Holmes. "The prints on the window frame will be from the servants and from Charles, who said he opened the window. No prints from anyone entering the window is what we expected, but none on the knife – what do you make of that Holmes?"

"It's what you would expect if the intruder wore gloves as Charles stated. However, since we agree there was no intruder, it means either the killer wiped their fingerprints from the handle, or the killer also wore gloves. May we see the clothing now, Inspector?"

Gregson undid the knots and unwrapped the parcel of clothes. Holmes spread them out carefully on the desk, and then examined them for some minutes, finally turning to the Scotland Yarder.

"Will you go first, or shall I, Inspector?"

"I am happy to follow your reasoning Mr. Holmes," replied the inspector genially.

"Very well. You noticed that there appears to be far more blood on the clothes than one would expect?"

"I did. If the lad was sitting here on the sofa, and Carter had his throat cut over here – well that's over ten feet away, and I can't see even the strongest of arterial spray accounting for the amount of blood visible on the waistcoat and shirt."

"I agree," said Holmes. "You can see on the carpet and on the table near where Charles was sitting, that the blood spatter at that distance is nothing like the coverage on the clothes. Also, there is more blood on the right arm of the shirt and right side of the waistcoat than there is on the left. What can we infer from that?"

"That Charles had his right side facing Carter when the bloodletting occurred?"

"Exactly. Carter's throat was cut from in front, not from

behind, by a much shorter right-handed person, lunging forward and upward to slash at him. The murderer was then instantly covered in a strong torrent of blood on his right arm and right side."

"Then as these clothes were being worn by Charles at the time of the murder, and Charles is much shorter than Carter was, and is also right-handed...."

"The conclusion is inescapable, Inspector," said Holmes darkly.

"Then what is your view of the case now?" asked Gregson. "It seems to be getting more and more complicated to me. We still have no motive."

"My view of the case, Inspector... is not complete," said Holmes. "May we interview the two other children, Arthur and Charlotte?"

Gregson looked at Holmes thoughtfully.

"I'll see what I can arrange, though the parents will again want to be present I should think."

Holmes nodded, and the inspector departed. As Holmes and I walked back to the morning room, I asked him about his theory. I knew he would be loath to share it with me or anyone else until it was proven to his satisfaction, but I wanted to know the clues upon which his theory depended.

"You have seen and heard what I have seen and heard, Watson," he said. "It is important to develop the skill to sift the important information from the extraneous. However, since you ask, it is my view that the case hinges on the bookmark, what Carter found behind the chest of drawers, and the real reason for the bruise on Charles's cheek."

I tried to unravel the meaning of these clues as we entered the morning room again and seated ourselves, but was unsuccessful. Suddenly I became aware of raised voices outside. The door opened and Gregson came in, looking decidedly flustered, with Lord Derringley immediately behind him.

"I repeat, Inspector," he was saying in a loud and forceful manner, "Charles was only a witness to this horrible crime. Arthur and Charlotte have nothing to do with it whatsoever. Why do you and Mr. Holmes need to interview them at all?"

Lady Derringley and Charles entered, and stood beside His Lordship.

"Yes Inspector, why are you doing this? Why are you still bothering my family? Why have you not found this man who entered the library and killed Mr. Carter?" she scolded.

"Because, Your Ladyship..." Gregson faltered, "because..." He looked beseechingly at Holmes.

"What the Inspector is trying to say, Your Ladyship," Holmes said coolly, "is that we have not found the man who entered the library last evening, because he does not exist."

There was a shocked silence. I glanced at everyone in turn. Gregson looked apprehensive, His Lordship appeared stunned, his wife put her hand to her open mouth, but Charles – his expression was inscrutable.

"What are you saying, Holmes? That my son is a liar?" roared Lord Derringley.

"Indeed, I believe so Your Lordship," said Holmes. "But unfortunately, worse than that, he is also a murderer."

This seemed to be too much for His Lordship. He shook his head in disbelief, and sank into an armchair.

"I'm sorry, sir," said Gregson, "but Mr. Holmes and I concur. The evidence is strong against Charles, and I must now arrest him and –"

"No."

We all looked at Lady Derringley.

"No," she said again, in a firm tone. "You will not need to arrest Charles. I killed Mr. Carter."

It was Gregson's turn to be stunned into silence, but Holmes I noticed, regarded her with a thoughtful but unsurprised gaze.

Lord Derringley finally found his voice.

"Constance?" What is the meaning of this? You couldn't possibly –"

"I'm sorry, Henry. It's true. The best thing you can do now is take Charles and leave us. I will tell the inspector and Mr. Holmes what really happened."

"I agree, Your Lordship," said Gregson. "It's best for now that you take Charles while we interview Her Ladyship."

Lord Derringley looked overwhelmed, but he took Charles by the arm and walked towards the door.

"I shall telephone Mortimer – our family lawyer," he said, ushering Charles out of the room and closing the door.

"Now then Lady Derringley, please be seated and then tell us the truth about the events in the library," asked Gregson, seating himself as he spoke.

"I will, Inspector, but first I need to tell you what happened this afternoon. I was in the conservatory, and chancing to look out into the garden I saw Charles and Arthur talking near the hedge. I then saw Carter approach them. He spoke to the boys for a minute, and it seemed to me he got quite angry. Arthur and Charles then ran off, and Carter then walked back into the house. I went and found Charles to ask him about the incident. He told me that Carter had spoken angrily to him several times, and had even hit or slapped him on occasion, for no reason that he understood. You can understand that I was very disturbed by this, and promised Charles that I would speak to his father about the matter, who would certainly give Carter his notice.

"With one thing and another I did not get a chance to speak to my husband before we dined. After dinner, Henry and Arthur went to the drawing room, and Charles said he was going to the library. My housekeeper wanted a word about some domestic matter, and so after a few minutes I went to the library myself, hoping to speak further with Charles about why Carter might be persecuting him. As I entered, I saw Carter and Charles standing in the centre of the room. Carter was holding a knife. He turned towards me, and Charles took advantage of this by hitting him sharply on the arm holding the knife. It flew on to the floor and skidded towards me, ending up near my feet. I picked it up as Carter uttered an oath and jumped towards me. I was in a panic, I just – lashed out, catching him in the throat. It was horrible. Charles and I were both covered in blood."

"And what did you do next, madam?" asked Holmes, as Gregson scribbled furiously in his notebook.

"I was in shock, as you can imagine gentlemen. I first thought to seek my husband's advice, but then Charles said, 'They don't hang women do they Mother?' I realised then I was in a difficult position, where it might not be believed that I acted in self-defence, and there was also the scandal to consider. Even if I weren't charged, I didn't want my husband's distinguished family name linked to a murder; people would talk, the press would have a field day. So I swiftly concocted the story that Charles has told you, about the intruder. I was sure he, a mere child, would be more easily believed, and the police would then look for this fictitious assailant. Once I was certain Charles had memorised the story, I wiped the knife of my fingerprints and instructed him to call for help in a few minutes. I then left the library via the other door so as not to meet anyone in the corridor. I made my way unseen to my room, quickly changed and washed, then burnt my bloodied dress in my fireplace."

"So you freely admit that you killed Carter, lied to the police, instructed your son to also lie to the police, and destroyed evidence?" asked Gregson.

"Yes, and I will accept any punishment the courts may see fit to pronounce – but it was an accident, I assure you," replied

Lady Derringley.

"Are you satisfied, Mr. Holmes?" said Gregson, turning to my companion.

"Almost, Inspector," he replied. "I would just like to clear up one or two points. Would you excuse me please?"

He strode swiftly to the door and left us.

**********

Gregson and I were in the hall when Holmes rejoined us some thirty minutes later. We had left Lady Derringley in the morning room with a constable on guard.

"Ah, Holmes, there you are," said Gregson, a trifle impatiently I thought. "Is your investigation complete? Can I make an arrest now?"

"Yes, Inspector, I am certain of my case, and you can make an arrest. However, if you will indulge me, I have asked His Lordship and Charles to join us, and I would like to go through a number of aspects of the case before you employ your handcuffs. It would also be advisable to have your constables in the room."

The inspector and I looked at each other, both sensing that there was a final act to this drama.

"Very well, Holmes. Here are Lord Derringley and Charles coming now."

We and two constables summoned by Gregson followed His Lordship and his son into the morning room, and the inspector bade them to sit. Lord Derringley looked pale and distraught, but Charles exhibited a remarkably composed demeanor.

"Why are we here, Inspector?" asked His Lordship gruffly.

"Mr. Holmes would like to say a few words before I, er – that is, before the matter is cleared up. Mr. Holmes?"

Holmes had remained standing, pacing back and forth in

front of the fireplace. He continued to pace, and then started to speak.

"This has been a difficult case. I will go through my reasoning and deductions based on the evidence the inspector and I have gathered, which I believe leads to an irrefutable conclusion. I beg all of you to listen without interruption; I will answer any questions you may have at the end.

After our initial survey of the library, the inspector and I agreed that there was no evidence of any intruder. The flowerbed outside the window was unmarked, the bookmark still in the book indicated Charles had not been disturbed in his reading, and it was unlikely any miscreant would attempt to enter a house at such an early time with the lights on indicating people were still about. Also, the angle of Carter's fatal wound indicated that it had been inflicted from the front by a shorter person than Carter, not by a person of similar height from behind, as Charles had stated. This meant that Charles had fabricated the story of the man who killed Carter. Whether that was to protect himself or another was still to be determined.

Our interview with the governess, Miss Jones, gave me some indications as to the characters of the children. This is not evidence, but her observations do bear on the mystery, in a manner which I can explain later. We then listened to Charles's statement concerning the events in the library. He gave such a clear and detailed description of the sequence of events, and of the intruder, that the inspector and I were loath to believe it had emanated from a frightened child who had just witnessed a gruesome murder. Witnesses to crimes are generally confused and uncertain as to what they have seen, and do not usually notice important details. His account sounded to me like a story he had learned, not something he had seen."

I glanced at Charles, and was surprised to see a mocking half-smile on his face. Holmes continued.

"The maid, Sally, gave us some new information, saying that while helping fit curtains in Charles's room earlier today, Carter appeared to find something behind a chest of drawers which moved him to swear, something he was not in the habit of doing. I was not quite sure if and how this fitted into our puzzle, but my intuition told me it was significant.

"We then learned that there were no fingerprints indicating someone had entered through the window, and that there were also no fingerprints on the knife. This was inconclusive. However, an inspection of the clothes Charles wore at the time indicated that he had been much closer to Carter than he had said, when his throat was cut. Close enough to have possibly murdered him, and certainly not ten feet away sitting on the sofa.

"As the circumstantial evidence was strong, the inspector was about to arrest Charles, when Your Ladyship confessed to the crime. However, to my ears, your version of events was quite improbable, for several reasons. That you should find a servant menacing your son with a knife, a servant whom Charles told you had recently taken to assaulting him for no apparent reason, a servant whom Sally had told us was of a kindly and helpful disposition – this did not ring true. That Charles should knock the knife from his hand, and that you should then pick it up and use it on Mr. Carter as he advanced towards you – this also seemed very unlikely. And finally, I have just learned from Sally that due to the pleasant summer weather of late, there has not been a fire laid in your room for more than a week. There is no ash of any sort in the fireplace, so your story of burning your dress is thus disproved. I therefore rejected your confession as an attempt to protect your son."

Lady Derringley opened her mouth to say something, but Holmes held up his hand.

"No protests please Your Ladyship, your confession is palpably untrue. Now let me finish by stating what I believe to have happened, based on the evidence and some surmise based on the balance of probabilities. Firstly, the events of this afternoon. One part of your story was true, Lady Derringley – you did see Arthur and Charles from the conservatory, talking near the hedge. What you did not see, which I have confirmed by a short interview with Charlotte, is that Carter and Charlotte were on the other side of the hedge. Carter was helping her look for her missing cat, and they both overheard the boys talking. Charlotte says she clearly heard Charles say he was going to kill Arthur. When Carter heard this, he went around the hedge and must have rebuked Charles, perhaps not for the first time for bullying or threatening Arthur.

"After this incident, a short while later Carter was helping Sally with the curtains. In trying to locate the dropped curtain ring, I believe he found a knife hidden behind the drawers. This brought home to him the seriousness of the threat he had heard Charles make earlier, and he swore in a moment of disbelief. Then I believe what he muttered to himself was something along the lines of 'he must be stopped.'

"He then decided to make one last appeal to Charles. Finding him reading in the library after dinner, he asked to speak to him. Charles replaced his bookmark and placed the book on the table. Carter then produced the knife and I've no doubt begged him to leave Arthur alone, or he would have to take the matter to Lord Derringley. This infuriated Charles, and because of this and the fact Carter had been so bold as to rebuke him earlier for threatening Arthur, he attacked Carter, somehow gaining the knife and the bruise on his cheek in the process.

"Charles, I'm sorry to say, then slashed Carter's throat. At this point, Lady Derringley entered the library and realised what her son had done. We know, Your Ladyship, that you are reluctant to admonish Charles for any misbehaviour, and I believe that you are quite aware of his criminal tendencies even though he is very young. Thus, when he suggested he fabricate a story to account for Carter's death, you went along with it.

When the inspector and I didn't believe his story and he was about to be arrested, you confessed to try to save him. What I would like to know now, Your Ladyship, is this: Has Charles told you what Arthur told me a few minutes ago – the reason for him wanting to kill his brother?"

Lady Derringley fixed Holmes with a steely gaze, but remained tight-lipped.

"Very well. Inspector, your Lordship – I trust I have proved to you that Charles killed Carter, a faithful servant who tried to prevent a tragedy, and in doing so became the subject of a tragedy himself. However, Carter's death has brought to light the truth. Arthur has told me that time and again Charles has threatened to murder him in order to remove the heir to the Derringley estate. He is filled with bitterness that he is the second son, and desperately covets the wealth and title which will be Arthur's one day. That one so young is capable of such feelings and such deeds is a monstrous thing, and also casts doubt upon his mental stability. I am not aware of any prison, hospital, or asylum that is suitable to keep one his age under control; but that is not a matter for me to decide. My work is merely to unmask the perpetrators of crime, and this I have done."

A slow, measured, hand-clapping filled the room. We all turned to see Charles slowly applauding, a beaming smile on his face. His eyes, however, were cold, unfeeling.

"And very good work it was too, Mr. Holmes," he said. "You are completely correct in all your deductions and surmises; in describing what happened; and my motivations for acting as I did. Arthur is a good person, but he was in my way. And I always get my way."

\*\*\*\*\*\*\*\*\*\*

A short time later, Holmes, Gregson and I were sitting in the morning room discussing the case. The constables had taken away Charles and his mother. Lord Derringley, stupefied at discovering that his young son was capable of murder without showing a shred of remorse, had planned to murder his other son, and that his wife was complicit in the matter, had taken to his bed, tended to by Marston. Arthur and Charlotte were in the care of the governess, who was trying to get them to sleep. Even though it was now gone midnight, the intense interest which the case had generated had banished all thought of sleep from my mind.

"It's amazing, Holmes. I can't quite believe it even now," the Inspector was saying.

Holmes puffed at a cigarette several times before replying.

"Yes, I can scarcely credit it myself. But we all saw the way Charles behaved. I don't believe he has the slightest sympathy for any other human being, save perhaps his mother to a small degree. It is as I said to Watson earlier; there are some behavioural traits common to certain types of criminals. I have seen some killers who show a similar lack of emotion and refuse to comply with society's usual moral standards, but they were adults. In one so young – well, there are many people who will not believe it possible."

A thought occurred to me.

"Holmes, is Charles the way he is because of his mother? All three children presumably had the same upbringing, and Arthur and Charlotte appear to be normal, so is his criminality a result of those hereditary factors of which you spoke?"

"In part, I am sure," Holmes replied. "Her Ladyship knew Charles exhibited some bad behaviour, which no doubt worsened over time. She refused to correct this behaviour, then went so far as to lie to cover his murder of Carter. She was even happy to face imprisonment for the crime herself, in order to spare him. She may not have a murderous nature, but her behaviour has hardly been exemplary."

"If only there were some indicator, some sign forewarning us that a child might turn out this way," I said. "We could perhaps prevent further similar evils from occurring."

"Perhaps there is, Watson. I will need to research further, and the lack of examples of children like Charles will make it difficult, but perhaps there is."

"What do you mean, Holmes?" I asked.

"I mean, Watson, that based on a rather distressing suspicion, I instituted a search by the gardeners and footmen with lanterns, while I spoke to Arthur and Charlotte. They discovered Charlotte's cat behind a little-used outbuilding in the corner of the grounds. Its throat had been cut."

# THE CURIOUS DEATH OF AMOS AMBERDALE

Upon looking through my notes, I find that it was an early autumn morning in 1890 when Holmes and I learned of the murder of Mr. Amos Amberdale. As it was a case which vexed the police, excited the press, and presented my friend with an opportunity to exercise those powers of deduction and reasoning for which he was famous, I think it begs to be added to those chronicles of cases I have laid before the public. Here then, are the facts of the matter.

My wife Mary, being of a kindly and caring disposition, had deserted me yet again, this time to tend to a sick friend in Portsmouth. As she had telegraphed to say that her presence there would be required for some two weeks, I had, as I had done oftentimes before in her absences, moved temporarily back into my old rooms with Holmes. He was pleased to see me, and we soon settled back into our old, congenial ways.

One day after breakfast, we were engaged in reading the early editions of the papers when Mrs. Hudson knocked and entered.

"There is a police constable to see you Mr. Holmes," she said. "He says he has a message from Inspector Lestrade."

Holmes threw down his paper and rubbed his hands together.

"A case! And it must be urgent, Watson, to send a messenger rather than a wire. Send him up Mrs. Hudson."

A few moments later, our doorway was almost filled with the large bulk of the constable, helmet in hand.

"Good morning Mr. 'Olmes, and to you, Doctor Watson," he said respectfully. "PC John Hartley is my name, and Inspector Lestrade asked me to give you this message Mr. 'Olmes sir."

He handed Holmes a note, who quickly read it and passed

it over to me.

"One of the best! Hah! What do you make of it, Watson?" he asked. The note read as follows:

*Please come at once. This is the type of case which presents an opportunity for the theorist, of which you are one of the best. A man has been impossibly murdered in a locked room.*

*G. Lestrade*

"It sounds most intriguing, Holmes."

"Indeed, Watson. The writing shows considerable agitation. That, and the wording – surely, for 'opportunity for the theorist' we may read 'I am out of my depth' – suggests Lestrade has made no progress in the case. Is this not so, PC Hartley?"

"The inspector is in a right state, sir, that's true. There be no clues, no motive, and a man stabbed to death inside a room locked and bolted from the inside."

"Then let us see what light we can shed on this mystery. You are free, Watson?"

"Certainly, Holmes. I would wish to come even if I were not free, as it sounds a most fascinating case. My practice is quiet at present, and my neighbour will handle what few patients I might receive today."

"Capital!" cried Holmes. "I assume you have a carriage waiting Hartley? Wait downstairs, we shall be with you in five minutes."

\*\*\*\*\*\*\*\*\*

Having dressed quickly, in less than the time stated we climbed into the carriage that had brought Hartley and Lestrade's summons and set off for Hampstead. This was the location of the home of Mr. Amos Amberdale and the scene of the crime, as the constable explained to us. It turned out to be a large three-storey house set in a couple of acres of gardens. A sign on the gate proclaimed the property to be named Applegrove House, and this was justified by two dozen or more apple trees that lined the driveway. We alighted from the carriage, and a constable at the front door told us that Inspector Lestrade was awaiting us in the room where the body lay.

"This way sirs" said Hartley, and we followed him up the main staircase to the top floor, down a corridor to a door which had obviously been opened by force, as the frame was splintered in two places, where the lock and a bolt had been. Inside, Lestrade was at a desk writing in his notebook, but our attention was immediately drawn to the body of a man between the door and the desk, lying face down on a rug with the haft of a knife protruding from his upper back. Lestrade looked up as we stood in the doorway.

"Ah, Mr. Holmes and the good Doctor! Thank you for coming. I'm sure with your assistance we can clear up this matter in short order. Shall I give you the basic facts before you conduct your examination of the room?"

"Please do, Inspector," said Holmes. "Perhaps out here would be best."

Lestrade got up and joined us in the corridor..

"The murdered man is a widower, Mr. Amos Amberdale, who prospered as an antique dealer before coming into a large inheritance five years ago which enabled him to buy this estate and live comfortably. He still owns the antique business, but the day-to-day operation is now controlled by his daughter and youngest child, who still lives here. He also has two sons, one of them married, who live elsewhere – I have sent constables to inform them of their father's death and to bring them here for questioning. An amusing point here is that Mr. Amos Amberdale seems to have been a little obsessive about the letter A, if you ask me. Perhaps because of his own name and the fact his wife was named Anne, they have named their children Agnes, Albert and Alfred, and when he bought this property he renamed it Applegrove House. What do you think of that?"

"Slightly odd, but not suspicious," replied Holmes. "Now tell us of the circumstances surrounding the murder."

"Of course. This is Mr. Amberdale's retreat, I understand," said Lestrade, gesturing towards the room. "A room where he kept his own private collection of antiques. It was always kept locked, and nobody was allowed in unless he was also present. When he was in the room alone, the door was also locked and bolted, so the servants tell me. He seems to have been a somewhat secretive fellow. Anyhow, he was in there last night; went in after dinner his daughter said, about eight o'clock. She and the servants all went to their beds at their usual hour, and it wasn't until he didn't come down to breakfast that he was missed. A search was then made. His bed had not been slept in, and having exhausted all other places he might be, Miss Amberdale got to thinking her father must be still in this room, having either fallen asleep or become ill. She got Harry, their gardener and a strapping young man, to shoulder the door in, whence they discovered his body as you see it. The window is snibbed tight, the door was locked from the inside with the key still in the lock, and the bolt was drawn as well. There doesn't appear to be any trapdoors in the floor or the ceiling, or any other way into the room. Yet he is lying there with a knife in his back, which I feel must rule out suicide."

"Well-deduced, Lestrade! Yes, in my experience it is rather difficult to stab oneself between the shoulder blades," remarked Holmes. "Very well, I will now examine the room."

Holmes entered the room, his eyes darting everywhere. I watched with Lestrade from the doorway. The room was of moderate dimensions, with the desk roughly in the middle. There was a window in the wall opposite us, behind the desk. The remaining wall space on both sides was taken up with glass-fronted cabinets, containing all manner of antiques: china vases, urns, jugs, bowls and tea sets; silverware of all shapes and sizes; small bronze busts and figures; glass and crystal vases, pitchers, goblets and decanters; and other various items of wood, pewter and even the gleam of gold occasionally. The desk had several books and a writing set upon it. Light was provided by a pair of lamps either side of the window, and another pair either side of the doorway. The ceiling looked to be undecorated plaster and the floor of polished wood, broken only by the rug in front of the desk, where as we had seen earlier the body of the unfortunate Mr. Amberdale lay prone.

Holmes first examined the body, and especially the knife. He then turned his lens upon the door lock, turning the key back and forth to work the lock, looking inside the keyhole and then at the key itself. He drew the bolt across and back, then inspected the splintered frame where the lock and bolt had fitted. He crawled around the floor, rapping on the boards, ending up at the window.

"You said the window was snibbed tight, Inspector, and it is;" he said. "Moreover, the dust and grime upon the latch tell me it has not been moved in many a year, or the metal would show a shiny mark. The floor appears sound, although we need to check under the rug once the body has been removed. Have you examined the ceiling? Tapped it with a pole for example?"

"No, I haven't had time for that," Lestrade retorted. "After I secured the scene and sent Hartley to fetch you, I was interviewing Miss Amberdale and the servants. Have you found any clue to how the murderer made his escape after stabbing Mr. Amberdale?"

"I have not, Inspector – yet," said Holmes, "but as I said, I need to see under the rug and take a closer look at the ceiling. Perhaps one of these cabinets is hiding some secret entrance, though the thickness of the walls evident at the door would seem to rule that out. However, this murder weapon intrigues me. With your permission I would like to remove it from the body and examine it more closely."

"Very well, if you think it will further the investigation –" Lestrade stopped as the sound of a carriage arriving interrupted him. "That will be the victim's sons I hope. I shall go meet them and leave you to it."

"Thank you, Inspector," Holmes replied. "Watson – your assistance please."

Holmes knelt beside the body, and grasping the handle of the murder weapon with a handkerchief, slowly withdrew it from the back of the victim.

"Now Watson, what do you make of this? Rather unusual is it not?"

I looked at the weapon closely. Its handle appeared to be about six inches long, rather thin, circular in cross-section and made from bone. The extremely narrow blade was longer than the handle, some nine inches in all I estimated, and separated from the handle by a small circular hilt of a grey metal.

"I've never seen a knife like this before. It is remarkably long and thin," I said.

"Indeed, I would be surprised if you had seen one of these outside a museum," Holmes replied. "As you know, I have made a small study of edged weapons as they relate to their use in crime. This is a rondel."

"I have not heard the term. I suppose it has the shape it does for some particular purpose?" I asked, keenly interested.

"This sort of weapon was in use between the fourteenth and seventeenth centuries, Watson, designed to pierce and burst through chain mail, or slide through the joints in a suit of armour or the eyeslit in a helmet. When armour became obsolete due to the advent of firearms, the rondel also fell into disuse. And technically Watson, it is a dagger, not a knife – knives nearly always have only one edge on the blade, while daggers have both sides of the blade sharpened. It is a curious choice of weapon, but perhaps not entirely out of place in an antique dealer's residence. However, I don't see any other weapons on display in the room – if it were part of this collection we see, that would imply it was picked up in the heat of the moment and used to kill Amberdale. If the murder was planned, and the weapon brought to do the deed, it should tell us something about the murderer. Did you observe anything else about it?"

"No, I don't think so."

"Look at the handle again," Holmes said with a smile.

"You mean these longitudinal marks?" I asked.

"Yes. There are two marks along the length of the handle, on opposite sides. They look to me like slight abrasions, as if the handle had been drawn or rubbed across a rough surface."

"And what does that mean?"

"Watson, I have absolutely no idea! Perhaps nothing. Now, Doctor, what can you tell me about the wound?"

Holmes wrapped the dagger in his handkerchief, while I looked at the blood-soaked back of the victim.

"From the position of the wound just to the left of the spine, and the slightly upward angle of the weapon before you removed it, I would suggest that the long blade pierced the heart. Death would have occurred within seconds. Also, there is a circular indentation in the cloth surrounding the entry wound, which I suspect will match the circular hilt on the dagger."

"And what can we infer from that?"

"That it was driven into the body up to the hilt with some force?"

"Excellent Watson! In fact, if you will help me turn the body on to its side, I suspect – Mr. Amberdale being rather on the slim side – that the point of the rather long blade will have come out of his chest. Yes, there it is." he said, pointing to a bloodstain on the shirt with a small rip in the centre. "Now if you would be so good as to help move the body – I think we can just slide it on the rug – then I can check the floor."

We took hold of the rug and slid it with the body a few feet to one side, revealing the bloodstained floorboards beneath. Holmes examined them with his lens, rapped on them and then sat back, a disappointed look on his face.

"I was hoping there would be a convenient trapdoor under the rug. There is not, so we will have to start again, without any preconceptions, to discover how this man came to have a dagger thrust forcefully into his back and the assailant leave the room with the window and door locked."

We heard footsteps in the corridor, and moments later Lestrade entered.

"Have you finished, gentlemen?" he queried. "I have the sons and the daughter downstairs if you wish to join me in questioning them."

"Thank you, Inspector, I will join you," said Holmes. "But I have not yet finished with this room. I need to make a more comprehensive survey of the walls, ceiling and floor, and have a look around outside. But that can wait, let us see what the children of Mr. Amberdale have to say."

Lestrade hesitated, then leaned towards us and lowered his voice.

"I'll just warn you, though I'm sure your good manners will not allow you to show any expression which might be considered improper. Miss Amberdale and her mother were in an accident ten years ago – the trap they were travelling in broke a wheel and overturned. Mrs. Amberdale was killed, and her daughter suffered quite horrific facial injuries and broken bones. The scars have healed, but she is still much disfigured."

"Thank you, Inspector. Your warning is well-intentioned, but I'm sure we have seen worse in our time," Holmes said briskly. "Lead on."

Lestrade led us to the parlour on the ground floor and introduced us to the children of Amos Amberdale. Albert, the eldest, was a slim, dark-haired young man with a full black beard and moustache. His brother Alfred was also of slight build, clean shaven with short dark hair. Agnes too, took after her father and brothers with a petite figure, and had long, lustrous, jet-black hair. The disfigurement Lestrade had mentioned was immediately evident – even though Agnes tried to cover that side of her face with her hair, it was clear that her nose was awry and her left cheek, temple and jawline were deeply scarred. It was also clear that she had been crying. The three of them sat together on a sofa.

"Now then Miss Amberdale, will you please repeat for Mr. Holmes the events of this morning," asked Lestrade.

"Yes, Inspector," she said in a dead, mechanical voice. "Father had not come down to breakfast. I sent one of the maids to see if he had just overslept, but she returned to say that he wasn't in his room, and his bed had not been slept in. I had a look around the house with the maids, and sent the butler and footman to look outside. When we failed to find him, I suspected he must be still in his retreat, perhaps asleep or ill. I went up and knocked and called, but got no answer. I sent for Harry, who broke down the door and then we saw –"

She broke off, sobbing. Albert gave her his handkerchief, and Alfred put his arm around her.

"I couldn't go in – I just couldn't," she continued. Harry went over to him, and told me he was dead. We closed the door and I sent Harry for the police."

"Thank you. Any questions, Holmes?"

"Yes Inspector. Miss Amberdale, can you think of anyone who may have wished your father harm?"

"Not at all. He had neither friends nor enemies that I am aware of," she replied. "He had some acquaintances in the antiques trade, and sometimes went on buying trips, but he seldom went out socially. The only visitors here were friends of mine."

"I understand it was your father's custom to lock himself in that room when he was inside – do you know why that was?" asked Holmes.

"He never really said why – I think it was just his nature, and he didn't like being disturbed. He was a man inclined to privacy throughout his life."

"Yes that's right, isn't it Alf?" said Albert. "He never had much to say, did he?"

Alfred nodded. "Yes, he kept himself to himself."

"And I also understand that when he bought this house some years ago, he retired, and you now run the antique shop yourself?" Holmes queried.

"Well yes, I run it, but Father still owned it. Amberdale's Antiques was started by our grandfather in 1849."

"I see." He turned to the brothers. "And what are your occupations?"

"Alf and I are in business together, three years next month."

"Oh – antiques perhaps?" asked Holmes.

"No – we aren't really interested in antiques. We are both locksmiths."

Lestrade looked startled. "How interesting. Are you aware that your father was killed in a room where the window was snibbed shut, and the door locked and bolted from the inside? As professional locksmiths, is it possible that someone could have left that room and then locked the door, left the key in the lock on the inside, and then bolted the door on the inside?"

Albert Amberdale looked hard at Lestrade.

"Are you accusing us of something, Inspector?" he said

with an angry undertone. "Neither of us was here last night."

"Come now Mr. Amberdale, it was a natural question," interjected Holmes. "Inspector, I have a better than average knowledge of locks, and there is no technique or tool that I am aware of which allows one to lock and bolt a door on the inside when one is outside. I think the brothers Amberdale would concur?"

"Indeed Mr. Holmes, it can't be done," replied Alfred.

"That is my opinion too, sir," said Albert.

Holmes nodded.

"I would like to ask Miss Amberdale another question now – and I'm sorry if this distresses you – but this is the murder weapon," he said, unwrapping the dagger. "Have you ever seen this in the house before? Was it part of your father's collection?"

Miss Amberdale blanched and closed her eyes, then recovered.

"I don't think so, Mr. Holmes. He was not really interested in antique weapons. He collected silver, china and glass mainly. I am no expert, but it looks medieval to me."

"I agree madam, I think it is at least two centuries old. A strange choice of weapon," said Holmes. "Inspector, I think we can leave these people to their grief for the moment. I will carry out a further examination of the room, the rest of the house, and the garden, then I will need to speak to the gardener, Harry, and the other servants."

"Very well, Holmes. I will arrange to have the body removed," Lestrade replied.

We stood up and left the Amberdales in the parlour. I asked Holmes if he needed my assistance.

"Certainly, Watson, we'll look outside first."

We entered the back garden, and I followed Holmes as he looked around the lawn and then stood looking up at a window.

"That's the murder room, Watson. As I said earlier, that window appears to have not been opened for a long time, but I just wanted to confirm that it was not used to enter or leave the room. There is no ivy, no tree nearby, no adjacent drainpipe, and finally no indentations in the lawn to indicate a ladder was used. The window is therefore ruled out as a means of egress for the killer. Now let us continue."

We walked around the property, Holmes checking the walls at various points for any traces of an intruder, and looking into various outbuildings. The last one we examined was set up as a carpentry workshop, and there were small wooden toys and wheeled animals in various stages of construction lying around.

"An unusual hobby for a lady" remarked Holmes. "You can see all the footprints in the sawdust are of Miss Amberdale's size. These toys are quite well-made and evidence some skill in woodwork."

We approached the door to leave, when Holmes suddenly stopped, staring. He whipped out his lens and studied the back of the door intently.

"What is it Holmes?"

"See for yourself, Watson," he replied, handing me his lens and moving aside.

The door was of stout timber construction, painted a dark green. About four feet from the floor was a group of small marks. Through the lens I could count nine small, narrow indentations in an area the size of my hand.

"It looks as if someone has repeatedly struck the door with some sort of thin-bladed tool – perhaps this narrow chisel on the bench here" I ventured.

"Perhaps. Or something else. You counted the marks?"

"Nine I thought."

"Fifteen actually," Holmes corrected. "There are nine in

the central group, but here, and here, you see there are six others scattered over the door, and even one on the door frame itself."

"And you think this is important?" I asked

"I'm beginning to get a glimmer of something," he admitted. "But we need more data. Let us speak to the servants, and see if they can help us."

We left the workshop and went back to the house. Lestrade was in the kitchen drinking tea. He poured a cup for Holmes and myself.

"Have you found any clues, Holmes?" he asked, with an undertone of desperation.

"Nothing substantial. But I have a question: Do you know why Miss Amberdale makes wooden toys? Is it purely for recreation, or is there a purpose?"

"So you've seen the workshop then," replied Lestrade. "Yes, I noticed that. She tells me that she does it for charitable reasons. The toys are given to a local orphanage."

"Interesting," mused Holmes. "Now can we have the servants in please, one at a time?"

\*\*\*\*\*\*\*\*\*\*

Half an hour later, we had interviewed the butler; the footman; the cook; the housekeeper; Harry the gardener; the groom; the scullery maid; two housemaids; and Miss Amberdale's maid without, it seemed, enriching our knowledge of the case. But we still had the last of the servants to see, the parlourmaid. She came into the kitchen and curtsied to us, a red-headed girl of seventeen or eighteen named Susan. She related to us the facts that she had discovered that Mr. Amberdale was not in his bedroom, his bed had not been slept in, and that she had helped in the subsequent search of the house for him.

"One final question, Susan, which I have asked all the others," said Holmes. "Has anything happened in the house recently that you consider strange, or outside the usual routine?"

"Well sir –" she hesitated – "Not really sir."

"Ah Susan, there is something, I think. Please tell us."

"Please, sir, Mr. Albert and Mr. Alfred are very nice gentlemen, and I'm sure it don't mean nothing, but – it just looks bad for them, what I heard, and I don't want to get them in trouble."

"It's all right Susan," said Holmes soothingly. "Whatever it is, it may have a completely different interpretation from what you imagine. Go on."

"Well sir, it was, let's see, three days ago now, in the afternoon. Miss Agnes was working at the antique shop, and Mr. Albert and Mr. Alfred came to visit their father. They had asked for tea in the parlour, and when it was ready I went to take it in. I was outside the parlour door when I heard raised voices, so I thought it best to wait, and not interrupt like."

"Quite so," said Holmes. "And what did you hear?"

"The brothers were asking for a loan, for their business, and Mr. Amberdale had refused. He said he had lent them money to start the business, and it was up to them to succeed or fail. The brothers were angry I suppose; they were saying they knew he had the money, Albert had a wife and baby to support, and did he mean the business to fail for want of a couple of hundred pounds. But Mr. Amberdale wouldn't be swayed."

"That's all you heard?"

"Yes sir. The brothers came out of the parlour then, looking very upset, and left the house. I took the tea in to Mr. Amberdale, and he also looked quite upset. I think he realised I must have overheard them quarrelling, for he said not to worry about the disturbance, everything was all right. And then he said something I didn't understand sir; he said now he knew how King somebody-or-other felt."

"Indeed! You don't remember the name of this King he mentioned?" asked Holmes.

"No, sir, I'm sorry. It was a short name, but it's gone clean out of my head," Susan said sorrowfully.

"Thank you, Susan; you may go now."

"Well now," said Lestrade excitedly, "that's the first hint we have had of a motive. The brothers argued with their father over money, and they are both locksmiths. Even though they and you, Holmes, say nobody could have locked and bolted the door from the corridor, perhaps it is possible in some manner unknown to you."

"I suppose it is possible, Inspector," replied Holmes, "but I think it unlikely. However, as you say, the brothers do have a motive. Do we know the dispositions of Amberdale's will?"

"I did ask Miss Amberdale about that earlier," said Lestrade. "Unless he changed it without her knowledge, she believes the will he made shortly after his inheritance left the antique business and five thousand pounds to her, and this property and the remainder of any cash equally divided between the sons. Although there was a deed of entail which allowed her to live in this house until she married, or until her death if she remained single."

"So all of the children have a motive then. All stood to inherit money, and either a share of this property or the business. But the fact remains, Lestrade, I doubt any court will convict anyone of this murder unless we can show how it was done, and how the murderer escaped and then locked up the room on the inside."

"Yes, I think you're right there, Holmes," said Lestrade dolefully. "So what is the next step?"

"I still have to go over the scene again, more thoroughly this time," said Holmes. "Every wall, the ceiling and the floor of that room need examining from both sides for any secret means of entry."

"Well as that is your forte, I shall leave you to it and make my preliminary report back at the Yard. I shall return later to see if you have made any progress."

After Lestrade had gone, Holmes seemed lost in thought. I started making some notes, when Holmes suddenly started and said "I have been a dullard, Watson. I have broken one of the basic precepts of detection, which I'm sure you remember: when you have eliminated the impossible...?"

"...whatever remains, however improbable, must be the truth," I finished. "So what is your theory then?"

"My theory is, Watson... unproven. Would you go into the murder room please, and wait for any instructions I might give. I will be inspecting in turn the rooms either side, the room below and the attic above. We shall need a pole of some description – hah, here is a broom that will do nicely! Let us see if we can discover the improbable truth!"

\*\*\*\*\*\*\*\*\*\*

For more than an hour, Holmes banged and tapped at the walls and ceiling of the room where Amberdale had met his death, firstly from the rooms either side, and then from the attic, having procured a lantern from the butler. He would occasionally shout at me to tap somewhere with the broom, mostly on the ceiling. Finally, he paced out the distance to the retreat from the end of the corridor, and went down the stairs to the first floor. I soon heard his muffled voice from beneath me.

"Watson! Stand where the body was and tap on the floor please!" he shouted.

I gave the floor three firm taps with the broom at the place requested.

"Now stand just inside the door and tap!"

I move to the door and did so. There was silence for a

minute.

'Watson, can you tell where I am tapping now?" he shouted, and I heard three sharp raps on the floorboards, as if someone were knocking on a door.

"Again!" I replied, bending closer to the floor, whence there came three more raps.

"Got it!" I shouted. I stood on the spot, about six feet in from the door and slightly to the left of it.

"Good! Stay there please."

Holmes appeared a minute later, his face and clothes streaked with cobwebs and dust.

"You were rapping right where I am standing, Holmes," I explained.

Holmes motioned me aside and threw himself on to the floor to examine where I had stood. Suddenly he lowered his head and sniffed the floor, then crawled around the room systematically sniffing at intervals of about three feet. Eventually, he stood up and dusted himself off.

"Well, Holmes?" I asked. "What have you found?"

"The very improbable truth, Watson," he said in a serious tone. "Our case is nearly complete, just one or two details to confirm. Oh dear! Look at the time, you must be starving, dear fellow. Please go down and ask the cook to provide some sustenance for you. I will join you shortly."

Puzzled, I went downstairs and begged a sandwich, which I was just finishing at the kitchen table when Holmes entered.

"Ah Watson! Ready to continue the investigation?"

"Certainly Holmes," I replied, wiping the crumbs from my mouth.

"I have enquired of the housekeeper, Mrs. Worthy, about Miss Amberdale's whereabouts. She says her mistress is in the library, and I have a question for her, as soon as I have availed myself of the amenities in the scullery to restore my state of cleanliness."

When Holmes had washed and made himself presentable, we walked to the library, knocked on the door and entered.

Miss Amberdale had changed into mourning black, and was seated at a large desk with a pile of papers in front of her.

"Good afternoon, Mr. Holmes, Doctor," she said. "I was just trying to find Father's will. Inspector Lestrade asked me about it earlier. What can I do for you?"

"Of course," said Holmes. "Miss Amberdale, I would like to know if you have any assistants at the antique shop, and if they are there today."

"A strange question!, But yes I have an assistant, Parker by name. I sent the groom to the shop to tell him of my father's death, and that I won't be in for a few days. He is knowledgeable and trustworthy, and will manage the shop for me until I am ready to return."

"Thank you Miss Amberdale. I will bid you good day, and please accept my condolences on your loss."

She nodded, and we left her there.

"Watson, I need to go on a short excursion, but I shall return soon and then we shall see if we can clear up this matter."

\*\*\*\*\*\*\*\*\*\*

An hour later, Inspector Lestrade returned, disappointed to find Holmes absent. He brought with him several newspapers, which all had headlines on a similar theme – an impossible murder, and police baffled.

"I don't know how they get their material sometimes, Doctor," he said in a melancholy fashion. "I certainly have not given any reporters any information. It makes the Yard look inefficient, and my superiors are giving me disapproving looks. I hope Mr. Holmes has discovered some clues or leads to follow."

It makes *you* look inefficient is what you mean, I thought to myself.

"Mr. Holmes expressed some confidence that the solution was at hand," I said, "so you may take comfort in that. He shouldn't be long."

In fact, it was only ten minutes later that Holmes arrived. We had moved into the parlour, and had just been provided with tea and biscuits by the redoubtable Mrs. Worthy. I poured Holmes a cup as he sat down. His countenance was difficult to interpret; he looked slightly pleased and serious at the same time.

"So! The good doctor tells me you may have the answer to this riddle," said Lestrade, with undisguised eagerness.

"Yes, I have solved the case," said Holmes slowly.

"Then for Heaven's sake tell me!" implored the inspector.

"Of course. I was just getting it clear in my mind. I will take you through my discoveries and my reasoning, but I warn you now the conclusion may shock you."

Lestrade and I looked at each other, as Holmes continued.

"The first thing I noticed was the curious weapon used. Although it served its purpose well enough, to kill Amberdale, it is, as I explained to Watson, a late medieval dagger called a rondel. And even though it was perhaps not unusual to find an antique in an antique dealer's house, it gave me some disquiet. But I could not fit that part of the puzzle into the whole at the time.

Then there was the crucial feature of the murder; how did the murderer escape from the room after killing Amberdale, then lock the door, leave the key in the lock on the inside, and draw the bolt as well? The window was snibbed tight and not opened for a long time; there was no ivy, tree or drainpipe to climb up, and no marks on the lawn from a ladder. An inspection of the lock and splintered door frame convinced me that the door had been locked and bolted before Harry broke it down. My initial examination of the room revealed no evidence of any secret entrance. I therefore applied my dictum, 'eliminate the impossible.' If it was impossible for anyone to have killed Amberdale then escape leaving the room locked, then Amberdale must have been killed from outside the room."

"From outside the room!" exclaimed Lestrade. "But how? Surely that presents another impossible situation?"

"Not impossible, just improbable," said Holmes. "I conducted a more detailed search of all the rooms adjacent, above and below the murder room, looking for any small opening through which the dagger could be thrown or propelled into the back of Mr. Amberdale. And eventually, I found it."

"Where?" Lestrade and I shouted together.

"The room under Mr. Amberdale's retreat is a guest bedroom, rarely used. In my examination of it, I discovered a wooden chair, the seat of which bore unmistakable signs of being stood on recently. I then looked around for somewhere a person would need to stand on a chair to gain access. The top shelf of the wardrobe beckoned. I used the chair myself to climb on this shelf and discovered that installed in the ceiling above it was a craftily concealed removable panel, some three feet by two feet in size. I removed this panel to see the floorboards of the room above, and a small area of the boards provided with extra wooden supports and a large hinge in the middle, to enable a pivoting action. With Watson's help I determined where I was in relation to the floor of the murder room. I then returned to the murder room, and was examining the floor to see how I had missed this pivoting area of the floor during my first inspection, when I noticed a particular aroma. It was only faintly present in other areas of the floor, but strong around this tiny trapdoor. You remember, Watson, I then sent you off to have your lunch?"

I nodded.

"While you were dining, I went back to the guest bedroom, and lying on the wardrobe shelf I found that the extra wooden supports were removable, and obviously designed to maintain the integrity of the floor and prevent the boards from creaking or giving way should anyone tread on them. I then pulled the small trapdoor down and saw that it gave me a view into the murder room towards the centre, where the rug had been. This then, was the means of getting the dagger into the room, but how was it done?

"Lying on the wardrobe shelf, one could not throw the dagger through the opening, so I reasoned it must have been propelled, and with some force to bury it up to the hilt in the body. My first thought was a small bow, but I could not see how that would send a dagger with some accuracy into the room. An arrow yes, but not a dagger. I then remembered the characteristic thinness of the blade and handle of our murder weapon, and the abrasions on the bone handle, and I had an inkling how it was done.

"I rejoined you, Watson, and discovering that Miss Amberdale had an assistant at the antique shop, I visited the establishment to speak with him. I found Mr. Parker to be quite an expert in antiques, and also quite garrulous. I learned that about two months ago, Miss Amberdale had purchased at auction several boxes of antiques from a deceased estate. Parker had initially sorted through them, making an inventory. There was a collection of several antique swords, knives, daggers, pikes, halberds and other assorted weapons, amongst other things. I asked him about a particular weapon, and he confirmed that there had been one in the collection, but when I asked him to show it to me, he could not lay his hands on it. He believes there is only one person who might know where it is."

"Are you suggesting that Miss Amberdale used the missing weapon Holmes?" I asked. "And that she killed her own father?"

"Surely not," said Lestrade in disbelief.

"Yes, Watson, I'm afraid so," said Holmes lugubriously. "Let us now see if she is still in the library, and put a question to her which may resolve this matter."

He got up as he spoke, and Lestrade and I followed him to the library. Holmes knocked and, we all went in. Miss Amberdale was still seated at the desk.

"Gentlemen, come in. Inspector, I have just found Father's will; it has not changed, so what I told you this morning about its provisions were correct."

She must have seen something in our faces, for she stood up and asked anxiously "What is it? Has something happened?"

"Mr. Holmes has a question for you, Miss," said Lestrade hesitantly.

"Yes Mr. Holmes?"

"Just this," said Holmes. "What did you do with the crossbow?"

Panic, rage, fear and resignation flashed across her face in quick succession, and then she slumped back down into the chair.

"I see your reputation is well-deserved, Mr. Holmes," she said evenly. "You obviously know all."

"Not all, Miss Amberdale. I know the who and the how, but not the why. Was it really only to hasten your inheritance?"

"Only partly, I assure you. My father was not a nice man, as my brothers will also tell you. He was harsh, miserly, and demanding. I ran the shop for him for a pitiful allowance, no matter how much profit I made for him. Not that he needed it – he had £1,500 a year from investing his inheritance, which was more than enough to run this estate. But he loved his antiques more than he loved his children. We all hated him. But I especially had another reason to hate him. It was his penny-pinching that left our trap in a dangerous state, as he refused to pay to have it maintained. The wheel broke, my mother was killed and I was left in this wretched condition, destined never to marry. He stole my future, Mr. Holmes!"

She said these last words with much bitterness.

"So you decided to murder him to revenge yourself upon him, and not just to enrich yourself," said Holmes. "When you found the crossbow and the rondel in the new items you bought at auction for the shop, you realised the crossbow could be easily modified to fire it. Then you just had to find a way to kill him so that no suspicion would fall on you. However, your scheming mind soon devised a way so that suspicion could fall on no-one; an impossible murder in a locked room. Your skill at carpentry made it easy to cut out the ceiling panel, make the trapdoor in the floor above, and cleverly support it so it wouldn't give way."

Miss Amberdale smiled. "I don't think it immodest of me to say it was a plan that would have fooled most people, Mr. Holmes. But you are not most people, are you? What gave me away?"

"Once I had decided that it was impossible for anyone to have killed your father in the room and then escape leaving it locked in the manner it was, it was clear the dagger had somehow been propelled into the room from outside the room. That meant there must have been an opening. I found it by a process of elimination, and after I did two clues fell neatly into place which confirmed the method. Firstly, the marks in your workshop door – they were the result of your practice with the crossbow. There were several wide shots to begin with, but then you perfected your technique. Did you not note, Watson that the central grouping of indentations were clustered around a knot in the wood? It was an obvious target.

"The repeated test shots also caused the abrasions on the

bone handle of the rondel as it left the crossbow at speed. Then I noticed a particular scent emanating strongly from the trapdoor, but much more faintly from the rest of the floor. I enquired of the butler, and he produced a tin of floor wax which matched the scent. You had noticed in your testing of the trapdoor that after it had been opened, the wax and dust around its edges all disappeared, leaving it relatively easy to see. So the sequence of events was as follows. Your father went into his retreat after dinner. You went into the guest room, climbed onto the wardrobe shelf with your weapon, and waited until you judged his footsteps placed him where you wanted. You quickly opened the trapdoor, which is almost silent in its operation. You saw him there with his back to you, and you shot your father with the rondel fired from the crossbow.

"Then you went to bed, though how you managed to sleep is beyond me. In the morning, after Harry had broken down the door and you had sent him to fetch the police, you sought to disguise the trapdoor by repolishing that part of the floor, the wax filling in all the cracks rendered empty by the trapdoor's opening. But this fresh floor wax gave off a stronger smell than the rest of the floor, which had been polished probably weeks earlier."

"Yes, I see now that was a mistake. To think that I am to be hanged for polishing a floor! Very well Mr. Holmes, I give you best. The crossbow is hidden in an old wine crate in the cellar. If there's nothing else, it must be time for the cuffs, Inspector!" she laughed, holding her hands out.

\*\*\*\*\*\*\*\*\*\*

Lestrade had left with his prisoner, still seemingly unable to comprehend that Agnes Amberdale had murdered her father in cold blood, and in such a devious fashion. We were on our way back to Baker Street in a hansom, Holmes having been silent the whole trip. Suddenly he gave a curious, hollow laugh.

"What is it Holmes?" I enquired.

"After some pondering, it has just occurred to me, Watson! The king! Susan said that after arguing with his sons, Amberdale had remarked that now he knew how King somebody felt."

"Yes, I remember."

"How is your Shakespeare, Watson?"

"Of course! King Lear – I'm afraid I don't recall the exact quote, but I'm sure you do."

"Indeed, and it is a very apt one."

Holmes was a fine actor, and I still recall to this day how even above the noise of our hansom's wheels on the cobbles, he managed to recite the Bard's famous line in a dramatic yet poignant fashion.

"How sharper than a serpent's tooth it is to have a thankless child."

# THE CASE OF THE NERVOUS NEIGHBOUR

"Mr. Holmes, there is a Mrs. Marwood downstairs who thinks her neighbour might have murdered his wife. Are you able to see her?"

Holmes and I both looked up from our newspapers at this startling pronouncement from Mrs. Hudson, who had knocked and entered our sitting room with what appeared to be a certain amount of annoyance. The state of her apron and a streak of flour on her face made it clear she had been interrupted in her baking by the lady in question.

"Thank you, Mrs. Hudson, we are disengaged at present. Please send her up and return to your kitchen," replied Holmes, raising his paper to conceal a small grin.

Upon referring to my notes, I find it was a cool morning in the early spring of 1895 that Mrs. Marwood ascended our stairs to bring her suspicions to Holmes. As she entered, Holmes gave her one of his quick, appraising glances and bade her sit by the small blaze crackling away in our fireplace.

"My condolences on your recent loss, madam. However, it is well that these trying times are rendered more bearable by the comfortable situation you have been left in; so often these days widowhood is attended by poverty, and of course a treasured pet will always ease distress," he said.

Familiar as I was with his methods, I noted the newness and quality of Mrs. Marwood's mourning dress, hat and gloves, and the ginger cat hairs which had given rise to Holmes's remarks.

"You are right Mr. Holmes," she exclaimed. "I lost my dear Henry only two months ago, and he has left me with more than enough to see out my days. And yes, it's true, Tumblekins has been a godsend these past weeks."

"This is my friend and colleague Dr. Watson, Mrs. Marwood. Now pray tell us why you believe your neighbour has done away with his wife."

Mrs. Marwood was, I judged, in her seventies, with a diminutive figure. There was however, a sprightliness of step, a glint in her eyes, and a determination about the chin which indicated that her story should be treated seriously. She was not one given to imaginings or hysterics I thought, as she began to speak.

"My name is Amelia Marwood, Mr. Holmes, and I live at 23 Argyll Road in Kensington. As you surmised, I am now a widow; my husband, Henry, was a successful furniture importer for many years, and his passing has left me financially secure. I want to talk to you about my neighbours, Mr. and Mrs. Arden. They moved into number 25 about nine years ago now, and I have found them charming, polite and thoroughly decent in all ways. They are I suppose in their mid-thirties, and Mr. Arden – his name is William – is a solicitor, and his wife is named Grace. They have no children.

Your opening remarks Mr. Holmes, make it clear that your reputation for observation and deduction is well-deserved. I would like to think that I too, have a small gift of observation, and a much smaller one of deduction – I see by the small yellow stain on his tie that Dr. Watson has had eggs for breakfast, for example."

"Capital!" exclaimed Holmes. "A lady after our own heart, eh, Watson?"

"Indeed," I said, self-consciously trying to clean my tie with a napkin.

"A lot of my day is spent sitting doing needlework or reading in my bay window, observing what goes on in my street and making insignificant deductions about the characters or occupations of passersby. But I never know if I am right, of course. However, I will tell you what I have observed lately."

"Please do, madam, this promises to be most interesting," said Holmes.

"Today is Monday. A week ago exactly, I noticed a shabbily dressed workingman leaning on a lamp post across the street. I had not seen him before, and we do not get many people just loafing, so I was – well, not suspicious, but interested. He smoked two cigarettes in the twenty minutes I watched him, and he seemed to be looking at me a lot of the time. But then Mr. Arden left his house next door to go to work as usual; he takes the train at the Kensington Underground station on the High Street. The man instantly crossed the street and began to follow him, so I realised he had been watching the Ardens' front door, not me. I was curious as you can imagine, and even more so when in the evening, Mr. Arden returned from work, and a different man, much taller and slightly better-dressed, appeared to follow him home and take up the position across the street next to the lamp post, watching his house. I debated whether to let the Ardens know about these men, but in the end I decided to wait and see if the situation continued."

"And it did, I presume?" asked Holmes.

"It did, Mr. Holmes. The next day, the same man followed Mr. Arden in the morning, and the same taller man followed him home in the evening. I determined that the next day, Wednesday, I would tell Grace about it when we went on our regular shopping expedition to the market together. But when I knocked on their door at ten o'clock that day, there was no answer. Several times during the day I knocked, but to no avail. It was not like Grace to let me down like that, without a word. Also, Mr. Holmes, even if Grace were not at home, where was their maid, Angela? Why did she not answer the door? Later, when I saw that Mr. Arden had returned from work, I went to see him, and Mr. Holmes, he was a changed man."

"How so?"

"Well, he had always been polite and charming as I said; a man of friendly and cheerful disposition. But as soon as he opened the door, I could tell something was wrong. He was quite tense, and when I asked him why Grace had missed our usual shopping appointment, he looked very upset. He said she had suddenly been called out of town to visit her mother in Leicester, and he was sorry for not telling me earlier. I asked him where Angela was, and he said she had accompanied Grace to Leicester. He kept looking over his shoulder into the house as he spoke, and I would describe his demeanor as agitated and nervous. I was then going to tell him of the men I had seen following him, but he made an excuse and bundled me back out on to the street in a rush. It was most unlike him Mr. Holmes."

"Now Mrs. Marwood, did you observe the men following him to and from work on that Wednesday?" Holmes enquired.

"No, sir, they did not."

"Hah! That is important, said Holmes, sitting up. "Note that, Watson. Now, Mrs. Marwood, Your theory then, is that the polite and charming Mr. Arden has murdered his wife, and the men following him are – whom do you suppose?"

"I thought they might be plain clothes policemen, investigating him, perhaps trying to find where he has hidden the body. But now I say that out loud, it does seem most unlikely, as does William murdering Grace."

"Hmmm. When did you last see Mrs. Arden?

"It was on the Saturday before I noticed the men following Mr. Arden. We took tea at her home in the afternoon."

"And she was her usual self, you would say?"

"Certainly, she acted perfectly normally. But I have not yet told you all, Mr. Holmes."

"No? Do go on Mrs. Marwood," replied Holmes, slumping

back down in his chair.

"As I said, I saw Mr. Arden on Wednesday evening. The day after, he went to work at the usual time, with again no-one following him that I could see. But during the day, I heard noises next door. Footsteps mainly, and sounds like people moving furniture, some banging and thudding on and off, and once a loud crash as if something heavy had been dropped. I thought it very odd, as Mr. Arden was at work and Grace supposedly in Leicester with Angela. I was so curious that in the afternoon, I went and knocked on their door, but there was no answer.

After Mr. Arden had arrived home that evening, I took over a steak and kidney pie I had made, with the excuse that as Grace and the maid were away I wanted to ensure he ate well. Again he appeared nervous, but he thanked me for my kindness. I told him about the noises in his house I had heard during the day, and he just laughed and said it was some workmen he had employed to look at a problem with the drains. He laughed, but his eyes held a secret terror. Mr. Holmes, that man is frightened to death of something!"

Holmes looked thoughtful for a while, then he asked "these alleged workmen – did you notice any van or wagon outside the Ardens' house? Surely they must have come in a conveyance of some sort, with their tools?"

"No there was no tradesman's wagon Mr. Holmes, nor did I see anyone arrive at or depart from their house on foot all day, excepting Mr. Arden and a postman. The next day, Friday last, my maid Lizzie brought me my mid-morning tea, and she mentioned that there were workmen making some noise in the Ardens' back yard. I went upstairs and looked down at their yard from the window of my spare room, and indeed there were two men digging a trench. And I'm sure you can deduce who they were."

"No doubt the same two men you had seen following Mr.

Arden on Monday and Tuesday," Holmes replied.

"Exactly," said Mrs. Marwood with a smile. "Is this not an intriguing case, Mr. Holmes?"

"It is indeed, Mrs. Marwood," said Holmes, filling and lighting his pipe. "And what of the last two days – have you seen or heard anything?"

"On Saturday they were still excavating the Ardens' yard, making other trenches and holes, and even lifting some flagstones and uprooting some plants. Yesterday they were not outside that I observed, but the banging and crashing noises in the house returned. I don't know what they are doing, Mr. Holmes, but it certainly has nothing to do with the drains!"

"Quite," said Holmes, rising. "Your case has points of interest, and your detailed observations have provided much for me to think about. I should be happy to look into this matter for you. I shall do some research today, and call on you tomorrow. In the meantime, please do not visit the Ardens' house."

"You think there may be danger, Mr. Holmes?" said Mrs. Marwood keenly.

"Possibly," he replied. "I don't believe Mr. Arden is a wifc-murderer, but certainly something is happening in that house in which a woman of your years should not be involved. Good day, Mrs. Marwood. Watson, would you –" he gestured to the door.

After I had shown Mrs. Marwood down the stairs and found her a cab, I returned to our sitting room to find Holmes staring into the fire, puffing at his pipe.

"Well, Watson, this is a mystery! Ordinary folk being followed, a disappearing wife, workmen who neither arrive nor leave but make noises and dig holes, and a very nervous neighbour. Have you any thoughts?"

"It seems to me that if Mrs. Marwood has not seen these so-called workmen arrive or leave, and nor do they have a cart, then they must be living in the house. Honest tradesmen do not reside in one's house while working, so it is clear that Arden's story about the drains is a fabrication."

"Yes, I concur Watson – ah, here is Mrs. Hudson with our luncheon. After we have partaken of this cold beef, cheese and pickles, we shall commence our investigation!"

\*\*\*\*\*\*\*\*\*\*

A short while later we were in a cab ratting along to an address in Kensington, given to the cabman by Holmes. I put a question to him.

"Holmes, surely the simplest solution to this problem is to see this fellow Arden? He obviously knows what is going on – probably something to do with his wife, since she has not been seen – and it has changed his behaviour. He goes to work and returns home to give the appearance of normality, but he must know about these two men doing something noisy in his house and digging up his yard all day."

"True, Watson. Yet I think we must tread carefully, and attempt to discover the meaning of this riddle for ourselves before we apply to Mr. Arden."

"So will you see his employer as part of your investigation?" I asked.

"Not immediately, unless our first line of attack reveals nothing. I would suggest that his employer has noted that Mr. Arden is behaving a trifle oddly these last few days, perhaps distracted in his work on occasion, and Arden has made some excuse to account for it. But whatever he has said to them is not sufficient for them to allow him a leave of absence. I fancy we shall learn more where we are going."

"Which is?" I prompted.

"Barclay & Barclay, the nearest house-agent to the Ardens, and by chance also the largest in the area. There are others, but there is a reasonable probability they will have the information we need."

We pulled up to the establishment he had named a few minutes later, and after presenting his card to a clerk, Holmes and I were soon being ushered into the office of the manager, Mr. Shaw, a small, rotund fellow in his fifties.

"A pleasure to meet you sir. What can I do for the famous Mr. Sherlock Holmes?"

Holmes looked a trifle pained. "Famous? This is your doing, Watson; your literary efforts have preceded us."

"Indeed Mr. Holmes, I have read the good doctor's accounts of your exploits with interest," beamed Shaw. "Please sit down and tell me how I may assist you. Are you considering purchasing a house in the area, or are you –" he dropped his voice "–on a case?"

"We are indeed on a case, Mr. Shaw," said Holmes. "The house at number 25 Argyll Road; did your agency handle the sale to Mr. and Mrs. Arden, who I believe bought the place some nine years ago?"

"Oh yes, Mr. Holmes, I handled that sale myself as it happens. They were a nice couple, I remember – a solicitor wasn't he, with a very handsome and charming wife?"

"Your memory is excellent, sir. Now I will test it again. Can you tell us who owned the property before the Ardens?"

"Um, let me think. The name escapes me momentarily, but I will look it it up for you. However, I do remember the circumstances, as they were rather tragic."

"Tragic? How so?" asked Holmes.

He turned to a shelf behind him, selected a large ledger and started leafing through it before replying.

"The house had remained empty for some months before the Ardens bought it, I recall. The previous owner, was a single gentleman, a bank manager by profession. He was struck and killed by a runaway carthorse, a terrible accident. The house was left to a distant relative in the country, and I sold it on their behalf to the Ardens. Ah, yes, here it is. The gentleman was called Mr. Joseph Newman."

"Newman," said Holmes. "Yes, Joseph Newman. The name echoes in my mind for some reason. A decade ago, but – thank you Mr. Shaw, for your invaluable information. Come, Watson, we must be elsewhere!"

We returned to our cab, which we had instructed to wait for us. The cabman was one of our regulars, Jack by name, and like a great many of his fraternity, he knew that Holmes paid well. He might hire a cab for a short trip or a whole day; he might want another cab or private carriage followed; he might even leap out without paying and run after someone on foot; but the cabbies knew that if they went to Baker Street afterwards, Holmes would settle their account, with a decent bonus.

"Scotland Yard, please, Jack," Holmes called out as we jumped in.

"I think I see your reasoning Holmes," I said, once we were on our way. "You think these men in the Ardens' house are looking for something hidden by this previous owner, Newman, hence all the digging and the noises in the house, which are a result of them conducting a search. Do you have any idea what it is they are after?"

"Not yet Watson, but I think the records at the Yard will help us. It was clear to me that these men had followed Arden for two days to learn his routine. Then, sometime on the Tuesday night, they either broke in or inveigled their way in through some pretence by knocking on the front door; probably the latter. This is why Arden was not followed on Wednesday. It was also clear that whatever they wanted dated back to a previous owner of the house; if it was something the Ardens had hidden, I feel sure they would have divulged its hiding place to secure their release and get these men out of the house."

"And Mrs. Arden? Have they killed her?"

"I think it more probable that she is being held hostage within the house. If she were dead, Arden would have no reason not to go to the police while ostensibly at work. I think her life depends on him returning from work every day, and this accounts for his agitation when Mrs. Marwood has seen him. These men do not want enquiries made after him, so they could not keep him a prisoner as well, and had to let him continue his normal attendance at work."

"Whatever it is must be well-hidden, Holmes. This is the sixth day of their occupation of the house, and they must have turned the place upside-down by now, and searched the yard without any result. I shudder to think what state the house must be in by this time, and I also fear for Mrs. Arden; what condition must she be in after nearly a week of confinement? We shall have to hurry, Holmes."

"Yes, Watson, we shall. When I have dredged the name of Joseph Newman from the files at the Yard, we will know who and what we are dealing with. We can then enlist the aid of an inspector and some constables to resolve the situation."

\*\*\*\*\*\*\*\*\*\*

An hour later Holmes gave a triumphant shout, raising a file in the air. We were in the Records Room of the Yard, and Inspector Bradstreet and I had been helping Holmes look through the files for Joseph Newman.

"Here it is, Inspector! The London and County Bank robbery in '85!"

"Yes, by Jove, I was a sergeant at the time, though I don't recall the details," said Bradstreet.

"The Paddington branch of the bank was burgled on the night of Saturday the 21st November," said Holmes. "They got away with almost £4,000, and the theory at the time was that they had inside help. The manager of the branch, Joseph

100

Newman, was one of several employees to fall under suspicion, but nothing was ever proved against anyone in the bank. The three perpetrators, however, were arrested two days later on the information of one of their neighbours, who overheard them talking about what they had done. None of the money was ever recovered, and the three went to prison for twelve years. I was not involved in the case, but I followed it in the papers at the time."

"Let me see their names, Holmes, and I shall see what became of them," said Bradstreet.

Holmes passed the file to the Inspector, who looked up each man in another index.

"Mawkins died in prison in 1891," said the inspector. "Cartwright, the leader, was released for good behaviour some three weeks ago, and Hardy... the same, released three weeks ago. You think Cartwright and Hardy are the two men in the Arden's house, and that they are searching for the proceeds of the robbery?"

"I do, Inspector. Their man on the inside must have been Newman, and for some reason it was decided, possibly because he would be less suspected, that he would keep the money safe until the hue and cry had died down. So he took it and hid it. Then he was unfortunately killed in an accident, taking the hiding place to his grave. Cartwright knows, or at least hopes, that the money is hidden on the property and not elsewhere, so when they became free men they lost no time in devising a plan to occupy the house for a length of time sufficient to find it. We must now devise a plan of our own to gain entrance to the Ardens' house and rescue Mrs. Arden and possibly the maid. Arden himself will still be at work for another two hours I should think. It will be difficult, Mrs. Arden being a hostage, and her captors hardened criminals who are no doubt armed."

"What do you suggest, Holmes?" asked the inspector.

"We will need eight or ten men, all plainclothed, armed and aware of Mrs. Arden's presence in the house. Have them ready in a nondescript covered wagon, parked out of sight of the house, say about six houses eastward from the Ardens'. I think I should first see if Mrs. Marwood has any intelligence on the state of affairs next door; she is very observant and may know of something which may help us."

"Very good, Holmes. I shall organise a raiding party of men experienced with firearms, and do as you say. We should be there in thirty minutes."

"Excellent. Watson and I will see what Mrs. Marwood has to say, then join you to plan the denouement."

\*\*\*\*\*\*\*\*\*\*

We waited a few minutes until Bradstreet and his constables were ready, then we all left together for Argyll Road. The inspector was at the reins of a grocer's van, and we took a hansom. We both pulled up at the place agreed, short of the Arden and Marwood residences. Holmes and I got out and walked up to number 23, where we saw Mrs. Marwood reading in her bay window. She got up when she saw us, and opened the door immediately when Holmes knocked, bidding us enter.

"Good afternoon, Mr. Holmes, Dr. Watson," she said. "Something must be urgent, as you've come today and not tomorrow. What is it?"

"I believe, madam, that I have uncovered the main facts of the case. But please, as Mrs. Arden is in great danger, tell us if you have anything to report from your observations today."

"Just one noteworthy incident, Mr. Holmes. Mr. Arden went to work as usual, and there have been some noises next door, though far fewer than on the other days. But about two hours ago, the man I first saw following Mr. Arden came out of the house, hailed a passing cab and went off in it."

Holmes's brow furrowed. "He may have gone simply to

fetch more supplies; they have been here a week after all. Or, it may be that the situation has changed, though if they had found what they wanted they would presumably both have left. Can you show us your spare room, Mrs. Marwood? I would like to see their yard from its window. Perhaps that will tell us something."

"Up the stairs, first on the right, Mr. Holmes. It will be quicker if you go without me. My legs –"

"Thank you, madam," he said, bounding up the stairs. I followed as fast as I could. Once in the spare room, we went over to the window, and Holmes drew the curtains back a few inches so we could both see into the Ardens' back yard. It was immediately apparent that something was happening. There was a closed carriage in the laneway at the rear of the house, with the driver's seat empty. Even as we watched, there appeared from the rear of the Ardens' house two men, carrying a well-dressed blonde woman, either dead or unconscious, by the feet and shoulders. Holmes and I turned as one, and sprinted back down the stairs and then to the rear of the house. We burst through the kitchen, causing Mrs. Marwood's maid to scream and drop a pan she was carrying, then charging out of the back door into the yard, we ran down a short path to the gate providing access to the lane.

Holmes threw open the gate, and I followed him through it, just in time to see one of the men climbing into the driver's seat as the other was climbing into the carriage itself. They both saw us, and the driver immediately shouted and whipped up the horses, as we started to run towards them. The second man closed the carriage door then leaned out of the window, pointing a pistol at us. Then he fired, and as the carriage gathered speed, he fired again. Holmes, put his arm around my shoulders and dragged me to the ground, winding me. I looked up, and saw the carriage disappear from view as it turned out of the lane and into the roadway some fifty yards ahead.

I rose to my feet, and took a step forward to continue the chase, but Holmes held my arm.

"They're away, Watson, it's no use," he said bitterly.

"What are we going to do Holmes? They have Mrs. Arden, and surely they wouldn't have taken her body if they had murdered her? She must be alive."

"Yes, I fancy she was just unconscious, though why they took her escapes me. Perhaps we shall find a clue in the house. But first, Watson, in order for me to continue in this case, I must beg a favour."

His voice had a curious strained quality, and I turned to look at him. There was a large bloodstain on his left upper arm.

"One of your best field dressings, Watson, if you please... " he said, as he slumped into my arms.

\*\*\*\*\*\*\*\*\*\*

Fifteen minutes later, Holmes was sitting in Mrs. Marwood's parlour, sipping brandy while I finished cleaning and bandaging the wound in his bicep. Fortunately, the bullet had gone straight through the arm, and Mrs. Marwood's medicine chest had provided the alcohol to clean the entry and exit wounds, the lint padding, and the bandage. The maid Lizzie had been sent down the road to fetch Inspector Bradstreet, who had posted constables at the front and rear of the Ardens' house and sent the rest back to the Yard. I had asked him to refrain from entering the house, so as not to disturb any small traces or clues that the men had left, and he had agreed, knowing Holmes's methods.

"That was a close shave, Mr. Holmes," the inspector said, "though it was a lucky shot to hit you at all, trying as he was to hit a moving target from a moving carriage."

"Luck is a strange mistress, Inspector," Holmes replied. "As you say, it was a difficult shot, so am I unlucky to have been hit? Or having been hit, am I lucky it is not a more serious wound? No matter, it is more important now that I examine the house next door, to discover anything that may point us towards the motive for abducting Mrs. Arden, or, if we are lucky," and he smiled, "where they have taken her. We also need to ascertain the whereabouts of their maid, Angela, for as we now know, Mrs. Arden did not go to Leicester. Therefore her maid did not go with her, and I am wondering where she may be."

I opened my mouth, but closed it as Holmes looked at me.

"Yes, Watson, please spare me your remonstrances. I am aware of my less than optimum health, and that I should probably be in hospital or at least resting at home. But Mrs. Arden's fate is in our hands, and I cannot tarry while I recover fully. I will try not to exert myself unnecessarily, and I have you as my attending physician for any running repairs that may be needed."

"Very well, Holmes, I defer to the gravity of the situation, but please be careful."

"Always, Watson. Always," he said rising. He turned to look in a small mirror on the wall.

"Mrs. Marwood's excellent brandy has put the colour back in my cheeks, so let us proceed."

We all left Mrs. Marwood's and went to the Ardens' front door, which was locked. Holmes produced his small leather case of lockpicks, and in a time which left Inspector Bradstreet shaking his head and the constable on duty open-mouthed, the door was opened. We saw at once some of the results of the week-long search; all the paintings and prints which adorned the walls had been tossed aside, and some of the floorboards had been taken up. However, the hall table which had once been against the wall had been placed in the centre of the hall, and on it was placed a sheet of paper.

"They didn't mean Mr. Arden to miss this note," murmured Holmes, as he stepped into the hall and picked up the sheet.

"It is addressed to Mr. Arden," Holmes said, reading it swiftly and passing it to the Inspector. I stood next to him and we read it together.

*Mr. Arden*

*It is not safe for us here any more, so we have gone.*
*We havn't found the money. We want you to keep looking for it, and to make sure you do, we have your wife.*
*We will take care of her, but if you do not find the money it will be badly for her. Do not tell the police! We will be in touch soon.*

Holmes's voice came from inside the parlour.

"Please stay in the hall, gentlemen, until I have examined the ground floor rooms."

During the next hour, Bradstreet and I watched Holmes from doorways as he inspected every room in the house. They all presented the same features – furniture piled up so carpets could be pulled up to reveal the floorboards, floorboards pulled up to reveal the joists, built-in cupboards torn away from the walls, anything hung on a wall removed in a vain search for a secret compartment or cache of banknotes. After Holmes came down from the attic, I could see his efforts had taken a toll – he looked tired and pale.

"Sit down, old man," I suggested. "I'll get you a drink."

Bradstreet found an armchair on its side, and righted it for Holmes to sit. He placed a small table in front of it, and Holmes started to arrange on it a range of objects. I put a glass of water in front of him, from which he immediately took a long draught.

"I know what cigarettes these men smoke, the alcohol they prefer, which teeth are missing from one of their mouths, their heights, their hair colours and their boot sizes and shapes. Also, one of them has lice. But none of this information helps us find Mrs. Arden," he said, shaking his head. "However, I have not discovered, as I feared I might, the body of the Ardens' maid. I am hopeful that is a good sign."

I looked at the objects on the table which had revealed some of these things to Holmes. There were a number of cigarette packets, a gin bottle, a half-eaten apple, and some hairs.

Bradstreet picked up the apple and looked at it closely.

"Yes, I see from the bite impression the fellow who ate this is missing... yes, three teeth. But their heights and boots; you must have found footprints then?"

"Yes, the attic is very dusty and there are several perfect footprints from both men. Their stride lengths gives me the height of one as just over six feet, and the shorter is about five feet seven inches. But these measurements would be known from your prison records," Holmes said wearily. "The hairs I found in the makeshift beds they had been using, as well as several dead lice in one of them."

A sudden commotion came from the front door. Bradstreet went to find out the cause, and returned a minute later with a well-dressed but very distraught man. I recognised him from one of the photographs I had picked up from the floor in the dining room earlier.

"This is Mr. William Arden, gentlemen. Mr. Arden, this is Mr. Sherlock Holmes and Dr. Watson," said Bradstreet. "

"Mr. Holmes – the detective? You have to help me find Grace! The inspector says she has been abducted, in order that I should keep looking for their damned money!" he shouted.

"Please, Mr. Arden, compose yourself. Everything that can be done will be done. Another chair please, Bradstreet. Now sit down Mr. Arden, and tell us what has happened here in the past week."

"These two men – they knocked on the door last Tuesday night. Angela was washing the dinner dishes, so I answered the door and found myself facing a pistol. They came in and told

Grace and I that there was something hidden in the house that was theirs by rights, and that they would be staying until they found it. I was to keep going to work so as to not attract suspicion by my absence, and Grace was to be held here as a surety that I would return every night, and so that I would not inform the police.

"I asked them what would happen to Angela, and they said she would be in the way and I was to dismiss her, and send her away that night with five pounds in lieu of notice. I objected at first, but the taller man, who was obviously the leader, held the gun to Grace's head and told me to go do it. I had to go into the kitchen and tell poor Angela, a thoroughly good and reliable servant, to pack her things and get out for no reason. She did not understand of course, and cried bitterly. I didn't have a five pound note as it happened, so I was compelled to give her ten, but even that was little recompense for losing her situation. When this is over, I will rehire her instantly of course, but she must think very badly of me at the moment."

"At least she is safe then," said Holmes. "We were worried about her."

"Anyway, after she left the house, we were both locked in our bedroom, and threatened to keep quiet," Arden continued. "I only slept fitfully as you can imagine, and I could hear one of them outside the door all night guarding us. Then in the morning, they had Grace make breakfast for everyone, and I readied myself for work. And this pattern repeated every day except the Saturday and Sunday of course. Every night I returned home to see a greater level of destruction of the house or the back yard. I think their efforts were slowed by having to guard us at night; one of them got little sleep every night I suspect, which meant sleeping during some part of the day and leaving only the other to perform the search. They didn't talk very much in our presence, but I did once overhear one of them – not the man in charge, but his companion – talking in vulgar terms of what he would do with his share of the money when they found it. That is when I knew what they were after. Today I went to work as usual, and upon my return I find you all here – how did you come to realise what was happening?"

Holmes smiled. "Your very observant and kindly neighbour, Mrs. Marwood came to see me."

"Of course," said Arden, "She is a delightful woman. She came to see me twice during the week, and I'm afraid I was a little short with her."

"She will understand you were under duress, and in fact, your agitation was the very thing that made her worry enough to consult me. She had also noticed you were being followed by the two men earlier in the week."

"Goodness! Was I?" Arden exclaimed. "I certainly hadn't noticed. But now Mr. Holmes, Inspector; what are we to do? They have taken Grace and –"

"Of course!" shouted Holmes, rising from his chair. "Fool that I am, I have not yet checked the yard for any indications they may have left as they carried her away."

He walked swiftly to the kitchen and out the back door, and the three of us followed him to watch, Bradstreet from the doorway, and Arden and I from the kitchen window. Holmes looked carefully at the ground, using the flagstones to step on and avoiding the holes and the earth that had been thrown up. He went all the way to the gate, twice picking up something from the ground, looking at it through his lens, sniffing it and placing it in the little envelopes he carried for the purpose. He then went out into the lane and returned a few minutes later, looking much happier than he had been.

"We may have had a little luck, gentlemen," he remarked. "The newly turned earth has taken impressions well anyway, but they are deeper than they would have been as they were carrying a weight. The shorter man was the one who left the house earlier to fetch the carriage, and it is his footprints that have left small clumps of material brought here from other locations. I am hopeful this is to where they have returned with Mrs. Arden. I have also seen their carriage tracks in the lane; one of the wheels has been repaired and leaves a characteristic mark in its rut. If I see it again anywhere, I will know it is they."

"What is the material you found in the footprints?" asked Bradstreet.

Holmes went into the kitchen and emptied the contents of the two envelopes on to the table. They looked like two samples of soil; one dark and damp-looking, the other dryer, lighter in colour and with some fibrous material in it.

"Now then, Inspector, here is an object lesson in why the Yard should invest in the scientific study of soils. What do you observe and smell here?"

Bradstreet looked at the two little piles on the table, then bent over and smelt them. Holmes motioned for me to do the same.

"The dark sample is mud, I believe, with a peculiar aroma. The other reminds me of horse dung, which lies about London in great quantities on the roads," remarked Bradstreet.

"Your observations are correct, Inspector, but it is what we can deduce from our observations that is important. The mud is Thames riverbank mud; there are two tiny molluscs embedded in it, and the smell is that of certain chemicals used in tanning leather. I have seen and smelt this type of mud many times in my walks along the river at low tide, where the tanning factories pipe their waste into the water. The other sample is indeed dung, but I believe it comes from a cow, not a horse, though it is some time since I studied animal droppings. It also has small specks of what appear to be dried blood in it.

"My conclusions are, then, that the man who fetched the carriage went off in a hansom as Mrs. Marwood observed. He went to the Thames and took a boat across, stepping in the mud as he exited on the opposite bank. He then went to a location which I hope is their hideout, where he picked up the dung on his boot. There are not many cows in the metropolis, and I think that the only place he would tread on cow dung with blood in it is a slaughterhouse. These men need privacy and no inquisitive neighbours if they are to hold Mrs. Arden captive, so on the balance of probability I think they are in an abandoned slaughterhouse near a tannery, on the south bank of the river. I know of only one location which fits this criteria."

"Mr. Holmes, you are amazing!" cried Arden. "This exceeds all that I have heard about you. You have worked out where Grace is from bits of mud and dung. Let us go there now and –"

"Caution, Mr. Arden!" interrupted Holmes. "My deductions are only probabilities. But certainly, we must investigate the strongest chance first."

"How do you want to tackle this, Holmes?" asked Bradstreet.

"I think, with your permission, Inspector, that this is a situation where a covert survey is in order to first establish the lay of the land. I will go in disguise and wander about the area looking for any clues. We may need your armed constables, but it would certainly be safer for Mrs. Arden if we knew where all the parties were located."

"Holmes, you are wounded. And what of your own safety?" I asked, already anticipating his answer.

"Thank you for your concern, dear fellow, but a damsel in distress outweighs all other factors."

\*\*\*\*\*\*\*\*\*\*

An hour later, darkness was falling as Holmes and I stepped out of a hansom near a dilapidated warehouse. Inspector Bradstreet was again waiting just down the street in the grocer's van, with eight constables and Mr. Arden in the rear. We had raced back to Baker Street so Holmes could disguise himself as an old seafarer, and thence to this rundown district near the river. We had also taken the opportunity to arm ourselves.

"What is your plan then?" I asked in a low voice.

"To reconnoitre the area, to find out if those whom we seek are in fact there, and if so their disposition; and then to ascertain the best means of effecting the rescue of Mrs. Arden," Holmes replied. "You stay in this doorway out of sight, and I shall return when I am able."

"Good luck then."

He nodded, and vanished into the gloom of an alley.

The minutes ticked by. It seemed an eternity, but in actual fact it was only about twenty minutes later that I saw a dark figure coming down the alley. It was Holmes. He squeezed into the doorway with me.

"We are fortunate, Watson. I walked up to the main gateway into the slaughterhouse, and pretended to stumble. While on the ground I determined that the carriage tracks in the mud were fresh, and bore the mark of the repaired wheel. So I knew our quarry had taken refuge in there. I then moved more circumspectly around the property, and I heard them before I saw them. They are both well on in their drink, and quite garrulous. I was able to see through a crack that they are sitting around a brazier, and that Mrs. Arden is bound hand and foot lying on some rags not far away. I also discovered the carriage and horses in an outbuilding nearby, and this and their drunkenness has given me the idea of how we might proceed. Let us consult with Bradstreet."

We walked down the street to where the inspector waited. He listened to Holmes's plan, and agreed it was sound.

"We just need a horseman now, Inspector," Holmes said.

"Got just the man. Perkins has often told us of his youth

spent on a Sussex farm. He is a competent rider."

"Very well, let us arrange our forces. Instruct the constables that silence is of the essence."

We left Arden in the van, with instructions to remain there until fetched. Holmes, Perkins and I walked on ahead of the rest, Holmes rapidly explaining to Perkins his part in the raid. As we approached the building where the horses were stabled, Perkins and I hid in the shadows while Holmes went on ahead. He soon returned.

"Everyone is still where I saw them last," he whispered. "Perkins, you know what to do. Give us three minutes, then commence the diversion."

"Right you are, sir," Perkins acknowledged, checking his watch by the light of the moon, and then moving off. A few yards away, Bradstreet was silently directing his remaining constables to varying positions which he thought advantageous. I followed Holmes as we crept quietly to the door giving access to the room in which I could hear Cartwright and Hardy still talking. We took up positions each side of the door, drew our weapons, and waited. When I judged the time allotted Perkins to be nearly up, I braced myself.

With two armed and dangerous felons to deal with, the lady's safety in question, and ten other armed men operating in moonlit conditions, things could so easily have ended in bloodshed or even death. But in the end, Holmes's plan worked perfectly. Perkins suddenly appeared from the outbuilding, riding one horse and holding the bridle of the other, urging them to a gallop towards the main gate. The sound of their hooves on the paved yard brought the two men running to the door, which they threw open and then charged out, falling headlong as they tripped over our legs placed across the threshold. Both their pistols went skittering across the flagstones as they hit the ground, and in an instant Holmes and I ran up, pressed a knee into their backs and a gun to their heads. Bradstreet and his men arrived seconds later, and as soon as they had handcuffed the cursing prisoners, Holmes and I raced into their hideout and untied Mrs. Arden, who appeared to be unconscious.

"Quickly, Inspector," I shouted, "send a constable to bring the van here at once."

I had brought my medical bag with me and left it in the van with Mr. Arden, and I thought that both the bag and he would be needed; the former to revive Mrs. Arden, and the latter to complete the joy of her rescue for both of them.

As it happened, rubbing her chafed wrists and fanning her face brought Mrs. Arden to her senses before Arden and my medicines arrived. She had sustained some bruises from her ill-treatment, but these were temporarily forgotten when her husband rushed in, gave an inarticulate cry, and rushed to her side. We gave them some privacy for their reunion, and then Bradstreet came over to us.

"A good night's work, gentlemen. Two dangerous rogues off the streets and back into prison, and Mrs. Arden returned to her husband."

"She will need at least an overnight stay in hospital," I replied. "Just for a complete check and some necessary rest, which you now also need, Holmes."

"Yes, Watson, I must admit I am somewhat fatigued. Back to Baker Street then, for after something hot from Mrs. Hudson, a glass of something amber, and a good night's sleep, I intend to return to the Ardens and see if we can find what Cartwright and Hardy could not.

\*\*\*\*\*\*\*\*\*\*

"The task has been made easier for us, Watson, by the efforts of Cartwright and Hardy," Holmes remarked, as we pulled up in a cab outside 25 Argyll Road the next day just before eleven. "They have shown us where the money is not, and there can be few places left to search. But it must be either cunningly hidden, or not here at all. But the probability is that it is here somewhere; the telegram I received from Bradstreet earlier in answer to mine, confirmed that Joseph Newman was killed about two o'clock on the Sunday afternoon following the Saturday night raid on the bank. So he did not have very much time to hide it anywhere else other than on his own property."

Arden had intended to pass the night at his wife's bedside in hospital, and had given Holmes his key to enable him to get in and conduct his search. As we alighted, we noticed Mrs. Marwood was in her window as usual.

"Let her know that Mrs. Arden is safe, would you, Watson" said Holmes, "and that after we finish next door we shall supply her with all the details of the case she instigated."

A few minutes later we stood in the Ardens' hall.

"Now, Watson," he said. "Yesterday when I was here, I was looking for clues as to where they had gone, not a secret hiding place. I was also wounded and not at my best. This morning, in my refreshed state, I hope to find a clue to the whereabouts of the money. As I said, it seems to me that the majority of places have been searched already; under the carpets and floorboards in every room, behind all the pictures, in all the built-in cupboards, and the attic. The garden has also been thoroughly investigated. I intend to start with some of the more permanent fixtures, the kitchen range, and the kitchen and laundry trough, and the four fireplaces and their chimneys."

During the next two hours, I helped Holmes search all the nooks and crannies of the items he had named. Eventually, tired and grimy, we ended up in the parlour. Holmes stood glowering at the fireplace.

"If we don't find the hiding place in here, Watson, I'm beginning to think it must be in one of the walls and plastered over, and then we'll need a sledgehammer to demolish the house, brick by brick."

"Surely Newman would have wanted easier access to the money than that, Holmes," I said. "Remember Poe's story – it may be that the obvious hiding place is the best."

"You are referring to his story titled 'The Purloined Letter', where a stolen letter was not hidden at all, but was in full view of anyone in the room. Hmmm, perhaps you're right, and I have been approaching this search incorrectly," replied Holmes thoughtfully. He stood silently for a few moments.

"Open the curtains, would you please Watson. I need more light," he said, with an undercurrent of excitement in his voice.

I did so, and turned to find Holmes staring at the fireplace, a handsome structure covered with decorated tiles and surmounted by a marble mantelpiece. He squatted down and looked again, then moved nearer to it, beckoning me to join him.

"Can you see it, Watson?" he said, pointing. "This tile has a very slightly different shade of grout surrounding it, compared to the others. I think it was fixed at a later date than the other tiles, using a different grout, even though both would be called white by their manufacturers. We could procure a tradesman to carefully chisel it out, but – there is so much damage in the house already, would it make any difference? I think not. Let us be bold – here is a handy piece of floorboard with a large nail protruding, and if I strike the tile just so -"

The tile flew to pieces, revealing a cavity behind. It was filled with rolls of banknotes.

"Well done, Holmes! I congratulate you."

"Thank you, Watson, but I cannot claim too much credit for this discovery. It was not so much a deduction, as the application of the solution to a fictional mystery to our situation. Let us find a bag of some sort to hold our treasure. We will present it to Inspector Bradstreet on our way home, after we have seen Mrs. Marwood."

I found a grocery bag in the remains of the kitchen, stuffed the notes into it, and then we left the Arden's house and knocked on Mrs. Marwood's front door. She answered at once.

"Come in Mr. Holmes, Dr. Watson. I will just ask Lizzie for tea, and then you can tell me how you solved the case."

Sitting in her parlour, I recounted the events of the day before to Mrs. Marwood, in between sips of tea and mouthfuls of scone. I had just reached the part where we had discovered the villains had left the Ardens taking Mrs. Arden with them, having been unable to find the money they desired.

"You mean there is still the proceeds of a bank robbery hidden in their house somewhere?" she asked.

"Well, no. Mr. Holmes found it just now, and we –"

I stopped as she turned to Holmes with raised eyebrows and an innocent expression on her face.

"Mr. Holmes, did you find the money in the parlour fireplace, behind the tile three down from the top and two across from the left-hand side?"

Holmes looked at her for several seconds, then burst into laughter. I must have looked stunned.

"Oh, Doctor, I didn't know the money was hidden behind the tile, but I have taken tea in that parlour dozens of times, sitting in the chair opposite the window. Many times I have noticed that the surrounds of that tile are a slightly darker shade of white, but I just assumed it had been damaged and replaced at some point in the past."

"Mrs. Marwood, your observational skills are truly exceptional," said Holmes, still chuckling. "In fact, there is a reward for finding this money, and I will recommend to Inspector Bradstreet that you receive it. As I said, Watson, a lady after our own heart!"

# A CRY FOR JUSTICE

The mystery I am about to relate started off prosaically enough with a wire from Inspector Lestrade, delivered by Mrs. Hudson with our breakfast. Lestrade often brought cases to our attention, and though usually he visited to solicit Holmes's advice or assistance, it was not uncommon for him to also telegraph for aid. Holmes opened and read the telegram and then handed it to me, before attacking his ham and eggs with gusto. I read :

*Two murders on hand already. Third one all yours, difficult due to time elapsed. 21 Parfett St Whitechapel.*

*Lestrade*

"He is busy with two murder cases, and has now been assigned a third which he thinks is the most difficult to solve because of the passage of time since the murder occurred," I translated. "Therefore he passes it on to you. Have I read this right?"

"I believe so, Watson," Holmes replied. "I wonder how long ago this murder occurred? Clues start to degenerate or disappear after a week or two. But we have no data yet, so we must not theorise. If you are able, we shall take a look after breakfast."

"I have no plans or appointments," I confirmed.

Forty minutes later, we pulled up in a hansom outside the address given. There was a constable at the door, who touched his helmet respectfully as we alighted.

"Good morning, Mr. Holmes, Dr. Watson. PC Barton is my name. The inspector hoped you would come," he said. "This one's a poser all right. Follow me please."

He led us into the house and down the passage towards the rear. As we went through the kitchen, he turned to us.

"Just a quick word of explanation, sir. This is a property which is rented. As the last tenant left a few days ago, the owner took the opportunity to repair the drains which had been complained about, before re-letting it again. The workmen were here early this morning, and they found the victim."

We followed him out of the back door to the usual small walled yard. An area of the brick paving had been taken up and piled to one side, and in the ground thus revealed, a trench had been dug. The constable gestured for us to take a look, so we approached the trench, which turned out to be about two feet deep. At the bottom, poking out of the earth, was a human skull.

"This case might be an older story than I initially surmised, Watson," Holmes remarked thoughtfully.

\*\*\*\*\*\*\*\*\*\*

An hour later, the archaeologist and police surgeon summoned by Holmes were working together to remove the remains carefully from their makeshift grave. Dr. Hamilton was an acquaintance of Holmes's from the British Museum, and he was carefully removing each bone and other articles from the trench, bushing them clean and passing them to Dr. Morton for labelling and packing securely. The skull especially was of interest to Holmes, as when it was removed a large section at the rear fell away in pieces, and it was clear that the victim had suffered a tremendous blow from behind with a heavy, blunt instrument.

"Definitely murder, Watson," he said. "This man was killed and then buried in secret."

Earlier, I had asked Holmes if this could be a case for the antiquarian rather than the police, but he had drawn my attention to scraps of clothing still clinging to the body.

"These appear to be relatively modern clothes; see here the buttons on the shirt, the remains of an overcoat, and the boots.

No, this is no Roman, Saxon, or even a medieval burial."

"Here's something, Mr. Holmes," said Dr. Hamilton, straightening up from the trench and holding out his hand. "These were where you would expect the right trouser pocket to have been."

On his hand were four coins. Holmes, picked them up one by one and looked at them.

"A sixpence, a penny and two halfpennies, dated 1880, 1874, 1871 and 1875 respectively. That is helpful, as we now know this man could not have been buried here before 1880, or he could not have owned a sixpence of that date. So he has been here at most nineteen years. And since they were in his right trouser pocket, he was probably right-handed. We progress, Watson, do we not?"

The coins were placed in an envelope, and then in the box containing items other than the bones of the deceased. At this point, Constable Barton came up and said that the owner of the house had arrived, having been told by the workmen of the discovery. Holmes and I left the recovery to the two professionals and went inside. An elderly, balding man was in the hall, nervously twisting his hat in his hands. PC Barton introduced us.

"Mr. Holmes, Dr. Watson, this is Mr. Edward Darch, owner of this house for the last twenty-five years. Mr. Darch, Mr. Holmes is assisting the police with this matter, so please answer any questions he may put to you."

We went into the tiny parlour and sat down.

"Mr. Darch, I assume you have a list of the tenants who have occupied this house, and their dates of occupation?" asked Holmes.

"Yes of course, but there have been quite a few," he replied. "Mr. and Mrs. Morris were the tenants who just left, and they were here three years just gone. Mr. Butcher was here before them for some years, a single man he was. If you want the other names and dates I will have to check my records."

"Yes, we will need a complete list if you please. Now then, do you recall any of your tenants going missing?"

"Going missing?" Like a missing person you mean? Well no, not unless – well, unless disappearing because they were behind in their rent counts. That happens all the time in this neighbourhood, and it's happened to me two or three times. People get to owing a pound or two, and then suddenly – they've gone. But they're not really missing, they've just gone somewhere else."

"How do you know? Do you search for them?" asked Holmes.

"That would be a waste of my valuable time, sir," Darch replied. "But I see your point. One of my tenants might not have upped sticks, but might be that poor feller out in the yard."

"Indeed he might. On your list of tenants, please note those which did not just move out, but disappeared owing you money. You have a card? Thank you. We will call on you tomorrow morning for the list."

After seeing Darch out, we returned to the back yard to find the two professionals nearly finished in their task.

"Just about done, Mr. Holmes," said Dr. Morton. "The post mortem will take place this afternoon, and Dr. Hamilton and I will assist the pathologist. If you come round to the morgue at six tonight, we should be able to tell you something useful I hope."

"Thank you, Doctor; we shall see you at six. Come Watson, let us return to Baker Street; I need to smoke a pipe over this matter before we learn what this fellow's body has to say to us, calling out as it does from nearly two decades ago."

\*\*\*\*\*\*\*\*\*\*

After a cold lunch, Holmes charged his pipe with shag and sat immobile for nearly an hour, while I arranged and annotated some notes of recent previous cases. The interesting case of the retired colourman, as well as the truth concerning the death of the art dealer Charles Milverton may one day be published in these chronicles.

Eventually Holmes broke into my train of thought.

"Well, Watson, what do you think of the case so far?" he asked.

"It is difficult," I replied. "Lestrade is right is saying the years elapsed since the crime will not make it easy to solve."

"Indeed. But fortunately we have narrowed the possibility of when the death may have occurred. The coins give us the oldest date, and the shortest period of time needed to transform a body into a skeleton will give us another date. That time depends on factors in the soil, but I am hopeful the pathologist and Dr. Hamilton will be able to give us some approximation. The combination of the possible years for the murder with Mr. Darch's tenant list will give us a starting point. We will also need to interview the neighbours on either side of the house, as well as the residents of the house opposite and the house adjoining the rear of the property."

"What do you hope a skeleton will be able to tell us, Holmes?" I queried. "Your talent for the observation of trifles is based on the external appearance of a person, and their clothing. All that is gone in this case, save a few tatters of cloth."

"You are right, Watson, which is why I called on Dr. Hamilton. I recognised that his experience with the careful removal of bones and sifting of the surrounding earth would be invaluable in this case, to preserve any tiny clues which may be present as to our victim's identity and manner of death. I am of the opinion that a thorough and scientific approach to the examination of a murder victim will become more and more important. The pathologist does what he can when he has received a body, but we need specialised, scientifically trained people to first look for clues on the body and at the crime scene, before it is taken to the morgue. Many a clue has been erased by policemen blundering around a body."

I nodded in agreement.

"Furthermore, I have harboured a growing suspicion, Watson, that there is something in each of us that is a unique indicator of our identity. Barring identical twins, triplets and so on, I believe every person on this planet is a physiologically unique individual. I predict medical science will one day progress to the stage where we can tell one human being from another from the smallest trace of blood, hair, or skin – perhaps even just a few cells of our substance."

"It sounds a little like one of Mr. Wells's fantastic stories. But I agree, if what you say were possible, and if records could be kept of what makes each of us different, and then the traces at a crime scene compared against them, it should simplify detective work immeasurably. It would be especially valuable in cases like this one."

"Absolutely, Watson, though I don't think it will happen in our lifetimes. In my own small way I have brought science to bear on the art of detection, with my studies of cigar ashes, soils, footprints, and the chemical analysis of substances, but I foresee the future of detecting and solving crime lies in a far greater application of the sciences than happens today."

"Yes, Holmes, time marches on, and science and technological advancement with it. We already have mechanised motor vehicles they say will replace the horse, and I have read reports of the possibility of similarly powered flying machines. However, my immediate need is for Mrs. Hudson's skills in the science of tea-making and baking. Will you join me, before we go to the morgue?"

Holmes laughed. "Certainly, Watson, tea and cakes are in order. Please ring the bell."

\*\*\*\*\*\*\*\*\*\*

We were at the morgue a few minutes before the appointed hour. Dr. Masterton, a pathologist we knew from several of Holmes's previous cases, showed us into the room where the skeleton had been laid out, with all the bones in their relative positions. A table nearby had the remnants of the victim's clothing and other articles found in the trench. Dr. Hamilton and Inspector Lestrade were also present.

"Good evening gentlemen," said Holmes. "What have you to tell us?"

I'll start," said Dr. Masterton. "This is the skeleton of a man. The wear on the teeth suggests an age of around forty to fifty years. A calculation based on the length of his right femur gives an approximate height of five feet and eight inches. You can see here that his left femur has been broken at some point, and has been set not quite in line. This means his left leg was slightly shorter than his right, and he would have limped."

He picked up the skull and showed us the rear.

"He was killed by a single savage blow to the right occipital region of the head," he continued. "This crushed the skull and left this hole of about two inches in diameter. There were six small pieces of the skull detached by the blow, and they would have been driven into the brain causing immediate unconsciousness and death within a minute or two."

"And how long ago would you say that death occurred?" asked Holmes.

"There was no tissue of any kind left on the bones. The soil conditions were conducive to microbial and insect action, so I would estimate this man died fifteen to twenty years ago," replied Dr. Masterton. "There is one other thing, Mr. Holmes. You see these lesions and imperfections on the long bones here,

here, and here? They are indicative of advanced syphilis."

"With the attendant symptoms, no doubt. Syphilis attacks the brain and spinal cord, so I expect this man suffered from constant back pain, difficulty walking in addition to his limp, memory problems, irritability and possibly changes in personality. Thank you, Doctor, that is most illuminating," said Holmes. "Dr. Hamilton, have you made any discoveries which may help us?"

"I hope so, Mr. Holmes," he replied, turning to the table bearing the recovered pieces of clothing. "I have placed all the remnants into piles, and I believe this man was wearing an undershirt, a shirt, a short jacket, trousers, a brown sock and a black sock with these boots, plus a heavy overcoat with a pair of leather gloves in the inside pocket. It is hard to tell after years underground, but my impression is that all the clothes were of a quite coarse quality. There was also a woollen scarf and flat cap resting on his chest."

"Hah! That is interesting," remarked Holmes.

"Why is that interesting?" said Lestrade quizzically.

"Firstly, the gloves, scarf and overcoat indicate that the weather was cold when he was killed. So the murder occurred in the colder months. Secondly, poor quality clothing, mismatched socks and a flat cap denotes someone from the lower strata of society; a workingman or labourer, perhaps even a 'gentleman of the road,' as they are called. Thirdly, he was not wearing his gloves, cap or scarf. He had taken them all off, put his gloves in his pocket, and probably placed his cap and scarf on a hat rack. Thus he was inside when he was killed, and the murderer just threw his cap and scarf into the grave before filling it in. Anything else of interest, Doctor?"

"I'm afraid I've only found three items other than the clothes, Mr. Holmes. The four coins you already know about, but there was some broken glass and a cork in one of the overcoat pockets. I have placed the pieces in this box if you wish to inspect them or even try to reassemble them, though I think it's obvious it was once a small bottle."

Thank you, Doctor," said Holmes after a quick look in the box.

There was also this," said Dr. Hamilton, taking what appeared to be a necklace from an envelope and passing it to Holmes.

Holmes examined it with his powerful lens for a minute, then showed it to Lestrade and myself. It was a necklace, the like of which I had not seen before. It consisted of a thin leather thong, attached to a triangular piece of what looked like bone, via a metal clasp with a ring to take the leather. The bone had a small mass of black lines on one side. Lestrade shook his head, so I asked Holmes if he knew what it was.

"It is a shark's tooth, Watson; what species I am not sure, but I have seen them before, worn by sailors. The device on one side will hopefully clean up and reveal itself, though I suspect it to be a depiction of a ship. It is a process called scrimshaw, where lines are incised into a shark or whale tooth with a knife, then rubbed with lamp black to define them. Sailors often engage in it to while away the hours at sea when not on duty."

A sudden thought seemed to strike him. "Doctor Hamilton, was this leather thong as you found it, untied, or was it knotted around the neck of the victim?"

"It is as I found it, Mr. Holmes; untied and on the victim's chest, under the scarf and cap."

"Curious," remarked Holmes. "I wonder –"

"What's curious is," said Lestrade impatiently, "how we can ever expect to solve this crime from so few clues?"

"On the contrary, Lestrade, for a body this old we have done remarkably well."

"Really, Holmes! You can't expect me to find the murderer of an unknown man who died fifteen or more years ago, who had a gammy leg and a bad back. You can continue with this case if you like, Holmes, but I have to find out who strangled a milliner in his shop, and how a theatre lighting hand got himself stabbed behind the Boar's Head public house. Goodnight gentlemen."

And with that he strode out. Holmes chuckled.

"Poor Lestrade. Finding one murderer is hard enough for him, and now he has three on his plate. We shall have to solve this one for him, Watson. Thank you, Doctor Hamilton, Doctor Masterton. I will take the remains of the bottle and the necklace, to see if they might provide further clues. Come Watson, Mrs. Hudson mentioned game pie at seven, so we must hurry!"

\*\*\*\*\*\*\*\*\*\*

The next morning after breakfast found us on our way to see Mr. Darch, the landlord, to obtain the list of tenants he had promised. Holmes then planned to interview the neighbours, hoping that some of them at least had been there between fifteen and twenty years ago, and possibly held information pertinent to the case. Holmes was silent for most of the journey, but suddenly spoke up.

"I'm afraid, Watson, that I appeared more confident than I actually am in front of Lestrade last night. It's true we do know a fair amount about our victim. In summary: He is a middle-aged man from the working classes, probably right-handed, limps on his left leg and suffers from the symptoms of syphilis. He was killed by a blow to the head, most likely inside a house in the winter of any of the years between 1880 and 1885, then taken and buried where we found him, the killer throwing the victim's cap and scarf in after him before completing the interment. However, we do not know his name. If we could only identify him with some certainty, we could perhaps discover more about his life, his habits, his associates, and that might give us a motive."

"What about the shark's tooth necklace, Holmes?" I asked. "What does that tell you?"

"Yes, the necklace," Holmes mused. "Finding it on the victim's chest under the scarf and not around his neck leads me to believe it did not belong to him. Imagine, Watson, you have just killed this man. You decide to bury him, so the body must be carried or dragged to the gravesite. Surely to avoid discovery you would do this under cover of darkness? During the carrying or dragging of the body, and then picking it up to place in the grave, I think that the necklace became entangled in the victim's clothing, perhaps caught on a button, and thence was pulled from the killer's neck. In his exertions and in the darkness, the killer failed to realise his loss, threw the cap and scarf into the grave and buried it with his victim."

"It certainly sounds plausible, Holmes," I replied. "You said these necklaces are commonly made and worn by sailors – does this mean you expect the murderer to be a seafarer?

"Expect is too strong a word," he replied. It's an indication, a line of enquiry. But here we are – let us see if Mr. Darch's list of tenants can add to our knowledge."

A few minutes later, Mr. Darch showed us into his parlour, and once seated he produced a sheet of paper which he gave to Holmes.

"So, Mr. Darch, you have had nine tenants since you bought the house in 1874. Three of them absconded owing you rent. I am most interested in this man – John Fothergill, who lived there between May 1881 and February 1883, and then disappeared owing you two months rent. What can you tell me about him?"

"Mr. Fothergill was a commercial traveller, Mr. Holmes. He represented a firm that published maps, and he would travel around London and the country, trying to get stationers and booksellers to stock his wares."

"Can you describe him?"

"Let me see, he was a single man, in his forties I should guess. Average height and build, dark hair. I think he had a problem with the drink – every time I saw him, to collect rent or over some complaint about the house, he smelled of liquor. Oh, and he always walked with a cane; a childhood injury he once told me."

"And when you discovered he had gone, you made no enquiries about him?"

"No sir, I did not. I went to collect the rent one night, and he was not there. I assumed he was on one of his trips to the country, which usually lasted several days at a time. When he was not there the next time I visited, I asked the old couple next door and they said they had not seen him for over a month. So I cut my losses and rented the house to someone else."

"His clothes and effects – they were gone too?"

"Yes they were. The furniture belonged to me, but everything he owned was gone."

Holmes stood up. "Thank you, Mr. Darch. We'll be in touch if we need anything further."

We hailed a cab to take us to Parfett Street. Once inside and on our way, I questioned Holmes about the information Darch had given us.

"Surely it is not a coincidence Holmes, that this Fothergill is of the age and height of our victim, required a cane to walk, and disappeared in the winter of 1883?" I said.

"I think it may be just that – a coincidence, Watson," Holmes replied. "It's possible that our victim is Fothergill, and that his killer removed all his clothes and belongings from his house to give the impression he had fled. But why would he be dressed in such shabby clothes? He was employed, earned a reasonable wage; surely, he would not own such clothing as we found our victim wearing? That requires an explanation."

I was still pondering on this when we arrived.

"For no reason let us try the neighbour on the right side first," said Holmes, but he was soon disappointed. The lady of the house was home, but she, her husband and three children had only lived there for four years.

On the other side, however, lived the same old couple whom Darch had spoken to about Fothergill some sixteen years ago. Mr. Gibbs was well into his eighties and a little vague, but his younger wife said she remembered all the tenants who had lived next door. Over some tea she regaled us with several uninformative anecdotes about Mr. Fothergill, but she also confirmed some things Darch had told us.

"Yes, sir, he liked a drink did Mr. Fothergill, though he wasn't usually rowdy or obnoxious when in his cups. He did once get into some altercation at a public house, and spent the night in the cells for public drunkenness. But his brother got him out and brought him home the next day, a nice man he was, a tobacconist by trade if I recall."

"Did he ever mention having back pain at all?" Holmes asked.

"Back pain? No I don't think so. He had a cane to walk with, and he said that was due to an injury when he was a lad. But back pain he never mentioned."

"Thank you, Mrs. Gibbs. Your tea was delicious and your information helpful."

"Now then, Watson," he said once we were back on the street, "we shall try the house opposite, where I see by the sign in the window that there are rooms to let."

Mrs. Jacobson answered the door in response to my knock, and she turned out to be a respectable, elderly widow who took in lodgers. She had also resided there for twenty-one years, and remembered seeing Mr. Fothergill numerous times leaving or arriving home, but she had never spoken to him.

"I heard that he just up and left one day, which didn't surprise me," she said in a thin, reedy voice.

"Why was that, Mrs. Jacobson?," enquired Holmes.

"Because I know who he had dealings with. Many's the times I seen and heard Smilin' Joe or a couple of his boys at the door, and I thought to myself he'll have to do a runner or he'll be a dead 'un."

"Smiling Joe? You are sure of this?" said Holmes, showing great interest.

"Oh yes, everyone 'round here knows Smilin' Joe. Gawd help you if you get into his clutches."

"Indeed, I have heard of him myself Mrs. Jacobson, and it is certainly best not to become involved with him. Good day, madam."

"One more visit to make, Watson, then back to Baker Street," he said, striding briskly along the pavement. Left at the next street, then left again, seven houses along and we shall see if Mr. Fothergill's neighbour at the rear can help us."

"Holmes —"

"Yes Watson, you are going to ask me who is this Smiling Joe. He is a well-known moneylender of sinister repute. He is polite in the extreme, and will smile as he breaks your fingers due to your unpaid debt. If Fothergill owed him money, he immediately becomes a factor in the man's disappearance, though as I said I am not yet convinced that our victim is Fothergill."

We arrived at the house that Holmes calculated abutted the Darch property at the rear, a tired-looking, nondescript brick dwelling much like many others in the district. Holmes rapped on the door with his cane, and after a minute it was opened by a man who, although looking to be nearly seventy with white hair and beard, was nevertheless tall and well-built. Holmes proffered his card.

"Good day, sir. My name is Sherlock Holmes, this is Dr. Watson. We are assisting the police in the investigation of the unknown body discovered in the yard of the house behind you. If you were living here in the early 1880s, may we have a few minutes of your time, Mr.—?"

"Farmer is my name, George Farmer. I was born in this house, lived here all my life and I guess I'll die here. I saw you all digging yesterday, from my bedroom window. A body was it? Who's dead then?

"That is one thing we unfortunately don't yet know, Mr. Farmer."

"Come in then, though I don't see how I can help."

He led the way down the hall to the kitchen.

"You'll excuse the mess gentlemen, I don't entertain much," he remarked as we sat down around the table.

"Now Mr. Farmer, there has been a succession of tenants living behind you, but we are interested in one in particular, a Mr. Fothergill, who lived there between 1881 and 1883. Did you know him?" asked Holmes.

"Aye, we spoke occasionally. Map-seller wasn't he?"

"That's the fellow. He disappeared one day – do you know anything about that?"

"Not a thing. One day he was there, a few weeks later there was a young couple in the house. But if he disappeared, he must be the fellow you found in the yard?'

"As I said, the identity of the body has not been established," said Holmes. "Are you retired, Mr. Farmer? What was your employment?"

"I worked in a brewery nigh on forty years, retired five years ago, though why you should want to know that beats me."

"It is my job to collect information, Mr. Farmer. I may not know what turns out to be useful until later. Thank you for your time, sir."

Farmer nodded and led the way back down the hall to the front door. We said goodbye to Farmer on his doorstep and made our way down the street, Holmes deep in thought.

"Watson, I have a small excursion to make," he suddenly said. "Please go home and have your luncheon. Afterwards, if you require something to do, you can try to determine what the broken bottle might have contained. I will join you later."

And with that he hailed a passing hansom and was off. I took the next one, and made my way back to Baker Street, still trying to make sense of all that we had learnt during our morning's work. Mrs. Hudson provided some sandwiches and tea, and when I had satisfied my hunger I opened the cardboard box containing the glass fragments found on the body. I laid them out on a sheet of paper and tried to look at them analytically, as Holmes might.

One piece was obviously the bottom of a small bottle, and two further pieces formed the opening into which the cork fitted. As I picked up the cork, a faint aroma caught my attention. Putting it to my nose, I immediately recognised the scent, which the years underground had not managed to erase completely. Pleased with my success, I then remembered the necklace which Holmes had also brought home. I found it on the mantelpiece, and determined to be helpful, I got out my bottle of rubbing alcohol and a soft cloth and tried to clean it. The ingrained dirt fell away from the tooth, leaving a small but finely detailed illustration, with a single word incised underneath it. I was drying it off when Holmes returned.

"Hullo, Watson, you've been busy, I observe," he said

divesting himself of his hat and cane.

"Yes, Holmes, I have discovered what was in the bottle," I said.

"Was it a painkiller by any chance, Watson? Laudanum perhaps?"

"It was indeed laudanum," I replied, somewhat deflated.

"I deduced as much, once we learned that the victim had advanced syphilis. The back pain caused by that disease is quite often intolerable, I am assured. I would certainly not venture out without a supply of some opiate, if I was a sufferer. And what of the tooth? You have cleaned it I see."

"Yes, it's come up beautifully. It's a picture of a sailing ship, with presumably the name of the ship beneath. I believe it says *Isabelle*," I said, holding it out to him.

"*Isabelle!*" Holmes took out his lens and inspected the newly cleaned tooth, then sat down in his chair, with a thoughtful expression.

"Does this mean something, Holmes?"

"Yes it does, Watson. It means I will have to visit Lloyd's of London tomorrow, and then perhaps the docks. Meanwhile, I am pleased to say my researches have proved that the skeleton is most definitely not the remains of Mr. John Fothergill."

"How do you know that?"

"By following a line of enquiry provided by Mrs. Gibbs. She said, if you recall, that Fothergill had a brother, a tobacconist. A perusal of Kelly's Directory revealed that a tobacconist named Michael Fothergill still operates in Clapham. I have been to see him, and he is indeed the brother of John Fothergill, and he told me the unhappy story of his sibling.

"We knew he was afflicted with a love of alcoholic beverages, but he was also a gambler. He lost, as drunks often do, and then made the mistake of borrowing money from

Smiling Joe. He could not repay the loan, Smiling Joe was getting impatient, and he was also behind in the rent. To save his life and give him a fresh start, Michael Fothergill paid for his brother's passage to Canada, and one night he helped him slip away from his lodgings and saw him safely aboard the steamer. I'm pleased to say he has turned over a new leaf in his adopted country, and is now an abstainer, a bookshop owner, a husband and a father, and regularly writes to his brother from Toronto."

"That is well for John Fothergill, but it still leaves us with the vexed question of just whose body is it that we have found? What poor soul cries out for justice from all those years ago?"

"I don't know yet, Watson, but it is a cry I intend to answer, and tomorrow may find us a step closer to doing so."

\*\*\*\*\*\*\*\*\*\*

Holmes had breakfasted and gone before I rose the next day. After I had finished reading the newspapers, I spent the rest of the morning writing up my notes on the case. When I believed that John Fothergill was the victim, I had the title of my chronicle of the case already in my head – The Case of the Missing Map Seller. Now that we knew he was safe in Canada, I had to think of another title, but I failed to do so before I decided to lunch at my club. It was late afternoon when I returned, to find Holmes cross-legged in his favourite chair, smoke drifting lazily from his pipe.

"Ah, there you are Watson. Would you ring for tea?"

"I have already asked Mrs. Hudson on the way in."

"Very good. Would you like to hear the result of my efforts today?"

"Certainly, if you wish to discuss them."

"As I've remarked before, nothing clarifies a case in my mind more than restating it to you. Also, I hope to have a visitor tonight who will be able to help us, and you will need to be in possession of the facts to understand."

135

"I see. You were going to start at Lloyd's, you said yesterday?"

"Indeed. There I discovered that the brig named *Isabelle* was launched in 1845, and after several years on the South American run, the owners decided to search for new markets. So the *Isabelle* set sail in 1851 for the far East under a Captain Jackson, and spent three years sailing the Pacific and visiting China, Australia, New Guinea and India before returning to London.

"An interesting voyage no doubt, but -"

"Patience, Watson. I then spent five hours in the public houses near the docks, talking to old sailors. The Boar's Head was the seventh such establishment I visited, and I finally found a barman who told me of a regular customer who was first mate on that trip, a Mr. Jim Olney. No-one appeared to know where Mr. Olney lives, but all were confident he would be there later tonight. I instructed the barman to tell Mr. Olney when he arrives, that if he takes a cab here and provides us with some information, he shall receive two sovereigns plus the cab fare."

"Why did you want to find a member of the crew from that particular trip?" I asked.

"Because, Watson, one of the several pictures that adorned the kitchen walls of Mr. George Farmer's residence was of a brig with the name *Isabelle* clearly visible on the bow. The same ship depicted on the shark's tooth necklace! What can we deduce from that?"

"Let's see, he said he had worked in a brewery for nearly forty years, and retired – five years ago? Forty-five years ago takes us back to 1854 – when did you say the Isabelle returned to London?"

"According to Lloyd's it was in May, 1854."

"Then you think Farmer must have been on the *Isabelle* for those three years, then retired from the sea and found employment in the brewery?"

"Apart from a monstrous coincidence, I can't think of any other reason to have a picture of the ship in his house. But it also explains the necklace, a souvenir he probably carved himself while in the Pacific, kept as a reminder of his youthful days at sea."

"But did you not say that you thought the necklace belonged to the murderer?"

"I did, Watson."

"Hmmm. What do you think this Olney will have to say?"

"I am not sure exactly, but I am hoping it will bear on the mystery of the unknown skeleton. It is clear that Farmer is connected to the *Isabelle* because of the picture in his home. Whether he is connected to the murder via the necklace is still to be proved. I am hopeful Mr. Olney, first mate of the *Isabelle*, will be able to tell us something of these connections. And incidentally, Watson, while at the Boar's Head I learned something that may help Lestrade in his search for the murderer of the theatre worker behind that establishment."

"He will be pleased about that, I imagine."

Mrs. Hudson arrived with our tea, and told us that our dinner of Dover sole would be served at seven o'clock. Holmes informed her that we might possibly have a visitor during the evening. As it turned out, we had just finished our raspberry pudding when Mrs. Hudson brought him up, an elderly man whose calloused hands and tattoos proclaimed that he had been a seafarer for many years.

"Sit down, Mr. Olney," Holmes said in a genial fashion. "Thank you for taking the time to see us. Here are the two sovereigns I promised, and the cab fare – two half-crowns should cover it."

"Thank you sir, most kind," said Olney, pocketing the coins. "Though I'm not sure what I can tell you to earn it."

"Mr. Olney, I believe you were the first mate aboard the *Isabelle* on her voyage east between 1851 and 1854?" queried Holmes.

Olney chuckled. "That's right sir, but that's many a year ago now. Under Captain Jackson that was, a master mariner and a fair and decent man too."

"Was there in the crew of that ship a man called George Farmer?"

"Indeed sir, he was a bosun with us."

"Tell me about him."

"George was a good sailor, sir, a hard worker. But he was quick to anger, and the captain had to discipline him sometimes for getting into fights. But a good-hearted chap on the whole."

"I believe he left the *Isabelle*, and the sea altogether, when you returned to England. Do you know why?"

"No, I don't, sir. We were never particular cronies, and when he didn't sign on for the next voyage of the *Isabelle* I thought nothing of it. I assumed at the time he had found a better berth on another ship, but later I discovered from our third mate, Billy Towton, that he had gone to work in a brewery. Billy was a friend of George's on that Pacific trip, and stayed in touch with George afterwards. He got sick in the end, poor chap, and had to give up sailin'."

Holmes and I looked at each other.

"Billy Towton became ill, you say," said Holmes casually. "Do you know what he suffered from?"

Olney looked a little uncomfortable. "Well sir, you are both men of the world, and I'm sure you know how sailors behave when they reach a port after months at sea. Poor Billy got the syphilis bad. I used to see him regular like after he gave up the sea, at places where sailors meet. His back got very painful, then it affected his walking, and then it got into his brain.

And if that weren't enough, he broke his leg and they didn't fix it right. He wasn't the same Billy in the end. He did odd jobs here and there, but oftentimes I had to help him out with a couple of shillings for the painkillers."

"You said you used to see him regularly – what happened to him?"

"Well that's the odd thing sir – nobody knows. One day, must be fifteen or sixteen years ago now, he just stopped coming to the pub of an evening. I asked around, but nobody knew anything. I think maybe it all got too much and he threw himself into the sea. He did miss the seafaring life."

Holmes was silent for a moment. "Thank you, Mr. Olney. I'll just take your address in case we need you again."

Olney supplied the information, and I showed him to the door. I turned to Holmes.

"The skeleton is Billy Towton's."

Holmes nodded.

\*\*\*\*\*\*\*\*\*\*

The next morning, Holmes sent a wire to Lestrade, asking him to join us. We heard him stomping up the stairs just after ten.

"He's in a mood, isn't he?" I said to Holmes.

"Indeed, Watson, but we have information that will hopefully clear up not one but two murders, which should settle his temper," Holmes replied, smiling.

Lestrade knocked and entered in response to Holmes's invitation.

"Mr. Holmes, I trust this is not a waste of my time. You know I am busy with two murders to solve, and a third which you are investigating. Have you any progress to report?"

"Sit down, Lestrade, I am sure your time will not be misspent. Now, firstly, have you caught the killer of the theatre lighting hand, stabbed behind the Boar's Head public house?"

"No I have not, Mr. Holmes. It is proving a difficult case."

"Can you tell me – was the victim subject to robbery as well?"

"Yes, he was, as it happens. I've established that he had just been paid that afternoon, but there was no money found on him."

"In that case let me direct your attention to a sailor who drinks at the Boar's Head. He is about five feet nine inches tall, of burly stature, a scar on his right cheek and a tattoo of a sperm whale on his left forearm."

"Yes, I've interviewed him and the hundred others who were there the night of the stabbing. They all claim to know nothing," said Lestrade, somewhat testily.

"I was in the Boar's Head yesterday afternoon. That gentleman came up to the bar beside me to order an ale. He laid a shilling on the bar to pay for it, and my attention was drawn to it by the strong smell of burnt lime. As I'm sure you know, Lestrade, theatres use lime burnt with hydrogen and oxygen to produce a powerful light, usually focused on the principal actor. Limelight operators get this substance on them while they work, so the shilling must have been taken from the victim, who had handled the coins he was paid with and imparted the smell to them."

Lestrade had the grace to look impressed. "Thank you, Holmes, I shall re-interview that man and search him for more coins smelling of burnt lime."

"I'm sure that will prove fruitful," remarked Holmes. "Now, as to our investigation of the skeleton found at Parfett Street. There is a very high probability that the victim is an ex-sailor fallen on hard times called Billy Towton, and that he was murdered by a man named George Farmer, whose property adjoins the rear of where the remains were found. They were friends and served together on the brig *Isabelle* in the early 1850s. The murder occurred I believe in February of 1883, though I cannot provide a motive nor prove conclusively any of my hypothesis."

Lestrade looked at Holmes in astonishment. "How on earth have you discovered all this in less than three days? he asked.

Holmes gave Lestrade a quick sketch of how the investigation had proceeded.

"So," he concluded, "we know Billy Towton had syphilis and a broken leg, so it is highly likely that the skeleton belongs to him. We know that Towton and Farmer were friends and kept in touch after their sailing days were over. We know Farmer was easily angered and got into fights, and Towton's disease would have resulted in mood swings and irritability. So there is a recipe for an argument between them. According to Olney, we know Towton disappeared some fifteen or sixteen years ago, which takes us back to '83 or '84. We know that sometime in February of 1883, Farmer's neighbour Fothergill left his lodgings without warning, leaving his property empty and thus available for a covert burial. The shark's tooth necklace probably belonged to Farmer, who lost it while burying Towton, but we cannot prove that. It's all circumstantial, and unless he confesses when pressed, I cannot see this case being resolved."

"Well, let us go and press him then, and see what happens" said Lestrade.

"Very well, Inspector, but if he admits nothing, then we don't have a case."

\*\*\*\*\*\*\*\*\*\*

We pulled up a while later outside Farmer's abode, having discussed the case and how to tackle Farmer during the journey. Lestrade had agreed to let Holmes take the lead. I rapped on the door, and Farmer answered, looking at us with undisguised suspicion.

"Mr. Farmer, we have just a few more questions for you," said Holmes sweetly. "Inspector Lestrade from Scotland Yard is also with us this time."

"You better come in then," he said, looking worriedly at the official representative of the law. "We can go in the parlour if you like."

Farmer led the way and we all sat down. Holmes pulled an envelope from his pocket.

"Now then, Mr. Farmer. We have reason to believe that the body found in your neighbour's house is one Billy Towton, a sailor in his youth but who later became too ill to handle a seafaring life. Did you know him at all?"

"I'm sorry, but I've not heard of him or met him that I know of," said Farmer, shaking his head vigorously.

"Is that so? Then, Mr. Farmer, would you mind telling us why Mr. Olney, the first mate of the brig *Isabelle*, whose picture hangs upon your kitchen wall, tells us that you and Billy served on that ship together for three years and remained friends afterwards?"

Farmer opened his mouth, then shut it again. Holmes opened the envelope and withdrew the shark's tooth necklace.

"Have you ever seen this before, Mr. Farmer?" Holmes asked. "We found it in Billy's grave."

"No, it's not mine," he croaked, turning pale.

"Then why, Mr. Farmer" said Holmes, raising his voice, "why is there on the mantelpiece, a photograph of you, in your youth, with this very necklace around your neck!"

We all turned to see the photograph, a head and shoulders portrait of an easily identifiable younger George Farmer, the shark's tooth standing out against his tanned chest. We turned back to see Farmer sobbing like a child, tears rolling down his cheeks and losing themselves in his beard.

"I knew it would catch up with me one day," he whispered. "It's haunted me these many years. I didn't mean to kill him, but my temper got the better of me."

Haltingly, Farmer told us the story, which was much as Holmes had surmised. Towton had been at Farmer's house one night, and they had both been drinking. Towton had said something, Farmer had taken umbrage, and an argument ensued, which eventually graduated from words to blows. Farmer had then hit Towton over the head with a poker. Realising he was dead, he remembered that he had not seen Fothergill for some time, and, fearful of having Towton's body found in his own back yard, he carried it into his neighbour's yard and buried it under cover of darkness and a light drizzle. He had picked up Towton's cap and scarf on the way and thrown them in the grave with him. He had realised the next day that his necklace, which Holmes had correctly predicted was of his own making, had been lost sometime during the night. He considered looking for it in the grave, but was unable to do so as new tenants moved into the house that day. The new tenants had not noticed the grave, as he had carefully replaced the brick paving over it, and taken the excess soil to his own back yard in a barrow. Nobody had ever enquired of him as to the whereabouts of his friend in the years since.

"A sad story, Holmes," I said, as Farmer was taken away in a police wagon accompanied by Lestrade. The inspector had thanked Holmes for his handling of the case, even saying that if he found any further skeletons, he would certainly send them Holmes's way.

"Indeed, Watson. We were fortunate, however. When we entered Farmer's house, I was fully expecting him to deny everything, and that would have been the end of it. But as soon as I entered the parlour, I saw the photograph which provided the undeniable connection between Farmer, the *Isabelle*, the necklace and Towton's grave."

"He seemed almost relieved to have been caught," I remarked. "As he said, the murder had haunted him for years. But at least now Billy Towton can be laid to rest properly, his cry for justice has been heard, and his killer will pay the penalty under the law."

"It is a late justice, Watson, but better justice late than none at all."

# THE QUESTIONABLE EXISTENCE OF MRS. CARBERRY'S COMPANION

I had risen somewhat later than usual, and found Holmes breakfasting on soft-boiled eggs and toast while reading a newspaper propped up on the coffeepot. I rang for Mrs. Hudson to order my own breakfast, and started on *The Times*. A few minutes later, she knocked and entered with a tray.

"Good morning, Doctor," she said cheerfully. "Breakfast for you and a telegram for Mr. Holmes."

She handed Holmes the telegram, which he read quickly and passed to me.

"Thank you Mrs. Hudson, please arrange a reply in the affirmative," he said.

The wire was from a Jonathon Carberry, and ran as follows:

*May I see you about my mother's companion? Police unwilling to act. Will call at 10am tomorrow if convenient. Please reply.*

"Detail is wanting," I remarked, "but it may prove to be something. You haven't had a case for nearly two weeks now."

"Yes, it has been a little quiet of late. But I am intrigued by the phrase 'police unwilling to act.' This means they are unsure whether any crime has been committed, and as you know, Watson, several of our more interesting cases have been devoid of any legal crime."

"Yes, that's true," I replied, taking the top off my first egg.

"But for now," he continued, "we must put it out of our minds until Mr. Carberry arrives on the morrow."

\*\*\*\*\*\*\*\*\*\*

And arrive he did, punctually on the hour of ten. He was a slightly built man of some thirty years, with thinning fair hair, rather thick-lensed spectacles and a habit of blinking which made him appear continually astonished. Holmes bade him sit down, and I poured him a cup of tea.

"Well, Mr. Carberry, what can I do for you?" asked Holmes pleasantly.

"Mr. Holmes, I have just returned to England and found my mother perplexed by a situation which I would like to lay before you."

"Certainly, Mr. Carberry. You have been in India, I perceive, where you have been working in the colonial administration there for several years."

"Why yes, Mr. Holmes that's true. How –"

"Your tanned features tell me you have been in the tropics. Your poor eyesight prevents you from being a soldier, I feel, so I deduced a position in the colonial service. Your face is tanned to a degree that indicates lengthy exposure to a stronger sun than England provides, so your position must have taken you in the open air a certain portion of the time. Your snake ring is of obvious Indian workmanship."

"Correct Mr. Holmes. I have just spent three years in the Indian Civil Service as a district agricultural officer, and I often had to ride out to distant farms. However, a few months ago I became engaged to the daughter of a captain in the Indian Army. She has been in India five years, and the climate does not suit her well. So I applied for and won a good position with the Canadian Board of Agriculture, enabling us to come home to marry, introduce her to my mother, and then settle in Canada. We are due to leave England in five weeks"

"Your happiness and prospects seem assured then, Mr. Carberry, but your mother is perplexed, you say. Please tell us about it," asked Holmes.

"Very well. I returned to London with my fiancée on Tuesday. She is staying with relatives, and after seeing her settled there, I went yesterday to visit my mother, who lives at Elm House, just outside Horley in Surrey. My father died some ten years ago, Mr. Holmes, but he left my mother in a comfortable position. When I arrived there, she was in quite an agitated state. I must tell you first that three months ago, she decided that because she had lived alone too long and was also becoming infirm, she advertised for a companion. She received several responses, and from them she chose a Miss Sarah Greenwood to come to live with her. Miss Greenwood was a middle-aged spinster of some education by virtue of her father being a schoolmaster, and my mother says she has proved most satisfactory. But when I arrived, my mother told me this companion had apparently vanished the night before, not appearing at the breakfast table. My mother was upset after she told me this, so I went to ask the housekeeper, Mrs. Trott, if she could shed any light on the mystery."

At this point, Carberry stopped and looked uncertain.

"Go on, sir, what did Mrs. Trott have to say?"

"Mr. Holmes, Mrs. Trott maintains that my mother has never had a companion, and that as far as she knows, Miss Sarah Greenwood does not exist!"

"Curious," muttered Holmes. "Your mother is not given to delusions or hallucinations, I take it?"

"No, sir, she has always been a sensible, practical woman," Carberry replied.

"Nevertheless, you have not seen her for three years. Her mental faculties may have declined, perhaps?"

"I don't believe so. She is upset and mystified as to why Miss Greenwood has left, but she is not delusional in my opinion."

"Did you make any other enquiries about Miss Greenwood?"

"Yes. I went to Horley police station. The sergeant there

147

tells me that even though my mother says that Sarah often walked into the village, he has never met her nor heard of her presence at Elm House. I went to the village grocer, butcher and public house, and all the villagers I spoke to deny any knowledge of her."

"You said in your telegram the police will not investigate this. Obviously, they think it fruitless to look for someone whom they believe to be a figment of your mother's imagination. Therefore, we must investigate this matter ourselves," said Holmes purposefully. "When is the next train to Horley?"

"Thank you, Mr. Holmes. I intended to see you and return to Horley by the train that leaves Victoria in sixty-five minutes," Carberry replied, consulting his pocket watch.

"Excellent, we will return with you. You will come, Watson?"

"Of course, if I can help," I replied.

"Your expertise will be invaluable in first establishing Mrs. Carberry's state of mind, Watson. Once we are satisfied on that point, we can commence our search for Miss Greenwood."
*********

After we had cleared the South London suburbs then Croydon, it was but a short trip to Redhill and then Horley. Upon alighting at the station, Holmes asked Carberry how far away Elm House was, and discovering it was less than half a mile, he proposed that we walk in the September sunshine to our destination. A ten minute stroll found us at the gates of Elm House, a modest two-storey Georgian house set in some two acres of ground. Carberry showed us into the parlour and went to fetch his mother, and soon we were being introduced to Mrs. Artemis Carberry, a woman in her sixties I judged. She walked with a cane, and it was clear that her son had inherited her hair colour and eyesight, for she also wore spectacles of some strength. Carberry rang a bell and a stout woman with greying hair and a rather prominent mole on her chin appeared.

"Mrs. Trott, sorry for the late notice," he said, "but our guests will be staying for luncheon. Thank you."

"Now then, Mother," Carberry continued, "Mr. Holmes and Doctor Watson have come from London to help us solve the mystery of Miss Greenwood's disappearance. Please tell them all you know."

"Firstly, I must thank you Mr. Holmes, Doctor Watson for coming to my aid. It is most kind of you to spare me some of your valuable time."

"You are most welcome to any assistance we can provide, Mrs. Carberry," said Holmes. "Now, how did you come to employ Miss Greenwood?"

"About a year ago, the arthritis in my ankles and knees began to worsen until eventually I was compelled to use a cane to get about. As I don't keep a horse or carriage, I am now unable to leave the house, and I decided to advertise for a companion, to keep me company and perform little errands for me. I received several replies to my advertisement, but only one appeared suitable, so I selected Miss Greenwood. She was the unmarried daughter of a schoolmaster and granddaughter of a squire from Gloucestershire. She was well-educated and possessed all the attributes of a lady that I desired in a companion. We also had a common interest in porcelain and other small *objets d'art*. I have been exceedingly happy with her for the last two months.

"Until yesterday. What happened then?"

"I came down to breakfast as usual. I am always a punctual riser, Mr. Holmes, but Sarah was a little more flexible, and generally arrived after me. But yesterday she did not arrive to breakfast at all. I asked Mrs. Trott to discover her whereabouts, but she appeared confused and asked me who I was talking about. It then transpired that Mrs. Trott believes that there has never been a Miss Greenwood here at all, which is nonsense, as she has been serving Miss Greenwood and myself meals for these last two months. She has been an able replacement for Mrs. O'Leary, but now it appears that either she or I are having delusions about the existence of Miss Greenwood."

"So Mrs. Trott has not long been with you? Why is that?" asked Holmes.

"Mrs O'Leary, my housekeeper of many years, had to give me notice. She had to return to Ireland to look after her aged parents. I was most upset to see her go. I advertised the position in the village, and though she lived several miles away, Mrs. Trott heard of it through a friend of the local blacksmith's wife. I hired her about six months ago."

She looked earnestly at Holmes.

"Is it me, Mr. Holmes? Is my mind slipping away from me? Have I dreamt up a companion for myself?"

"I think it unlikely, Mrs. Carberry," said Holmes firmly. "Watson, your medical opinion?"

"It also seems unlikely to me. Although I have not examined you, you appear quite lucid and sane to me, Mrs. Carberry." I said.

"Very well. Mrs. Carberry, have you anything physical which may prove the existence of Miss Greenwood? Her application for the position perhaps?"

"Why yes, I have that somewhere in my bureau upstairs. I shall find it for you. And now that I think of it, she gave me that small bronze dog in the cabinet there for my birthday a few weeks ago. It is by Franz Bergman, an Austrian rapidly establishing a name for himself in bronzes. She knew I would like it, and it came with a note which I also still have."

"Excellent!" replied Holmes. "While you find those papers, we will talk to Mrs. Trott, and also, if we may, inspect the room Miss Greenwood occupied."

"Certainly, please go wherever you think necessary to resolve this matter. Go up the stairs, turn right, and her room is the second on the left."

"One more thing, Mrs. Carberry; could you give me a description of Miss Greenwood?"

"Easily Mr. Holmes, as I have seen her for several hours a day for the past two months. She is the same height as myself, slim of figure, with shoulder-length red hair, though she usually wears it up in a bun. She has blue eyes, and she told me that she was forty-six years of age."

"Thank you, Mrs. Carberry. Come, Watson."

We left the parlour and headed to the kitchen. Mrs. Trott had just taken a delicious-smelling pie from the oven.

"Steak and kidney, is it Mrs. Trott?" I asked, eyeing it hungrily.

"Indeed it is, sir," she replied.

"You are obviously busy with preparing our luncheon, Mrs. Trott, but we would appreciate it if you could answer a few questions for us?" said Holmes smoothly.

"I'll do my best, sir."

"You are aware that Mrs. Carberry believes that she has had a companion living here for the last two months, a Miss Sarah Greenwood. You believe that this is not so, do you not?"

"I know it's not so, sir," she said forcefully. "I've been here nearly six months now, but there has been nobody staying here in that time."

"So how then do you account for Mrs. Carberry's belief?"

"Well, sir, perhaps it's not my place to say, being new and all, but I can only say she must be imagining things. Maybe it's her age, or something not right with her mind, or even wishful thinking. But from what I know of her, I don't think she's deliberately making up this lady companion. I think she's a good and honest person, not given to lying, but she really seems to believe this Miss Greenwood exists, and that is sad –"

She broke off, choking down a sob. Holmes smiled at her reassuringly.

"There now, we'll find out what is going on. I asked Mrs. Carberry if she had any physical proof that Miss Greenwood existed, and I'll ask you a similar question – do you have any proof that she doesn't?"

Mrs. Trott thought for a moment, then went to a drawer in a large dresser against the wall. She took some papers out and presented them to Holmes.

"The only thing I can think of sir, is the fact that it is my job to buy the food for this household. These are the latest monthly accounts from the village grocer, butcher and baker, and I think you'll see that the food I buy would only feed two people, not three. We don't have a kitchen garden either."

Holmes studied the accounts for a couple of minutes.

"Yes, it does seem that the quantities listed here would only support two persons, if as you say you don't grow anything yourselves. Thank you, Mrs. Trott," he said, turning to leave.

I followed Holmes up the stairs and then to the room Mrs. Carberry had said Miss Greenwood had occupied. As we entered, I put a question to him.

"Holmes, is there a rational explanation in which both Mrs. Carberry and Mrs. Trott are right? They both seem so sure of their opposing viewpoints."

"If there is, Watson, I have not yet discovered it. At the moment, it seems that one of them is either lying or deluding themselves. I cannot see what either lady would gain by lying, and we are agreed that Mrs. Carberry appears to be of sound mind. And Mrs. Trott – I have come across a few cases where people have imagined they see something or someone that isn't there, but I have never chanced upon an instance of someone imagining not seeing someone that is there. But we will see what this room can tell us."

The room was furnished as a bedroom, but it struck me that it appeared more like a guest room or a hotel room, not a room a lady had lived in for months. I said as much to Holmes.

"Well-observed, Watson. When a person occupies a room for any length of time, they generally leave the imprint of their life and habits upon it. Just stand there, please, and I will see what I can find."

For the next twenty minutes I watched as he carried out a detailed examination of the room and furniture. He opened all the drawers, even taking them out and looking underneath them, but they were all empty, as was the wardrobe. He investigated the dressing table, even pausing to sniff its surface. He checked the window and its latch, the small writing desk and chair, the chest at the foot of the bed, and the bedside tables. He looked under the bed, and lay on the floor peering at the carpet. However, it was not until he probed the recesses of an armchair near the fireplace that he gave a small "aaah" of satisfaction. He picked up something with his tweezers and beckoned me over.

"It's only suggestive, not conclusive, Watson, but I am coming round to the idea that Miss Sarah Greenwood perhaps did at one time exist and inhabited this room. Whether she still exists, that is another question."

He held out his tweezers, in which was grasped a single red hair.

\*\*\*\*\*\*\*\*\*\*

Carberry came in just then to say lunch was served, so we followed him to the dining room. Holmes whispered to me on the way to tell no-one of our discovery, and during the meal he skilfully deflected any talk of the mystery, conversing at length on Mrs. Carberry's porcelain collection, and the wonders of the Great Exhibition of 1851. At the conclusion of the meal, Mrs.

Carberry handed Holmes Miss Greenwood's application for the position and the note that accompanied the birthday gift.

"I hope these will eliminate any doubts you may have, Mr. Holmes," she said.

"I'm sure they will be most helpful. Watson and I will now continue our investigations in the village and elsewhere. May I borrow the Bergman bronze Miss Greenwood gave you? It could be crucial, and I promise it will be returned."

"Of course, if you need it."

"Thank you, Mrs. Carberry. I will be in touch. Good day to you both."

Holmes studied the application and the note intently as we walked back to Horley, then folded them and placed them in his jacket pocket just as we arrived at the station. We discovered that there was a train to London in ninety minutes.

"That gives us time to conduct a few interviews in the village, Watson. Let us try the grocer over there first."

The grocer and his wife were affable country folk, and readily divulged that Mrs. Trott was a regular customer, and continued to buy the same quantities of food that Mrs. O'Leary had before her. They had never heard of or seen a Miss Greenwood. It was a similar story at the butcher's shop and the bakery. The bakery also provided teas, scones and a selection of cakes, so as we still had forty minutes to catch our train, we took tea and discussed the case.

"Doesn't the hair you found prove that Miss Greenwood exists?" I ventured.

"So you would think, Watson. But I have a suspicion that this whole affair is deeper than we imagine. Strictly speaking, the hair does not prove Miss Greenwood exists. It may not even prove that a red-headed woman perhaps once sat in that chair, as it is conceivable that someone placed the hair there for us to find. But also, Watson, if Miss Greenwood exists and has for some reason disappeared, how did she do so? The usual clothes and effects of a lady would entail considerable baggage – did she walk to Horley in the middle of the night, carrying off all her belongings on her back? Or –" he stopped, a pensive look on his face.

"But if Miss Greenwood does or did exist, then why does Mrs. Trott insist she doesn't? What is her motive? And Carberry said his mother had told him that Miss Greenwood often walked into the village, so why haven't any of the villagers seen her?

"As I said, this matter is deep, and also murky at present."

"What of the letter and note Mrs. Carberry gave you? Did they reveal anything?"

"The letter was written by a right-handed, educated Englishwoman using the language and grammatical structures one might expect in applying for the position of lady's companion. The note is in the same handwriting, and merely wishes Mrs. Carberry a happy birthday and hopes the gift will please her. It is signed simply 'Sarah.' There is one lead provided in the letter, which I will follow up once we are home. It is a long shot, however. But on the way back to London, we will try another long shot, and get off at Croydon."

"Why Croydon?" I asked.

"Because, Watson, I believe it is the nearest place to Horley where one might obtain a Bergman bronze. Come, our train awaits!"

\*\*\*\*\*\*\*\*\*\*

The Croydon stationmaster proved very helpful, and named two shops within walking distance where one could buy fancy porcelain, ceramic figurines, small bronzes and the like. We tried the nearer first.

"So you are endeavouring to ascertain who bought the bronze dog for Mrs. Carberry's birthday," I suggested as we strolled along.

"Exactly, Watson. Here we are, Arnoldson's Emporium."

Holmes asked for the manager, and his card produced a reverence and a willingness to assist which was most gratifying. Upon seeing the bronze, the manager agreed that he had bought four of them for sale in his shop, two had been sold already, and two remained on his shelves.

"I don't suppose you recall to whom you sold the two that have gone?" Holmes asked.

"Yes I do, Mr. Holmes. The first one I sold the day after I put them out for sale, to Mr. Tilney. He is often in here, and bought it for his wife."

"And the second?" prompted Holmes.

"It was a lady I have never seen before, or since. Some three weeks ago if I remember, she came in looking for a gift. I showed her several items, but she settled on the Bergman dog."

"Please describe this woman."

"Well, as I said she was a lady, well-dressed, well-spoken, average height. I suppose she might have been in her forties, though I'm not good with women's ages."

"Hair and eyes?"

"Her eyes I don't remember, and her hair was up and mostly hidden by her hat. But a few wisps had escaped, and it was quite a vibrant red colour."

"Thank you, Mr. Arnoldson. Your assistance has been invaluable."

"My pleasure, Mr. Holmes."

Once back out on the street, I immediately put it to Holmes that Arnoldson's description of the woman who bought the bronze tallied with that given by Mrs. Carberry of Miss Greenwood.

"True, Watson, Miss Greenwood now appears to have some substance, does she not? But we still have work to do. If she does exist, where has she gone? And why do Mrs. Trott and the villagers deny her existence?" It is quite a problem, which I shall tackle tomorrow. For now, back to Baker Street."

\*\*\*\*\*\*\*\*\*\*

Holmes sent off a wire early the next day, then spent the rest of the morning in a complicated chemical analysis. I made a few house calls, but returned punctually at one o'clock for Mrs. Hudson's Irish stew, one of my favourites. We had just finished dining when a telegram arrived. Holmes read it, then thoughtfully lit a cigarette.

"Good news, Holmes?" I queried.

"Some progress, Watson. Miss Sarah Greenwood did exist, at least in Gloucestershire," he replied. I wired the police in Tetbury in that fair county to clear up some points in connection with Miss Greenwood's ancestry, which she outlined in her letter of application. She claimed to be the daughter of a schoolmaster and granddaughter of a local squire living near Tetbury, and this appears to be true. An Inspector Mickle of the Tetbury constabulary, who knows the family, informs me that when Sarah Greenwood came of age, she went to work in London as a governess, for whom he does not know, but will endeavour to find out from the members of her family that remain in the area. The father and grandfather have now both passed on. He also states that Miss Greenwood would be forty-six years old now, and has red hair and blue eyes."

I thought for a moment.

"But Holmes, is there any proof really that this Sarah Greenwood from Gloucestershire is the same woman that Mrs Carberry hired as her companion?"

"Very shrewdly put, Watson! Yes, that is one possibility; that someone has stolen Miss Greenwood's identity and background to obtain a position she would not merit ordinarily. But to what end? If it were just to obtain a well-paid situation, why the disappearance?"

"What is your next move then?"

"I will smoke several pipefuls of tobacco and cogitate, while I await further information from Inspector Mickle," said Holmes, moving to the mantelpiece and selecting his favourite clay from the several pipes there.

\*\*\*\*\*\*\*\*\*\*

It was not until late the next morning that Holmes received another telegram from Inspector Mickle, and he appeared to be much pleased by it.

"Now we can get on, Watson, if you are free," he said briskly, throwing off his dressing gown. "We have information we can work on."

"Certainly, Holmes, where are we going?"

"To Chelsea, the home of the Debbingtons."

In less than ten minutes we had dressed, hailed a cab and were on our way to Chelsea. We pulled up outside one of a row of large terrace houses, and Holmes jumped out, asked the cabbie to wait, strode up the steps and rapped on the door. A solemn-faced butler answered, and Holmes presented his card and asked to see the lady of the house.

"I'm sorry, sir, but both Mr. and Mrs. Debbington are not at home today," said the butler. "I shall tell them you called."

"Perhaps you can help me in their absence. What is your name, my good man?" asked Holmes.

"My name is Mansfield, sir, but I don't –"

"Mansfield, I am engaged in a serious investigation, and it is very important that I determine the whereabouts of a Miss Sarah Greenwood, whom I believe is or was employed here as a governess."

"Miss Sarah, sir! Yes, she was governess here, but only for some eight or nine years. Master Tobias grew up and went to

Eton, sir, so her services were no longer required. She left us nearly twenty years ago now."

Holmes face fell.

"Please say you recall where she went?" he sighed.

"I do sir. The Debbingtons gave her a glowing reference, which enabled her to go straight into a new position as housekeeper for a Mr. Huntington, an elderly single man."

"Residing where?"

"He resides, sir, on a large property in Hampstead called Delphi Park."

"Thank you, Mansfield," said Holmes, and we returned to the cab.

"Cabbie! You know Delphi Park in Hampstead?"

"Yes guv, I knows it."

"Then that's our destination."

We got in and were soon on our way to Hampstead at a trot.

\*\*\*\*\*\*\*\*\*\*

Delphi Park turned out to be an impressive early-Victorian edifice, set in its own extensive gardens. Our cab approached the front entrance, where there was a waiting carriage. There was a well-dressed man talking to a woman on the steps, and they looked at us as we pulled to a stop. Holmes and I got out.

"Good morning, Doctor Jamieson!" Holmes called out.

The man looked startled.

"Do I know you, sir?" he asked politely.

"No, sir, we have not met, but the medical bag you are holding is embossed with 'Dr. A. W. Jamieson,' so the deduction was simple in the extreme. Sherlock Holmes, sir, at your service, with my colleague Doctor Watson."

"The detective? Pleasure to meet you, sir. You too, Doctor.

What brings you here?"

"We are here to speak to Mr. Huntington, but your presence implies he may not be in the best of health."

Doctor Jamieson looked at the woman, who nodded.

"This is Miss Johnson, the housekeeper," said Doctor Jamieson. "Yes, Mr. Huntington hasn't been in the best of health for a number of years now, and I'm afraid the end is not far away. A weak heart mainly, but cigars and alcohol have also left their mark. His age is against him too, seventy-five last month."

"Is he able to see us, do you think?"

"He is able, I should judge, but whether he will or not I couldn't say. He doesn't see many people."

Holmes turned to the housekeeper.

"Miss Johnson, would you take my card to your master and ask if he will admit us, please? It is an important matter," asked Holmes earnestly.

Miss Johnson nodded, took the card and went inside.

We conversed with Jamieson until she returned, saying Mr. Huntington would see us, but that we were not to excite him in any way. We bade farewell to Jamieson, and followed Miss Johnson up the staircase to the old man's room. She knocked on the door and entered.

"Mr. Holmes and Doctor Watson, sir," she said, then withdrew.

The room was in semidarkness, the curtains being drawn. An emaciated figure was propped up in the bed, looking every one of his seventy-five years. His eyes were bright however, and he looked at us curiously.

"I've heard of you of course, Mr. Holmes. Please sit down. What can I do for you?" he said, in a stronger voice than I would have anticipated.

"Good afternoon, sir, thank you for seeing us," said

Holmes. "We are endeavouring to trace a woman named Sarah Greenwood, whom I believe came into your service about twenty years ago."

"Miss Greenwood? Yes, she was my housekeeper until about, let me think, five or six months ago. She left me rather abruptly, and I employed Miss Johnson in her stead."

"She left abruptly, you say – what reason did she give?"

"None. It was most inconvenient, I can tell you. She had been here so long, she knew all my whims and fancies. She just gave a week's notice and just said it was something she had to do."

"You found her of good character and a satisfactory servant, then?"

"Well, yes, although she didn't seem to like the word servant being applied to her. She had an education, you see, and she told me once she was descended from wealthy landowners. She certainly spoke well, and we had many interesting conversations, about art and history mainly. I am fond of the ancient Greek culture myself, chiefly because my father also had the same interest, such that it even influenced the name he bestowed on me. Apollo Huntington, sir, that is my name. It's also the reason I called my home Delphi Park, after the oracle."

"I see. So you can tell us nothing about where Miss Greenwood went when she left your employ?"

"Not a thing."

Holmes stood up.

"Thank you again for your time, Mr. Huntington. Good day to you, sir."

Miss Johnson was waiting for us outside the bedroom.

"I'll show you out, gentlemen," she said, and we followed down the stairs to the entry hall. Here Holmes stopped.

"Miss Johnson, may I ask you a few questions if you have

161

time?"

"Yes, Mr. Holmes, I have time," she replied.

"You were employed here to replace the housekeeper who left, a Miss Greenwood. Do you know anything about her, why she left, where she went?"

"I never met her of course," said Miss Johnson, "but the other servants here have told me about her. Mr. Huntington has simple needs, but it is a large house, and there is a butler, a footman who doubles as his valet, a cook, three maids, a gardener and a boy. They have all said much the same thing about Miss Greenwood; that she was once upon a time a friendly and polite person, but in the last two or three years before she left, she did become quieter, less cheerful, even despondent I'm told. Mr. Huntington thought she needed some intellectual stimulation, so he allowed her the use of the library."

"I realise you weren't here, but do you know of anything that occurred that was out of the ordinary, anything unusual that might have made her want to leave?"

"There is only one unusual event I recall, although I would have thought it would make anyone want to stay here rather than leave. Mr. Huntington made a new will just before she left, in which all the servants were to receive two years wages upon his death."

"Interesting. That does seem like an incentive to stay. Who else benefits from this new will?"

"To understand that, you will need to know about Mr. Huntington's history. Yates, the butler, has spoken of it to me once or twice. It seems that Mr. Huntington's father was an educated but poor man. When Mr. Huntington was aged seven, his mother died three days after giving birth to a daughter, who also died within days. He and his father struggled to keep body and soul together, but in the end through sheer hard work, Mr. Huntington became owner of one of the largest brick factories in

England. With that came riches, naturally, and he bought this house and had his father live here in comfort in his declining years.

"Mr. Huntington senior passed on about fifteen years ago, and in his effects was found a letter to his son, to be opened after his death. In this letter, he revealed that our Mr. Huntington's sister had not in fact died after all. With his wife's death and a small boy to care for, he had been forced to give her up, so the infant had been left in a church. Well, Mr. Huntington became quite distraught as you can imagine, suddenly finding out he had a sister. He thought she should share in his riches, and he spent some years and a considerable amount of money trying to find her, but there wasn't much in the way of clues in his father's letter. He gave up in the end, but when he realised his time was nearly up, he made the new will, leaving small amounts to the servants as I said and the remainder of his estate to his sister, if she could be found."

"And if she can't?"

"If his sister cannot be found within one year from Mr. Huntington's death, or it is determined she has also died, his estate is to be divided up amongst various charities. Yates overheard the lawyers who came here to draw up the will – the estate is worth some £60,000."

Holmes appeared to be thinking rapidly, then he spoke.

"Miss Johnson, do you think Mr. Huntington would mind if we spent a little time in his library? I assure you it could be of crucial importance to discovering the whereabouts of not only Sarah Greenwood, but his long-lost sister as well."

Miss Johnson looked astonished, as did I.

"If you can find his sister, I don't think he'll mind where you go, Mr. Holmes. This way."

She showed us to the library, which in its number of books was not extensive. I noticed that the majority concerned the

163

ancient Greeks; their civilisation, history, art and architecture, philosophy and literature. Holmes stalked around the room, looking at the books on the shelves, then he went to the desk, upon which there were several loose volumes. He flipped through these, then tried the desk drawers. One was locked. He looked up at Miss Johnson, who smiled.

"Yes, Mr. Holmes, as housekeeper I have a copy of all the keys," she said, selecting one from a score of keys on a ring and opening the drawer.

Holmes pulled a large book from the drawer and placed it on the desk. I could see from where I was that it was a old King James Bible, with a heavily decorated cover. He opened it to the title page, then flipped through it, but when he reached the last page he stopped and studied it. Suddenly, he bent over so his face was nearly touching the pages. When he raised his head, his eyes were twinkling with excitement.

"Miss Johnson! Is Mr. Huntington a religious man?"

"No sir, he is not, more's the pity. A man at the end of his life should make his peace with God, but many times I've heard him say he has no time for religion."

Holmes stood up, grabbed me by the arm and steered me towards the door.

"Come, Watson! Thank you, Miss Johnson!" he shouted back over his shoulder.

\*\*\*\*\*\*\*\*\*\*

Instructing our cabbie to drive us to Victoria Station, we left Delphi Park. Holmes was deep in thought, and though I still did not understand what had happened in the library, I was loath to interrupt his thoughts. He remained silent until we arrived, where we discovered that the next train to Horley was due to leave in fifty-five minutes. As it was now mid-afternoon, we retired to the station cafe for sandwiches and tea. Half-way through his second cup, I remarked that he had obviously found a clue at Delphi Park.

"Watson, I must confess that when we arrived there I was hoping purely to find out more about Miss Greenwood. But Miss Johnson's revelation about Mr. Huntington's past provided an unexpected insight into this mystery, and I believe I now have most of the threads in my hand."

"Indeed! I don't suppose you would care to share them with me?

"Very well, I will tell you those facts of which I am reasonably certain. Here is what I think happened, a story which started seventy-five years ago when Mr. Huntington was born. His father, enamoured of the Greek civilisation, christened his son Apollo. Seven years later, his mother gave birth to a daughter and died shortly thereafter. The young Apollo was told his sister had also died. Through his determination and hard work he rose from his penurious childhood to become a wealthy man, but fifteen years ago his father died. Wanting his son to know the truth, he had left a letter telling him that in fact his sister had not died, but because he was then father of a young boy, without the help of a wife, and still poor, he was compelled to present her as a foundling into the care of a church.

"In the meantime, however, in the days between his daughter being born and his decision to give her up, he had done what is common practice in many families, and recorded her birth in the family bible, on the last page in this instance. The bible in Huntington's library was published in 1768, and there are several generations of the Huntington family listed in it. The last entry though, records that on the 18th of July, 1830, a girl was born and given the name of the Greek god Apollo's sister, Artemis.

"Artemis! But that's –"

"Exactly, Watson. I believe Mrs. Artemis Carberry is Apollo Huntington's sister."

"That's extraordinary, Holmes. But how does that connect with the disappearance of Miss Greenwood?"

"Did you notice, Watson, during my examination of Miss Greenwood's room at Elm House, I became aware of a lingering scent on the dressing table."

"Yes, I remember now, you sniffed its surface."

"When women sit at a dressing table and spray a perfume about their face and neck, a large residuum of the scent droplets fall to the surface. It was still discernible to me, and although it was not one of those I am familiar with enough to give it a name, I filed the scent away for future reference. I have just discovered the same scent in Mr. Huntington's library."

"The bible! You sniffed at the last page!" I cried.

"Yes, Watson, this proved to me that Miss Greenwood had handled the bible, and left a trace of her perfume on it, probably from her wrists. So, as we have heard, she was originally happy in her position with Mr. Huntington, but after many years became dissatisfied. Her education and family connections made her think she was entitled to a better life than she had at present. Huntington allowed her the full use of his library in an effort to give her intellectual fulfilment, but this was not the cause of her unhappiness.

"In the library one day she picked up the family bible and discovered the secret of Mr. Huntington's sister. For some reason we'll never know, Huntington's father had not revealed her name or any details fifteen years earlier, but now Miss Greenwood had a name and a date of birth. Not being a religious man, Apollo Huntington had probably never opened the bible; or if he did on rare occasions, he had not looked at the last page, and so has never discovered what Miss Greenwood now knew.

"Huntington had just made a new will leaving the bulk of his fortune to his sister, if she could be found, and it occurred to Miss Greenwood that if she could track down the sister, and somehow ingratiate her way into her life, there might be some money in it for her. Perhaps her plans were a little unformed at this stage, but track her down she did, through the church records I imagine. So she left Huntington's employ and moved somewhere near Horley, to investigate and acquaint herself with the life and habits of Mrs. Artemis Carberry, nee Huntington."

"And then she discovered that Mrs. Carberry wanted a companion," I said. "Do you think she secured the position with the intent of living on the largess of Mrs. Carberry? Once Mr. Huntington had died and she had somehow alerted the estate's lawyers of his sister's whereabouts, Mrs. Carberry would be a wealthy woman."

"Possibly, Watson. But I suspect she had other, more sinister intentions, which I cannot share just now."

"But even so, none of this explains her disappearance and Mrs. Trott's assertion that she never existed. We have proved beyond doubt that she does, have we not?"

"We have, Watson. And I hope to reveal the solution to the mystery when we reach Horley. There is our train, I believe!"

\*\*\*\*\*\*\*\*\*\*

The journey to Horley was uneventful, and upon our arrival Holmes excused himself for a minute and dashed into the police station. We then set off on foot to Elm House. It was a delightful walk in the late afternoon sun, and in ten minutes Holmes was knocking on the door. Mr. Carberry answered.

"Mr. Holmes! And Doctor Watson. It's good to see you, gentlemen, come in. Do you have news?"

"Indeed, Mr. Carberry, I think we may clear up this mystery shortly," replied Holmes. "Is your mother in the parlour? If so, we'll join her there, and if you could ask Mrs. Trott for some tea I would be most grateful, for it has been a long day."

"Certainly, Mr. Holmes, Mother is in the parlour, do go

through, and I will see about the tea."

Mrs. Carberry greeted us warmly.

"Welcome, Mr. Holmes, Doctor. Have you made any progress?"

"I believe so, but I first need to confirm one or two details. I do beg your pardon in advance, madam; I know in polite society it is in poor taste to discuss a lady's age, but it is necessary in this case. I assure you, it would be of immense help to me to ascertain your date and year of birth."

Mrs. Carberry gave a small frown, but then shrugged and smiled.

"Very well, Mr. Holmes, if it helps. I was born on July the 18th, in the year 1830."

"Thank you, Mrs. Carberry. One more thing, and again I apologise if this touches on a sensitive matter, but do you know the circumstances of your birth?"

Mrs. Carberry paled.

"You obviously know, Mr. Holmes, but how? And what has my birth do with Miss Greenwood's disappearance?"

"All will become clear, Mrs. Carberry, but I can tell you, the fact that you were left to all intents and purposes an orphan in a church, is directly responsible for Miss Greenwood's presence in your home."

Mrs. Carberry looked astonished, as well she might. She turned to look at me.

"Doctor Watson, in the desk behind you, in the right-hand drawer, you will find a pale blue envelope. Would you pass it to me please?"

I found the envelope and handed it to her. She opened it, and withdrew a single sheet of folded notepaper, handing it to Holmes. He glanced at it and passed it to me.

"I was abandoned in a church as a baby, only a few days

old," said Mrs. Carberry. "This was pinned to the basket I was in."

The note read:

*Please look after her, for I cannot. Her name is Artemis, born 18th July, 1830. Thank you.*

At this point, her son came in.

"Tea will be here shortly Mr. Holmes. What's this? Mother, why are you showing them that note?" he said with some concern.

"It's all right, dear. Mr. Holmes needed to know our family secret as part of his investigation."

"I don't understand –"

"Then let me make it clear Mr. Carberry," Holmes interrupted. "You hired me initially to determine if such a person as Miss Sarah Greenwood had existed here as your mother's companion, and if she had, why she had suddenly disappeared without trace."

He got up and started pacing about the room.

"The case was complicated by the fact that although Mrs. Carberry believed that Miss Greenwood had lived here for two months, her bedroom was completely empty of her clothes or belongings. It was also true that your housekeeper denied ever seeing her, and no-one in the village knew of her existence either. Also, the food bought for the household was only sufficient for two persons, Mrs. Trott and Mrs. Carberry.

However, the clues which I have found, and the leads I have followed now enable me to answer those initial questions – ah, here is Mrs. Trott with our tea."

He opened the door, and Mrs. Trott entered bearing a tray, which she placed on the tea table.

"I can now assure you both that Miss Sarah Greenwood does exist, and lived here for two months," Holmes continued.

"As to where she is now –"

He sprang forward and grasped Mrs. Trott's grey hair, which came away in his hand, a cascade of red falling about her stunned face. Holmes reached towards her again, and he plucked the prominent mole off her chin.

"Mrs. Carberry, I'm sure when she removes all the padding about her dress which completes her disguise, you will recognise your companion, Miss Sarah Greenwood?"

Both the Carberrys sat open-mouthed in disbelief. Miss Greenwood gave a hoarse cry and moved towards the door, but Holmes headed her off.

"Please don't try to escape, Miss Greenwood. The police will be here soon, after I asked them to give me a thirty minute start. Just sit down, and if you wouldn't mind clearing up a few details for Watson's records?"

Miss Greenwood looked sullenly at each of us in turn, then sank into a chair.

"Mrs. Carberry, I realise you have had a shock. Please have some tea, for I have another shock for you, albeit a more pleasant one. You recall I said that you being found in a church was the cause of Miss Greenwood's presence here?

She nodded slowly, while her son poured her a tea and gave it to her.

"I'm afraid to say your mother died shortly after giving birth to you, and your impoverished father did not have the means to care for you, as he already had a son. That son, who is your brother, and yourself were named after the Greek god and goddess who were also brother and sister, Apollo and Artemis. Your brother, Mrs. Carberry, eventually became a wealthy industrialist. He is still alive, but is ailing and has not very long to live. His will leaves his house and most of his fortune to yourself, the sister he never knew."

Mrs. Carberry put her hand to her mouth in surprise.

"Miss Greenwood here worked for your brother," Holmes continued, "and discovered information which led to her being able to ascertain your name and whereabouts. She moved near here six months ago with the intention of somehow finding a way into your life and getting hold of at least some of the money you would soon inherit. In what appeared to be a fantastic stroke of luck for her, when she arrived you were advertising for a housekeeper. As this was a role she could play easily, she applied for the position but in the guise of Mrs. Trott, already planning to one day appear as herself in some other role and then disappear."

"But why?" asked Carberry.

"Her plan was – and you can correct me if I'm wrong, Miss Greenwood – to make your mother believe she was going insane, by insisting on the existence of a companion, which Mrs. Trott would deny ever being here. Was it not Mrs. Trott who suggested that you needed a companion, Mrs. Carberry, or at least encouraged you to advertise for one?"

"You are right, Mr. Holmes! I mentioned one day that I needed someone to talk to now that I couldn't get about, and she – Mrs. Trott, that is – strongly suggested a companion would be ideal."

"Her plan was aided by your poor eyesight, and with a wig, some padding and a large mole to distract the eye from the other facial features, Mrs. Trott became your housekeeper. After a settling-in period, she convinced you that a companion was needed. As she now knew you well, her application was easily the most suitable, even mentioning a love of porcelain, and then Miss Greenwood, lady's companion, came to live here. It must have been quite difficult, playing both roles for two months, but you recall, Watson, that Miss Greenwood was invariably late down to breakfast? Mrs. Trott was the early riser, cooked the breakfast and served it, then quickly shed her disguise and appeared as Miss Greenwood.

"This pantomime was re-enacted at other mealtimes, and I'm sure she would always be your intermediary to deliver messages to Mrs. Trott because of your infirmity. So you never realised that you had never seen them together in the same room. When she said she was walking into town, she just became Mrs. Trott, and never appeared in the village as Miss Greenwood. The food requirements never changed, as there was only ever two people in the house. Then when she knew your son was arriving, she cleared out and cleaned her room the night before, and failed to appear at breakfast that day. Her clothes and effects are I imagine in Mrs. Trott's room?"

Miss Greenwood nodded.

"She planned to reappear once Jonathon had gone to Canada, probably confusing Mrs. Carberry by saying she had never left, and having Mrs. Trott now acknowledge her existence. With her son in Canada, she hoped that making Mrs. Carberry appear to not be of sound mind would enable her to obtain a power of attorney over her affairs. Then she could control the money legally. But if that failed, you had another plan in reserve, did you not, Miss Greenwood?"

"You'll never prove that," she said, shrugging her shoulders.

"Perhaps," said Holmes. "But if after she had inherited, you could convince Mrs. Carberry to make another will in your favour, well I would not be at all confident of her enjoying a very long life. With her unsteadiness of gait, an accidental fall down the stairs would be simple to arrange."

Just then I noticed through the window that two policemen were arriving in a trap, so I went to let them in, showing them into the parlour.

"Sergeant, thank you for your punctuality," said Holmes. "Here is your prisoner, Miss Sarah Greenwood, the charge will be attempting to obtain money by deception."

The Carberrys, mother and son, seemed to have somewhat recovered their composure, after learning in short order about the machinations of Miss Greenwood, the existence of Mrs. Carberry's brother, and the fortune he planned to bequeath her.

"Mr. Holmes," said Mrs. Carberry. "I would like you and Doctor Watson to be my guests tonight, and then tomorrow could I impose on you to introduce me to my brother, and Jonathon to his uncle? The money is not really important to me at my age, but it will secure my son's future. You won't have to go to Canada now, will you dear?"

"We'll see, Mother," he smiled.

\*\*\*\*\*\*\*\*\*\*

After dinner that night, prepared by Mrs. Carberry with Jonathon's assistance, Holmes filled in the details of his investigation for them.

"Once I had discovered the red hair and the scent in Miss Greenwood's room. I was sure she existed. Her being seen purchasing the bronze confirmed it. That meant Mrs. Trott was lying, but to what end? She was very quick to point out to us that she had not been buying food for three, a fact which I confirmed at the village shops. Mrs. Carberry definitely existed, as did Mrs. Trott. If Miss Greenwood also existed, then the only solution I could think of where three people only eat like two people, is that there are in fact only two people, and one of them was acting in two roles. Miss Johnson gave us the motive for the deception, and the bible provided the information possible for Miss Greenwood to carry it through. A very convoluted plot in the end."

"And brilliantly unravelled by you, Holmes," I said, raising my glass.

Mrs. Artemis Carberry spent the next seven weeks at the bedside of her brother, Mr. Apollo Huntington. They had two lifetimes of experiences to talk about, and he then passed away a very happy man. Delphi Park is now the home of Mr. and Mrs. Jonathon Carberry and his mother. However, Miss Sarah Greenwood managed to avoid a prison sentence.

"Unfortunately, Watson, people cannot be punished for what they might have done, only for what it can be proved they have actually done," said Holmes, after reading of the trial. "What did Sarah Greenwood do? She obtained the position of lady's companion, and fulfilled that role for two months. That is not a crime. She then vanished abruptly. That is also not a crime. She disguised herself as Mrs. Trott and worked as a housekeeper. Nothing criminal there. We know her intentions were malicious, fraudulent and possibly murderous, but there is no proof. The judge censured her, but she is free to go about her life."

"She might find it difficult to obtain employment now, which is something," I observed.

"Perhaps, Watson. As I remarked at the beginning of this matter, some very interesting cases have no crime attached to them, but I think here we can be satisfied that we have at least prevented a crime."

"Which is all to the good," I said emphatically.

# THE ADVENTURE OF THE BENEVOLENT THIEF

I had been sharing our Baker Street rooms with Sherlock Holmes for about two years, when all London was gripped by a mystery which caused much speculation in the press and much disquiet at Scotland Yard. A young woman faced the gallows, and amongst the public there was both belief in her innocence with consequent sympathy, and belief in her guilt with a desire for punishment. Officially, at least, the case was not resolved satisfactorily, and so after this remove of years I wish to place on record the truth concerning the matter the newspapers almost universally described as the "modern-day Robin Hood."

There had been three instances of robbery in the streets and one of burglary before Holmes became involved in the case. We had read of these in the papers of course; on three occasions wealthy gentlemen had strayed into dark places late at night and been divested of their cash at gunpoint. In one case, the amount stolen was £25, and the next day, a man dressed in black with a black scarf around the lower part of his face walked into an orphanage and threw an envelope containing £30 on to the desk of Mrs. Reid, the head of the establishment. The man then ran off without saying a word.

The confused Mrs. Reid notified the police, and the gentleman who had been robbed the night before advised the police that the money might possibly be his. However, he hastily withdrew his claim when there was an outcry over the relative positions in society of himself and the orphanage, and together with the fact the amount given to the orphanage differed from the amount stolen, the orphanage was allowed to keep it.

A week later, a well-dressed gentleman had £65 taken from him in the early hours of the morning, also at gunpoint by a man dressed in black with a scarf over his face. A constable on the beat, on turning a corner had happened upon the incident

175

occurring across the street, just as the thief took the money and disappeared down an alley. He gave futile chase, and returning to the scene of the crime it transpired that the gentleman did not wish to press charges or give his name. The constable attributed this to the fact that he wore a wedding ring, while his much younger and rather gaudily dressed companion did not. The next day, £60 in an envelope was delivered by a messenger to a charity which aided the blind.

A few days later, another of the landed gentry was relieved of some £40 in notes and coins in an alley near his club. The thief was a man of average height, dressed all in black, with a scarf hiding his features and carrying a pistol. This amount was never recovered nor heard of again, and the press speculated that it had perhaps also been given to a worthy cause, which had chosen to remain quiet about the gift lest it be taken from them.

In the fourth instance, the youngest son of an earl had his apartment burgled whilst he was out for the evening and his valet and housekeeper had the night off. Approximately £150 was taken, he thought – the young aristocrat said that he had so much money that he was never completely sure how much he had in cash lying around at any given moment. This statement did not endear him to the public; and so when £170 was found in the offertory bag of a local church active in helping the poor, the general opinion was that even if the money did belong to the Honourable James Phipps-Chattington, it would be put to far better use by Father Martin.

Holmes and I were discussing the case one morning, Holmes noting that the thief displayed some intelligence in stealing only cash, when in all four cases jewellery and other valuables were available for the taking.

"He obviously does not want to raise further money by either pawning items which may be traced back to him, or selling goods to a fence who may later betray him," Holmes remarked.

"He is also rapidly attaining the status of a folk hero," I replied. "According to *The Guardian*, he is a modern Robin Hood and many people are of the opinion that the police should not try too hard to apprehend him."

"Indeed! One could argue that is what the police are doing, as Lestrade has been assigned the case," Holmes said with a chuckle.

Just then, we heard a carriage pull up outside and moments later a knock on our front door. A further minute later, Mrs. Hudson knocked and entered, proffering a tray with a card upon it. Holmes picked it up.

"Mr. Oliver Webster, Accountant," he read out. "Send him up, Mrs. Hudson."

Mr. Oliver Webster turned out to be a slim young man, dark-haired, clean shaven and well-dressed. His worried expression told of some burden in his life, which after introducing me, Holmes invited him to divulge.

"I have been advised to come and see you, sir. My sister has been arrested for murder by Inspector Lestrade, but she is innocent, sir, and you must prove it!"

"Please compose yourself, Mr. Webster," said Holmes, "and tell me the facts, in order, and I will endeavour to assist you."

"Yes, of course. I apologise for my disconcertedness." He took a deep breath.

"My sister is Julia Webster, and she is the manager of The Society for Housing and Employment, a charitable organisation she founded herself some three years ago. Its object is to provide aid to the poor of the East End, in the form of finding housing and jobs for the destitute, which hopefully keeps them from having to enter the workhouse. She has the day-to-day running of the charity, with assistance from several volunteers, and she also applies to various businesses and wealthy individuals, asking them to become donors in order to maintain the charity. She takes no wage herself, you understand; she still lives with our parents in some comfort. Father is the owner of several haberdashery shops, and is happy for her to spend her time helping those less fortunate. I myself keep the books for the charity, without charge – I am employed by day at Eversley & Johnson, Chartered Accountants.

"I had just arrived at work this morning when I received a telegram from Julia, urgently asking me to meet her at the charity's headquarters. I begged leave from my employer, and took a cab straight there. I found Julia in her office, counting a large sum of money. She said that she had found it in an envelope pushed under the front door when she arrived that morning. I have counted it twice, she said, and there is exactly £1,000, enough to keep the charity afloat for some time and perhaps even extend its range of operations. She then asked my advice as to how to proceed.

Just then Inspector Lestrade and two constables came in. He at once saw the money on the desk, and he said because of that and two eyewitness accounts, he had to arrest her for the theft of the money and the murder of a Mr. Elias Davies the previous evening. We were both stunned as you can imagine.

"Now I cannot tell you the full story, Mr. Holmes, as Inspector Lestrade would only let me speak to Julia for a minute before he took her away to interview her. She told me that she had indeed visited Mr. Davies last night, and they had even argued, but she had not killed him of course. As the inspector was taking her away, one of the constables, seeing I was distressed, took me aside and said that you have a reputation for solving difficult mysteries, and gave me your address."

"Who is this Elias Davies? Do you know him?" asked Holmes.

"We have never met, but Julia has mentioned him to me

on several occasions," replied Webster. "He is a landlord with a reputation for extreme meanness. He owns dozens of properties, and rents them to the poor. They are all squalid, poorly maintained, and overcrowded, and he has no hesitation in throwing families onto the street for being a day or two late with the rent. For this reason, he is known throughout the East End as 'Eviction' Davies. I have no doubt Julia visited him to argue on behalf of some tenants of his; she has done so before."

"Very well, Mr. Webster, I will look into this matter for you. I will first go to Scotland Yard; Lestrade owes me one or two favours, so I think he will let me speak to Miss Webster. I have your card, and I will be in touch. Rest assured, I will do everything in my power for your sister."

"Thank you, sir, I'm sure you will," said Webster with obvious relief. "Good day to you, and to you, Doctor."

Holmes filled and lit his pipe as Webster's footsteps receded down the stairs. He then looked at me with a twinkle in his eye.

"You look like a man with something to say, Watson," he remarked.

"Well yes. A large amount of money has been stolen from a rich man, and given to a charity. Do you not think this is another example of the work of the mysterious Robin Hood?"

"It is certainly possible, Watson, but if it is he, he has progressed to murder this time. Or there could be another explanation entirely. We have not yet ascertained all the facts. We need to hear Miss Webster's story, and also speak to Lestrade about these two eyewitnesses he mentioned. A visit to the scene of the crime is also required. Let us bestir ourselves and make haste to Scotland Yard!"

\*\*\*\*\*\*\*\*\*\*

We arrived at the Yard by hansom within half an hour, and asked for Lestrade. A constable showed us to his office, where we found him busy writing in his notebook.

"Ah, Inspector! I trust you are not putting the final touches to your report on the murder of Mr. Elias Davies?" said Holmes with a smile.

"And what if I am?" said Lestrade suspiciously.

"I am acting for Miss Julia Webster, and I would just like to satisfy myself as to her guilt or innocence before you put the noose around her neck, if I may."

"She's guilty all right, Mr. Holmes, and no mistake. The butler showed her in to see Mr. Davies, and he heard them arguing. She then left the house in a temper, also seen by the butler. Ten minutes later, Constable Porter, on the beat which runs past the dead man's house, saw Miss Webster, whom he knows by sight, coming out of the gate of the Davies residence. She appeared upset and flustered, and Porter flagged down a cab for her and saw her safely away. This morning the butler sent a messenger to us to say his master's been killed. The French window to the study is open, Davies is dead and the safe is open and empty. I went to the charity where she works because she was the last person we know of to see Davies alive, and I found her with a large sum of money on her desk. Easiest case I've ever handled," he said, leaning back in his chair.

"Yes, very easy. So you think she left the house then returned, entering through the open window and murdered Davies? How was he killed?"

"He was coshed on the back of the head, a simple matter as he was sitting at his desk with his back to the open window."

"And Miss Webster, having dispatched him, then displays her safe-cracking skills and robs him?"

"No, the safe was open already. The butler, Holywell by name, noticed that when he said goodnight to Davies, after Miss Webster had left."

"I see. Come Inspector, do you not entertain the slightest

doubt that a young woman of good character who voluntarily runs a charity for three years, suddenly bludgeons a man to death in order to steal from him? Does this sound likely to you?"

"I follow where the evidence leads," said Lestrade loftily.

"Then I don't think you have found all the evidence. May we see Miss Webster please?"

"Very well, Holmes, as you've been of some help to me once or twice I will allow you to see her. But I think you're on the wrong track this time."

He led us to the cells, and indicated to the police matron that we were to spend fifteen minutes with Miss Webster, no longer. The matron opened the cell door, bade us enter and locked it behind us. Miss Julia Webster rose to meet us, a pretty young woman of perhaps seven and twenty years.

"Sherlock Holmes, madam, at your service. This is Doctor Watson. Your brother has engaged us to investigate this matter, as he believes you are innocent of these charges."

"I am Mr. Holmes, I am," she said earnestly in a pleasant contralto. "I can see that it looks black against me, but I assure you I did not kill Mr. Davies, nor steal any money from him."

"Please sit, madam, and tell me concisely what happened last night. We have only fifteen minutes."

"Certainly. I was working late last night, as I am compelled to once or twice a week. About eight o'clock, two men asked to see me. They were tenants of Mr. Davies, living in the same dwelling house. They had both just been visited by an agent of Mr. Davies, to say that if their rent was not paid by noon on the morrow, they and their families would be evicted. I say agent, but in truth he is just a thug, an enforcer of the brutal policies of Mr. Davies. One of the men has been ill for a week, and the other had been laid off a few days ago but had found new employment that day. For these reasons they had not been able to pay their rent on the due date.

"I determined to see Mr. Davies and plead for leniency on their behalf. I have tried before and usually failed, but twice I have gained an extension for his tenants by begging. So I took a cab to his house and asked to see him. It was quite late, and perhaps improper under normal conditions for me to visit him unaccompanied, but the matter was urgent. The butler showed me in to his study, where Mr. Davies was drinking brandy and writing in a ledger. I made my case to him, but he refused to listen. I actually got on my knees Mr. Holmes, but he kept shaking his head. He then went to the safe and opened it, being careful to shield the combination from me with his body. He pointed into the safe, where I could see there was a lot of money, and started shouting at me to the effect that he didn't make this amount of money by letting people stay in his houses rent-free.

"I'm afraid I lost my temper, Mr. Holmes, and I rebuked him for his greed and lack of compassion. He then said he was tired of arguing and ordered me to leave, and as I opened the study door to do so, the butler was just coming towards me. He had obviously heard the argument and was concerned for his master, but I brushed past him into the hall. I heard Mr. Davies say to him that everything was all right, and then I left the house.

"When I got outside, I stood there fuming for perhaps five minutes. I calmed down somewhat, and decided to make one last effort. The house was all in darkness however, save for the study. I walked across the lawn to the study window, which was open. Davies was slumped at the desk, and I thought he had fallen asleep. I called to him, but he did not stir. I then noticed that safe was still open, but that all the money had gone. I'm afraid I panicked and ran to the gate and then into the street, where a constable I know was coming towards me. He could see I was upset, but I think he assumed it was because it was late and I was alone. He hailed a cab for me, and I went to my home."

"You didn't think to ask the constable to investigate if Mr. Davies was all right?" asked Holmes.

"No. I'm sorry Mr. Holmes, but even as I stood there on the street, I realised that I might be blamed for what had happened. I didn't know if Mr. Davies was dead or not, but I knew his safe had been emptied and I thought to my eternal shame that he deserved to be robbed, after gloating like that. It was wrong of me I know, and now my not telling Constable Porter makes me look guilty. But that's what happened, I swear to you."

She dissolved into tears as she said these last words. Holmes stood up and put his hand on her shoulder.

"Do not fear, Miss Webster. I will undertake to see you through these difficult times," he said gently. "Come Watson, we have work to do!"

\*\*\*\*\*\*\*\*\*\*

After obtaining a note from Inspector Lestrade giving his grudging permission to examine the crime scene, we travelled to the residence of Elias Davies, a large villa set in its own grounds. We knocked, and the door was opened by the butler, a middle-aged, dark-haired man with a grave expression.

"Holywell, I presume?" said Holmes.

"Yes, sir, can I help you?" the butler replied.

"My name is Sherlock Holmes, this is Doctor Watson. We are here with the permission of Inspector Lestrade to investigate the murder of Mr. Davies; here is his authority for us to do so."

Holywell read the note, then ushered us in to the hall, taking our hats and canes. A constable was sitting in a chair drinking tea, but he hastily rose and came over to see us.

"These gentlemen are here to investigate the death of Mr. Davies," said the butler, showing the constable the note.

"Very good, sir. This way please," the constable said, leading the way to a door off the hall. Holmes stood in the doorway for some moments, taking in the scene, before

183

commencing his examination. Knowing his methods, I waited in the doorway and watched him.

The study was not a large room, but well-appointed. A mahogany desk stood in front of the French windows. There were bookshelves with few books, side tables, drawers and an open safe in the corner. The floor was carpeted. Holmes examined everything closely, eventually sitting at the desk and looking at the ledger.

"Anything of note, Holmes?" I ventured.

"Not a great deal, Watson. The carpet has too short a pile to retain any impressions. The window lock has not been forced, so it was opened from the inside. The killer entered quietly through the open window, then struck Mr. Davies in the head with an unknown weapon. Davies then slumped forward; here you can see the bloodstain on the ledger, and on the desk where his head rested. The blood has worked its way across the desk and dripped off the edge here. There is one thing which may help us – this ledger indicates that there was more than £3,400 in the safe, however, Miss Webster had only £1,000, which Lestrade found when he arrested her. If she stole the contents of the safe, where is the remaining £2,400?

"A good question. Lestrade did not mention finding any other cash – I suppose he will say she has hidden it at her home overnight."

"Perhaps, though I am unsure if he even knows how much was stolen. But –"

He stopped suddenly, sniffing the air. His gaze fixed on a goblet on the desk, containing about half an inch of a dark amber liquid. Picking it up, he raised it to his nose and then walked over to a table where various decanters and glasses were arrayed. He took the stopper out of each decanter and sniffed the contents, then brought the goblet over to me.

"What do you think this is, Watson?" he asked.

I sniffed at the liquid.

"Smells to me like a very fine brandy, Holmes," I said.

"To me also, Watson. You recall Miss Webster saying that Davies was drinking brandy when she was shown into this room last night. However, look at the colour – there is nothing like it in any of these decanters, which judging by their aromas I believe contain, gin, port, Scotch and two types of sherry."

"What does that mean, Holmes?"

"I'm not sure. Let us ask the butler – it's time we interviewed him in any case. Would you get the constable to find him please?"

I sent the constable off, and he returned a short while later with Holywell behind him.

"Ah Holywell! Thank you for coming, I just need to hear from you what happened here last night. Start from when you admitted Miss Webster. What time would that have been?" asked Holmes.

"Well sir, I didn't look at the clock, but I should estimate it was around nine or just after when Miss Webster arrived."

"She asked to speak to Mr. Davies?" Holmes prompted.

"Yes, sir. I asked Mr. Davies if he would see her, and though he seemed a little put out by the lateness of the hour, he said to show her in. Which I did, then left."

"And a short time later you heard them arguing?"

"I heard raised voices, so I went back to the study in case I was needed. By the time I was approaching the door, I heard Miss Webster chastising Mr. Davies for being greedy. He then shouted at her to leave. The door opened as I got there and Miss Webster came out, looking very angry, and started walking over to the front door. I went into the study, where Mr. Davies was sitting at the desk. He said not to worry, everything was alright. I left the study just in time to see the front door close as Miss

Webster left."

"And whilst in the study, you noticed that the safe was still open, and the money was still in it?"

"That is correct, sir."

"Was the window open at this time?"

"No, I don't believe so, sir. I would have noticed."

"Now then, Holywell, this goblet on the desk contains the brandy Mr. Davies was drinking at the time he saw Miss Webster. But there is no decanter of brandy in this room. How did Mr. Davies obtain it?"

"He asked me to fetch it, sir, just before Miss Webster arrived. It is kept in the billiard room, where it is – I mean, was – Mr. Davies's custom to spend time after dinner, enjoying the brandy, and cigars that complement it. So I went to the billiard room and brought him a glass."

"I see. A simple explanation! Now, after Miss Webster left, what happened?"

"After I had locked the front door, I returned to the study to see if Mr. Davies required anything further. He didn't, and said I could retire for the evening. I checked all the windows and doors, then went to my room. I did not see or hear anything unusual until I found Mr. Davies in the morning, at about 7:30 a.m."

"Are you aware that Miss Webster has been arrested for the murder of Mr. Davies?" Holmes inquired.

Holywell looked surprised and somewhat discomfited.

"No, sir, I was not. I told the inspector that Miss Webster was here last night, and he said he would have to go and speak to her. But he's arrested her you say?"

"The inspector found Miss Webster with a large amount of cash on her desk, which she claims was pushed under the door of her charity. She admits that after you saw her leave, she stood

186

outside for some minutes, trying to regain her composure. She then states she decided to see Mr. Davies again, and seeing as the house was dark except for the study, she went across the lawn to the study window. It was open, the safe was empty and Mr. Davies was lying slumped on his desk. She panicked and ran, seen on the street by a constable. The inspector's version is that she returned to the study, killed Mr. Davies, emptied the safe and then ran to the street."

"I wouldn't have thought Miss Webster capable of hurting anyone," Holywell said, frowning. "She has been here several times, and once while waiting for Mr. Davies she related to me the importance of the work her charity performs. A good Christian lady in my opinion, sir."

"My belief also. That is why I am attempting to ascertain the truth and prevent a miscarriage of justice. Thank you, Holywell."

The butler left, and Holmes stood looking around the study.

"So if Miss Webster is telling the truth," I said, "then the murderer took the very small opportunity between Holywell leaving Davies in the study, and Miss Webster going to the open study window to find Davies dead and the money gone. Furthermore, while the murder and theft were taking place, Miss Webster was standing outside the front door recovering her temper, and heard and saw nothing."

"And the time period involved cannot be more than five minutes," replied Holmes. "That is certainly enough time to hit someone on the head, stuff three thousand pounds into a bag and leave. But if the murderer were watching the house for such an opportunity, he must have seen Miss Webster leave and then stand near the door. Surely he would wait until she had left altogether, before making his move? No, something is not right..."

He continued to probe the room with his searching gaze. Suddenly he strode over to the desk.

"I think we have learned all we can here, Watson. Meanwhile, it is a pity to waste such a fine brandy."

He picked up the goblet, drained it and walked out of the study, a thoughtful look on his face.

\*\*\*\*\*\*\*\*\*\*

Holmes hailed a cab, and gave Scotland Yard as our destination. He remained pensive the entire journey, so I did not interrupt his thoughts, even though I was puzzled as to why he had finished the dregs of the victim's brandy. When we arrived, he asked to see Inspector Lestrade again, who was in a good humour having, as he thought, solved a capital crime within an hour of being summoned.

"My dear Inspector," Holmes started, "have you given any thought to a theory whereby Miss Webster is telling the truth, Mr. Davies was murdered before she saw his body from the study window, and that the killer is this man whom the newspapers call the modern-day Robin Hood?"

"No I have not Mr. Holmes," replied the inspector with some asperity. "What proof is there that anyone else other than Miss Webster killed Davies?"

"There is the missing cash for one thing. Did you not see that the ledger on the desk attests that there was more than £3,400 in the safe? Miss Webster only had £1,000 when you arrested her; where is the remainder, if she stole it?"

Lestrade looked a little nonplussed.

"She must have hidden it. I will have her house searched immediately."

"Of course, but I don't think you will find it. Tell me, Inspector, as I have not seen the body, what of the head wound on Mr. Davies?"

"It appears to have been a single violent blow, by something triangular in cross-section, the pathologist said."

"Interesting. Not a round piece of wood or pipe, then," remarked Holmes, "the usual choice of thieves and murderers generally. And what became of this triangular weapon, and did Miss Webster have the strength to inflict such a wound as Davies sustained?"

"The weapon has not been found. No doubt she disposed of it either on her way home by throwing it out of the cab, or after she got home. As to her strength, that is difficult to say. As you know, Holmes, anyone is capable of an exertion beyond their usual ability in times of stress or anger."

"That is true, Inspector. However, Miss Webster was no longer angry, having left Mr. Davies and regained her composure outside."

"If you believe her."

"I do, Inspector. Now, these robberies and the burglary committed by this thief who gives his illegal booty to charitable organisations – have you the files to hand, and may I see them?"

The inspector hesitated a moment, but then shrugged and passed over the four files from a stack on his desk. Holmes read them quickly.

"Thank you, Inspector. There is little in them, excepting that the three victims robbed in the street agree on the description of the thief – a middle-sized man, dressed all in black, with a black scarf over his face so only his eyes could be seen. He doesn't say much, just menaces them with a pistol and in a rather hoarse voice asks for cash."

"Yes, there is not much to go on," agreed Lestrade.

"A thought, Inspector – I believe this benevolent thief did kill Davies, and robbed him of £3,400 of which £1,000 was given to Miss Webster as she says; if then further amounts adding up to £2,400 were discovered to have been given to the doers of good works, would that change your mind about Miss Webster's guilt?"

"I doubt it, Mr. Holmes. Any other cash given to charity could have come from other robberies we don't yet know about, not necessarily from the safe of Mr. Davies. Or they could be just ordinary donations by well-meaning persons."

"Well, we'll see Inspector. We shall take our leave now, thank you for your help."

We returned to Baker Street stopping on the way at a telegraph office, where Holmes wired Oliver Webster to reassure him that although we had no evidence yet to free his sister, we were making progress. We then had a late lunch, after which Holmes settled in his favourite chair and lit his pipe. I picked up my notebook to record the details of our morning's work, and when I had finished I looked up to find Holmes asleep. I quietly changed and left to spend the rest of the afternoon and the evening at my club.

\*\*\*\*\*\*\*\*\*

The next morning, Holmes had already breakfasted and was reading the papers when I came down. I asked him what his next move in the case would be.

"I have already instigated the next stage of my investigation," he replied. "I have set the Irregulars a task, and we will see what they can find out. Meanwhile, there is an interesting article in the first edition of *The Times* this morning. There is a clinic in the East End, where the poor may receive free medical treatment. It is run by several volunteer doctors and nurses."

"Yes, I have heard of it," I said, pouring myself a coffee.

"Last night a young lad walked into the clinic, and said to the nurse that a man in the street had given him a shilling to deliver an envelope to them. He produced the envelope, inside which was –"

"A large sum of cash," I finished.

"£400 to be exact, Watson."

"You surmised this would happen. There is still about £2,000 unaccounted for from Elias Davies's safe; is this what the Irregulars are looking into?"

"Yes. It's possible that some of the donations may not make it into the papers, and I wish to find out about as many of them as I can."

Just then Mrs. Hudson appeared with my kedgeree, to which I devoted my full attention for the next twenty minutes. Afterwards, I read the news of the day, whilst Holmes brought the latest volume of his commonplace books up to date, pasting in articles he wished to keep and indexing them. Shortly after lunch, one of the Baker Street Irregulars, Bracken by name, came to report.

"We 'ad some luck, sir. Found three places wot have just got a lot of tin given to 'em."

He named three charitable guilds which dealt with widowed young mothers, injured miners who could not work, and crippled children. They had all received cash donations from an unknown source in the amounts of £400, £250 and £500 respectively.

"Thank you, Bracken. How many of you were employed on this matter?" asked Holmes.

"There were eight of us, sir."

"Very well. Here are eight shillings. Well done."

"Thank you, sir."

He scampered off down the stairs, as I performed a calculation in my head.

"So that's another £1,150 accounted for, which leaves some £850," I said to Holmes, who nodded.

As the weather was fair, I suggested a walk. Holmes

191

acquiesced, so we strolled about for an hour, stopping on the way back at the tobacconist to replenish our supplies, and thence to the newsagent for the earliest editions of the evening newspapers. Upon our return, we went through them over tea and scones. It was I who made the discovery in the *Evening Standard*.

"Here it is, Holmes. They have reported the gift of £500 to the Society for the Advancement of Crippled Children which we knew about, but also another donation of £250 to a fund for the education of deaf children. The reporter does not seem to have made the connection between these donations and the murder of Elias Davies."

Holmes looked up from his edition of *The Echo*, his eyes flashing.

"Lestrade is a fool!" he said contemptuously.

"What is it?" I asked.

"This article states that he has found out about these new donations, and instead of seeing them as a strong indication that Julia Webster did not steal Davies's money, he has arrested Oliver Webster as an accessory after the fact to the murder of Davies. He thinks Mr. Webster has made these donations from the stolen money in order to make the police believe that the real murderer and thief is still at large."

"Holmes, is it at all possible that Oliver Webster is the Robin Hood we read about, responsible for all the robberies, the burglary and the death of Davies? And that his sister does not know?" I queried.

"I don't believe so, Watson. If he has alibis for the time of Davies's murder, and for any of the other thefts as well, that would eliminate him as a suspect. I think we need to see Lestrade again, and see what Oliver Webster has to say."

We put on our hats and coats, picked up our canes and made our way down to the street, where we hailed a hansom to take us to the Yard. This time, Lestrade did not appear to be in such a good mood, and he groaned when he saw us.

"What now? If you've come to tell me Oliver Webster is innocent of any wrongdoing, save your breath. He spent last night at his club, verified by various other club members. We have found the cabbie who drove him home and the cabbie who drove him to work this morning, where he has spent the day in full view of his colleagues. He couldn't possibly have spent last night or today giving out sums of money to charities. He also has an alibi for the night Davies was killed; he dined at his sweetheart's house with her parents, and did not leave until nearly ten. I had to release him an hour ago. I should never have arrested him!" he finished disconsolately.

"No, you should not have, not without more investigation," Holmes said severely. "And the same goes for Miss Webster. Have you released her also?"

"No, I have not. She is still the main suspect in this matter. She was the last to see Davies, he foolishly perhaps showed her the money, and they had an argument, to which the butler was a witness. PC Porter than saw her leaving the property in an agitated state some five or ten minutes after Holywell saw her exit via the front door. I then found her in possession of at least some of the stolen money. I think we have enough to convict. Unless you have some cast-iron evidence or a confession to show that someone else is responsible?"

Holmes pursed his lips and looked at Lestrade for some moments before replying.

"No, I do not, Inspector. But when I do, you will be the first to know," he said forcefully, striding out the door.

Standing outside the Yard, I asked Holmes what he intended to do now.

"Now, Watson, I intend to return to the scene of the crime and there I hope to solve this mystery. Cab!"

\*\*\*\*\*\*\*\*\*\*

Darkness was falling as we arrived at the Davies' residence. Holywell admitted us to the study, saying that the constable on duty that day had just been taken away by a sergeant. The sergeant had told him that he could now clean the room, Lestrade believing that no further evidence could be gathered.

"I was going to attend to it after my dinner, sir, if you think that will be all right?" he said.

"I will let you know," said Holmes. "It's possible I may find something which the inspector will need to see tomorrow."

"Very good, sir," he said, bowing and leaving us alone.

"What are you looking for Holmes?" I asked.

"I'm not sure, Watson. Something I missed when I first examined this room, to provide corroboration for the theory I have formed," he replied, slowly walking around the desk. He circled the desk twice, then suddenly ran his hand along the edge nearest the safe, adjacent to where the trail of now-dried blood had run over the edge and formed a small pool on the carpet. He drew out his powerful lens and examined this area intensely. He then stood up, his eyes shining.

"What is it?" I said excitedly.

"You recall, Watson, that the pathologist had said that the head wound was caused by a weapon triangular in section, which I remarked was unusual?"

"Yes, I remember."

"Look at the edge of this desk. It is a ninety degree corner, and if a person's head were to contact it at an angle, the resulting wound would look...""?

"Triangular!" I exclaimed. "But there is no blood or hair on the edge of the desk to indicate that's what happened."

Holmes passed over his lens.

"Look at where the blood has dripped over the edge of the desk."

I knelt down and looked closely at the area indicated.

"You see where the blood trail has worked its way to the edge, it is smooth? But at the edge, the dried blood is not only slightly uneven but there are some small hairs trapped within it?

"Yes, I see that. So you think –"

"I think that Mr. Davies hit his head on the edge of the desk with sufficient force to kill him, leaving a triangular-shaped impression in the skull. His body was then placed in the chair, leaning over the desk. The blood escaping from the wound trailed across the desk, and by chance reached the edge and dripped over at the exact place his head had collided with it some moments before. The unevenness and hairs at that place indicate there is a small piece of Mr. Davies's scalp stuck to the edge, right where the blood later covered it."

"Amazing, Holmes!"

"What is amazing, Watson, is the carelessness I exhibited in not seeing this yesterday, as like Lestrade I assumed Davies had been struck while sitting in the chair. It is a lesson I intend to learn for future cases, Watson. Never take a crime scene at face value."

"So then, you believe that Davies's death was accidental? But who was it who placed him in the chair and removed the contents of the safe?"

"I am certain, Watson, that Davies's death was an accident. As to the other actor in the drama, there is only one person it could possibly have been."

"It was an accident, sir. Of that I can assure you," came a voice from behind us. We turned to see Holywell in the open doorway.

"I believe you," said Holmes. "You only meant to rob him,

195

hence the fast-acting sedative you put in his brandy."

Holywell nodded.

"Indeed sir. When I returned to the study after locking the front door, he was sitting down slumped over the desk, and I thought he was asleep. I already knew the combination of the safe, as he had absentmindedly opened it a few days ago in my presence. He thought I was preparing him a drink, but I had chanced to see and note the combination. As it happened however, the safe was open, so I was putting the money in my pockets when I heard him get up behind me. I turned, and he came at me with a raised fist. I pushed him away, and in his drugged state he stumbled and fell back against the edge of the desk. It was part of my original plan that it would look more natural that someone had come in through the window behind him and struck him. So I put him back in the chair and opened the window, finished taking the money and left."

"And your original plan was to sedate him, wait until he fell asleep, then open the safe and force the window," said Holmes. "When he awoke, he and the police would think that the thief had just taken advantage of his slumber to rob him. But in your no doubt distressed state at being the cause of his death, you just opened the window instead of making it look like someone had broken in."

"Exactly sir," replied Holywell. "I had just given him the brandy, when Miss Webster arrived. If I had known of her visit, I would have waited until after she left of course. I wasn't to know she would return to the study from the outside and see Mr. Davies dead, which made her a suspect in the eyes of the inspector."

"But if you took all the money from the safe," I cried, "you are the one who has been distributing it to the charities! You are the Robin Hood of whom the public and the papers are so enamoured!"

"Indeed I am, sir," Holywell smiled. "I delivered the £1,000 to her headquarters later that night, not realising that would also increase her appearance of guilt. But it was her explaining the necessity of her good works that gave me the idea of the whole thing in the first place, so I gave her the lion's share of my plunder, as it were. There was also the fact that my master was a particularly nasty human being, not only to work for but in the way he treated his tenants. I thought my thievery and subsequent generosity would offset some of his behaviour, and when I learned the combination to his safe, it seemed right that he should also suffer some monetary loss as had the other rich gentlemen I had robbed. Though as I say, I didn't intend to kill him. But if someone has to hang for his death, better it be me than Miss Webster."

"I don't know that you would suffer that punishment, as it was an accidental death," remarked Holmes. "But it was still a death which occurred during the commission of a robbery, so I believe there would be a long term of imprisonment involved."

"But Holmes, surely the fact that Holywell gave all the fruits of his thefts to aid the unfortunate of our city would tell in his favour?" I questioned.

Holmes was silent for a moment.

"The law does not take into account what you do with the money you steal, Watson. People have been transported and imprisoned for stealing a miserly few shillings to buy food for their starving children. "The only hope is that you get a lenient judge who may impose a lighter sentence, but the fact that you stole only from the rich to give to the poor, the disabled, and the orphaned will make no difference to your guilt in the eyes of the law. However... it does make a difference to me. Your intentions were good, and your victims were able to afford their loss. You did not intend to kill your master, but there will be few who mourn the passing of 'Eviction' Davies. For these reasons, if Watson agrees, I feel imprisonment is inappropriate in this case."

Holmes and Holywell looked at me.

"I am happy to see Holywell go free, Holmes," I said at last, "but what of Miss Webster? Lestrade is determined to see her punished."

"Yes, our client must be exonerated. Here is what I propose. We will tell Lestrade that when we arrived here, Holywell had fled, leaving a confession to all the robberies and describing how Davies met his death. I will tell him of the evidence of the drugged brandy, the blood, and how the desk edge was responsible for the wound. He will then be compelled to release Miss Webster. Do you have any of the stolen money still in your possession, Holywell?"

"Yes sir, I still have nearly £300 I planned to give away tomorrow."

"A goodly sum to make a new life for yourself in a distant land."

"But sir, I did not steal it for myself! I couldn't –"

Holmes smiled. "Your scruples are impeccable, Holywell. But if you are to go free and Miss Webster to be released, you must disappear. Use whatever money necessary for that, and then donate the remainder to a charity in your new home."

"Very well, sir, if you insist. I have a brother in Australia who will help me, I'm sure."

"Lestrade may discover that fact, and trace you there. I suggest you go to South Africa or India, for a year or two at least, and then make your way to Australia."

"Very good, sir. Thank you for your help and generosity. I shall always remember it."

"You are welcome. Now let us draft your confession, then tomorrow Watson and I will visit Lestrade. Miss Webster has spent long enough in a cell."

\*\*\*\*\*\*\*\*\*

Lestrade was naturally unhappy at having a suspect in a cell replaced by one on the loose. He had accepted the confession and Holmes's other evidence with bad grace, and ordered the release of Miss Webster.

"Now I will have to set wheels in motion at all the ports in the country, I suppose," he grumbled.

Not necessarily, Inspector," said Holmes. "We found his confession in his room, but in the kitchen we found this newspaper in a bin. It is yesterday's *Times*, and it has been folded in such a way that the topmost page shows the list of departure times for boats to the Continent. I surmise he is heading to Europe."

"That will narrow the search," Lestrade conceded. "Well, I had better get on with tracking him down. The commissioner will not be pleased that he is on the run."

"Look on the bright side, Inspector. There is no need for my name to appear in this matter. You can tell the commissioner that at least you have identified this modern-day Robin Hood, and there will now be no further robberies of rich men by Holywell. And you have saved an innocent young lady from the gallows."

Lestrade nodded lugubriously, and Holmes and I rose.

"You're welcome, Inspector," said Holmes sweetly over his shoulder as we left.

\*\*\*\*\*\*\*\*\*\*

We had returned from Scotland Yard and were discussing the case over a pipe and scotch. I asked Holmes what had put him on to Holywell as a suspect.

"Several small pieces of evidence, Watson, each by themselves not conclusive, but together they had a cumulative effect. Firstly, the window had not been forced, so no-one had broken in that way. However, it was conceivable that Davies had himself opened it. Secondly, it was highly improbable that someone was in the garden during the exact few minutes there was an open window, a man seated with his back to them and the safe open. But also, if there were such a person, he would surely have seen Miss Webster and waited for her to leave before committing the crime. After talking to Holywell, it occurred to me that he had had the most opportunity of anyone to kill Davies and rifle the safe. I then remembered Miss Webster had stated that during their argument, Davies had said he was tired of arguing and ordered her to leave. She then saw him through the window, slumped over the desk, but thought he was asleep. I wondered if perhaps Davies had meant he was literally tired. A sedative instantly suggested itself, and the obvious means of administering it was the brandy he had been drinking. To test my theory, I finished the brandy, and even before we arrived home I could feel it working on me. Not long after we returned, I fell asleep. It took longer to affect me than Davies because I had only a small amount of brandy, whereas Davies drank most of the goblet. As Holywell had supplied the brandy to Davies, my suspicions rested on him."

I nodded, and gazed into the fire for some minutes.

"Holmes," I said, "do you not have any reservations about taking the law into your own hands?"

"Oh yes," he replied instantly. "It is wrong to break the law, and to let guilty parties go free without recourse to the judicial process. It was also wrong of me to gain your collaboration in the matter. But I believe it would have been a greater wrong to imprison Holywell for many years for what he did, and my conscience is clear for choosing the lesser of two evils. Are you having second thoughts?"

"I was a little uneasy about it," I admitted, "but now you have put it that way, it seems a fair result. Though I hope we never have to do it again."

"My thoughts exactly, Watson. Let us hope that Holywell

will repay the trust we placed in him by building an honest and respectable life for himself, wherever he ends up."

"Which certainly won't be Europe," I smirked. "That was a nice piece of misdirection you gave Lestrade."

And we both roared with laughter.

# THE CASE OF THE STOLEN ALMA-TADEMAS

In looking back through my notes on the hundreds of cases that it was my good fortune to share with Sherlock Holmes, I am surprised that I have not hitherto prepared for publication the following narrative. It concerns not only a major crime of interest in itself, but it was the first time that Holmes became aware of the activities of that master criminal whom he would eventually defeat at the Reichenbach Falls, the story of which was published as "The Final Problem." I speak of course of Professor James Moriarty. As I believe this might be of interest to the reading public, I hasten to rectify this omission, and present this case with an apology for its lateness in seeing the light of day.

It was a crisp, cool day in the early autumn of 1886. Holmes had read *The Times* after breakfast and moved on to other newspapers, so I was now perusing its pages. There was little of a criminal nature excepting one article, and I asked Holmes if he had noticed it. It concerned the theft of a painting from the Royal Academy the night before last, and said Inspector Gregson was investigating the crime with his usual vigour. Holmes lowered his paper and yawned.

"Yes Watson, I noticed it. Gregson is coming along as a detective, but I would not be surprised if we see him soon for a consultation. The painting is a valuable one, the artist well-known, and there will therefore be pressure to recover the painting and apprehend the thief quickly."

"It says in the article that all the paintings in the exhibit are newly painted by members of the Academy," I said. "How then do you know the stolen one is valuable, if it has never been sold?"

"Because Watson, it is by Lawrence Alma-Tadema. Have you not heard the name?"

"Now that you mention it, I believe I have seen his name once or twice in the newspapers. I do not normally keep up with art news, however. What do you know of him?"

"He is of Dutch descent, but has lived in this country for a number of years. He has become famous for his depictions of Roman life, but also paints other historical scenes from Greece and Egypt. He is popular with both the public and the critics, and is reputed to be spending a fabulous sum on renovating his new house in St. John's Wood. I have an article in my commonplace book from last year, which if I recall correctly stated that a painting of his titled *The Triumph of Titus* sold for $20,000 to a wealthy American. That would be the equivalent of around £4,000, so any new painting from his brush could be expected to be valued in the hundreds if not thousands of pounds."

Just then we heard a knock on the front door. Mrs. Hudson answered its summons, and then Holmes cocked his head as a light but purposeful step made its way up our stairs.

"As I said, Watson… ah, come in, Inspector Gregson! Please sit down and tell us the details of the stolen painting."

The inspector smiled as he sank into the chair nearest the fire.

"Very good, Mr. Holmes. You have read in the papers that I am investigating the theft from the Royal Academy, and so you deduce that I am here to discuss it with you."

"Is that not so, Inspector?" asked Holmes.

"Only in part. Yes, I am here about the theft of a painting titled *An Apodyterium* – I hope I pronounced that right – by an artist called Lawrence Alma-Tadema, from the Royal Academy two nights ago. But we have received information this morning from the local police that two nights ago another artwork was stolen from Hammerton Hall in Yorkshire, the home of Sir Forster Winstanley. The painting was called *An Audience at Agrippa's*, also by Alma-Tadema.

Holmes raised his eyebrows.

"The Yard received another wire this morning," the inspector continued. "Again, two nights ago, two paintings were stolen from the mansion of Henry Marquand, director of the Metropolitan Museum of Art in New York. Normally we wouldn't expect to hear of a theft in New York, but the police department of that fair city thought it advisable to let us know on this occasion as the paintings" – here he consulted his notebook – 'titled *Amo Te, Ama Me* and *A Reading from Homer*, were by a British artist named –'"

"Lawrence Alma-Tadema," I breathed. "This cannot be a coincidence."

"Of course not, Watson!" said Holmes trenchantly. "Four valuable paintings by the same artist stolen from different locations on two continents on the same night – that is a well-planned operation carried out with considerable organisational skills. Were any clues left at the scene of the Royal Academy theft, Inspector?"

"Not really, Holmes. It appears to be a very professional job. I would appreciate you accompanying me to the Academy to see for yourself what –"

"Yes, I think I'd better. This promises to be an exceedingly interesting case!"

\*\*\*\*\*\*\*\*\*\*

We took a growler to Burlington House, Mayfair, an impressive Palladian edifice, and home of the Royal Academy. Gregson took us to a rear entrance in a service yard.

"This is where I think the thieves gained entry," he said.

Holmes inspected the lock with his lens.

"Agreed. The lock has been expertly picked. What are the dimensions of the stolen painting, Inspector?"

Gregson consulted his notebook.

"It is 17-½ inches by 23-1/8 inches."

"So not large enough to require a conveyance to move it, but large enough to be suspicious if one tucked it under one's arm. The paved yard retains no traces of a cart or carriage, but I would think a job like this would need one, to take the picture and its thieves away in secrecy and safety. Which means there was a driver, perhaps a lookout, and I think two more to complete the theft. So a team of at least three, perhaps four. What is the most direct route from this entrance to where the painting hung?"

"This way, gentlemen," said Gregson, striding off down a corridor.

Holmes followed, head down, examining the floor as he went along. Another corridor and a flight of stairs later, we arrived at a gallery with many artworks adorning the walls. Gregson led us to a conspicuously empty section of wall. Holmes brought out his lens again, looking at the wall where the picture had hung, and the floor immediately in front of it. At one point, he produced his tweezers from a pocket and plucked something from the floor.

"As you said, Inspector, not much in the way of clues. There are no discernible footprints, but I have found this."

He held up a short fibre in his tweezers.

"What is it Holmes?" murmured Gregson.

"I believe it is from a reasonable quality wool blanket, placed on the floor by the thieves. They then removed the picture from the wall, putting it on the blanket and wrapping it. Whoever desires these pictures is minimising the risk of any damage from the moment of the theft."

At this moment, a constable appeared in the gallery and walked over to us.

"Message from the Yard, Inspector," he said crisply, saluting with his right hand and holding out a piece of folded paper with his left.

Inspector Gregson read the message, then looked up at us, shaking his head despairingly.

"There is a Lord Keyworth who lives in Keyworth Castle, Nottinghamshire. He has not been in his library for two days, but this morning he had occasion to do so, and discovered his painting called *Welcome Footsteps* by Lawrence Alma-Tadema has been stolen. So that's five now. What does it mean, Mr. Holmes?"

"From the fact that the stolen paintings are all by the same artist," said Holmes, "we can deduce that there is someone behind this who is a serious collector of Alma-Tadema, and who has no scruples in how he obtains them. Either they have organised the thefts themselves, or have paid someone with the planning expertise and manpower to do their thieving for them."

"Why were all these thefts carried out on the same night?" I asked. "Surely that is more difficult and requires so many more men."

"True Watson, but if these thefts had been carried out over a period of weeks or months, after three or four had occurred anyone owning an Alma-Tadema would have either increased their security or perhaps rendered their paintings safe in a bank vault. This would make stealing them much more difficult. Obviously, all these stolen paintings were highly desired, and whoever it is that wants them did not want to chance them being more difficult or even unavailable to steal. I think is quite possible that we still have not heard of all the thefts that occurred two nights ago."

Inspector Gregson looked crestfallen.

"I shall need a special force at this rate. I can't be in all these places at once," he groaned.

Holmes smiled.

"No you can't, Inspector. But with your permission, I will

take a trip to Yorkshire via Nottinghamshire, and see if I can make anything of the crime scenes there. Fancy a breath of country air, Watson?"

"I would be happy to assist any way I can," I replied.

"I should come with you, really," said Gregson lugubriously.

"You may of course accompany us if you wish," said Holmes. "But there is a line of investigation in London that needs following up if you would like to stay."

"And what is that?" asked Gregson.

"As I said earlier, I believe that there is an Alma-Tadema collector behind these thefts. It occurs to me that he probably started off collecting in the usual legitimate fashion; by buying artworks from auction houses and galleries. I think it behooves someone to visit Sotheby's and Christie's, and any art gallery which has sold an Alma-Tadema, and determine who has been buying them. Perhaps more importantly, it would be useful to know who has been unsuccessfully bidding on them, as it's possible that not being able to obtain particular paintings legally may have prompted the urge to steal them."

"Yes, that sounds reasonable," conceded the inspector. "I shall stay in London and see what I can find out in that regard. I'm sure you will discover anything worth discovering at the crime scenes, using your methods."

"It might also be useful to contact the New York police and get any information you can from them about the theft there; any clues they found and the *modus operandi* used. We should be back in a couple of days, and we will compare notes then," said Holmes. "Please notify Lord Keyworth and the victim in Yorkshire – Sir Forster, wasn't it? – that we will be acting as your agents and visiting them soon. Come, Watson, back to Baker Street to pack our bags, thence to the Midlands!"

\*\*\*\*\*\*\*\*\*\*

Darkness was falling as we pulled up in a hired trap at the inn recommended by the driver, in the small town of Keyworth. The journey had necessitated us getting out at Plumtree, a town some five miles south of Nottingham, and then the trap to Keyworth, with only train station cafe sandwiches to sustain us, so I at least was looking forward to a hot and nourishing meal at the inn. Holmes had wired Lord Keyworth from Nottingham, advising him of our visit on the morrow. We had not discussed the case very much on the train, as we had little data as yet, so after a satisfying meal and an ale, we had an early night.

The next morning found us on the road to Keyworth Castle, Holmes driving us in a trap hired from the innkeeper. We rounded a corner and saw the imposing gates of the estate ahead. A gatekeeper emerged from the small lodge and opened the gates for us, touching his cap and saying we were expected. As we approached the main building, it was clear that it was not a true castle, but a large seventeenth century building with a turret at each corner. We pulled up at the entrance to find the butler awaiting us.

"Good morning gentlemen," he intoned. "His Lordship had your telegram concerning your visit, so if you'll follow me please."

He showed us into the library, saying Lord Keyworth would be with us shortly. A few minutes later, a maid came in with a tea tray, and then just as I poured a cup, His Lordship strode in, a man of some fifty years with a frank and friendly countenance.

"Good morning, Mr. Holmes, Doctor Watson. Thank you for coming. Sergeant Preston in Keyworth is a competent fellow, but this matter is a little beyond him, I fear. However, Inspector Gregson assures me he has every confidence in you."

"Thank you, Your Lordship. I shall endeavour to do what I can to return your painting to you," replied Holmes.

"I have read that other paintings by Alma-Tadema have been stolen; even two in the United States," continued Lord Keyworth.

"That is correct, sir. It seems Mr. Alma-Tadema's works are in high demand among the criminal fraternity at present. Now what can you tell me about the theft of yours?"

"You can see where it was hung, of course," said Lord Keyworth, turning to point. "Right there, between those windows. I had not been in here for two days, but when I did come in yesterday morning after breakfast, I immediately noticed its absence. I sent a groom to fetch Sergeant Preston, who came at once. It was he who found where the thieves effected their entrance; that last window on the right has had its lock forced. He said he would report the theft to Scotland Yard and make some enquiries, which seem to have borne fruit. He sent me a message late yesterday to say that he has discovered that a station porter saw four men catching the first train from Loughborough to Leicester the morning after my painting was taken. One of the men was carrying a large flat package wrapped in brown paper."

"Where is Loughborough?" asked Holmes. "And what is the size of your stolen painting?"

"It is a small town some ten miles south of here, Mr. Holmes. The picture is 16-½ inches by 21-5/8 inches – here is my receipt I located yesterday for the sergeant," answered Lord Keyworth, handing over a small piece of paper.

Holmes looked at the receipt, then handed it back.

"Your Lordship, I would like now to examine this room for any clues if I may."

"Certainly, Mr. Holmes. I'll leave you to it."

He left us, and Holmes immediately went to study the window which had been forced. He inspected the latch and frame with his lens, then opened the window and leaned out, looking at the ground outside. He used his tape to measure something on the ground, bending right over to do so. He then walked around the room, stopping in front of the other artworks which adorned the walls, finally ending up in front of the space where the Alma-Tadema had hung. He stooped and picked up something from the carpet, then looked at me.

"A small clod of soil, which appears to be the same as the soil outside the window," he remarked. "There are some boot impressions in the ground outside, and the window was opened by the use of a crowbar to lever it up. The frame damage on the outside is distinctive. And apparently the thieves allowed themselves to be seen carrying the painting and boarding a train. All-in-all, not quite as professional a job as the Royal Academy theft. But I suppose if you have a large number of criminals employed on a job, one or two of them are likely not to be as skilled as the others."

"What will you do now?" I asked.

"I think I have gleaned all that I can from this crime scene, but I would, if possible, like to talk to the porter at Loughborough. Let us take our leave of Lord Keyworth."

We found a footman who went to fetch his master while we waited in the hall. Lord Keyworth joined us in a few minutes.

"Any luck, Mr. Holmes?" he asked.

"I have a few indications and a lead to follow, your Lordship. We will return our trap to the inn and then make our way to Loughborough, then after that we have another crime scene in Yorkshire to examine."

"Hmm. Getting to Loughborough might be difficult. Would it help if my coachman followed you in my trap to Keyworth to collect your bags, and then took you to Loughborough?"

"That is exceedingly generous of you, sir. It would be most helpful," said Holmes.

"Think nothing of it. You are trying to recover my painting after all," Lord Keyworth said airily. "Take a seat and I shall arrange it. Good day to you both."

We waited some ten minutes and then we heard the trap pull up on the gravel outside. We went out, spoke to His Lordship's coachman, Albert, then set off back to Keyworth with him following. Half an hour later, having settled our bill and loaded our baggage on to the trap, we set off for Loughborough at a trot. Albert dropped us off at the train station, where we asked the station master about the porter Sergeant Preston had mentioned.

"Ah yes, that would be James over there," he said, pointing out a figure at the far end of the platform.

James added a few details to what we already knew. He had been on duty when the first train from Nottingham to Leicester had gone through, and he noticed the four men, one with a package, waiting for it. They were all in ordinary clothes, muffled against the cold, so he could not give any descriptions apart from one of them being a bit taller than the other three. It was unusual he said for a party of four to catch the early train, as generally there were few passengers getting on at Loughborough. He described the size of the package with his hands, and it matched the size of the stolen picture. Holmes thanked him for his time with a shilling, and we walked to the ticket office to see how we could get to York. Holmes also had a question for the ticketseller, concerning the tickets the four men had purchased. It transpired that they had not bought tickets that morning, but a man had purchased four tickets from Loughborough to Leicester the day before.

After we had purchased our tickets, Holmes returned to the station master's office and asked to see a map of the district. He duly obliged, and Holmes perused it for some minutes. He confirmed with him that the stations at Plumtree and Nottingham were both very much closer to Keyworth, but only Nottingham had several early trains. In fact, the train the thieves took at Loughborough had started from Nottingham some twenty minutes beforehand. He also asked him if he could see any advantage in travelling the extra miles to take the train at Loughborough, and the official said he could not. Holmes was deep in thought as we left, and nodded absentmindedly when I suggested soup and sandwiches at a cafe opposite the station while we awaited our train to York.

"You are puzzled about something you learned at the station," I observed, finishing my sandwich.

"Yes Watson, I am," Holmes replied, thumbing tobacco into his pipe. "I am puzzled as to why the thieves chose to take the early Loughborough train, necessitating a drive of some ten miles, when they could have taken a train at Nottingham, about seven miles from Keyworth."

"Perhaps they were afraid that Nottingham, being a larger and busier station, would have more people about, witnesses to their departure," I suggested.

"Or, perhaps – I wonder! We still have fifteen minutes before our train," he said, looking at his pocket watch. "Time enough to send a wire to Gregson, There is some investigation to be done here in Loughborough, Watson, but Gregson can handle it – I need to get to the Yorkshire crime scene while it is still, I hope, relatively fresh. To the telegraph office!"

\*\*\*\*\*\*\*\*\*\*

We spent the night at an inn in York, and the next morning after a large country breakfast, we took the train that went to the picturesque village of Knaresborough. However, we had travelled only about halfway there before we had to get off at the nearest point to Hammerton Hall, a half-mile walk away.

Upon our arrival, we were ushered into the study, where Sir Forster Winstanley greeted us warmly. He was an elderly man with a fringe of white hair and a straggly white beard.

"Morning Mr. Holmes, Doctor Watson! I had a wire from Scotland Yard to say you would be coming, and to give you every assistance. What would you like to do first?"

"Please may we see the room the painting was stolen from, Sir Forster?" inquired Holmes.

"Certainly, this way gentlemen, it was hung in the first floor gallery."

We followed Sir Forster to a long gallery, windowed on one side and paintings hung on the other, with statuary and porcelain scattered along its length. He stopped in front of an empty section of wall.

"You have had the painting a number of years, Sir Forster?" questioned Holmes.

"Why yes, about ten I think. How did you know?"

"The wallpaper is darker where the picture hung, protecting it from the light. It looks to be about three feet by two feet in size," remarked Holmes, looking at the floor then crossing to the nearest windows. "This wooden floor will not help us with footprints. Where did the thieves gain entry?"

"That we don't know," admitted Sir Forster. "None of these windows or their latches is broken, and all the doors were found locked on the morning after the burglary."

"Hmmm. I will check all the external doors later. Sir Forster, can you tell me anything about the night the painting was taken? Last Tuesday night, or early Wednesday morning more likely, is that not so?"

"Yes Mr. Holmes. I heard nothing in the night, nor did any of the servants. I walked down the gallery mid-morning on Wednesday, noticed it was missing, and notified the local constabulary. This is a quiet and law-abiding district as a rule, and the odd case of public drunkenness is all they usually have to deal with. But now we have had a major theft and a murder in the area, on the same night."

"A murder!" Holmes exclaimed. "On the same night? Please tell me about it."

"I only know what I've heard from a neighbour. The blacksmith at Upper Poppleton, a village on the way to York, was found in his workshop on Wednesday morning, dead from a head wound."

"You do not think it a coincidence, Holmes?" I asked.

"I think it highly unlikely, Watson," he replied. "Sir Forster, we came here by train and then walked, so we have no transport. How can we get to Upper Poppleton?"

"If you think investigating this murder will help recover my painting, I would be happy to offer you the services of my coach and driver for the day."

"That is most generous, thank you. If you could arrange that, I will check the doors before we go."

Sir Forster went off to have the coach made ready, and I followed Holmes about the house as he examined each door for signs of being picked. The results were negative until we came to the tradesmen's entrance leading to the scullery and kitchen.

"Yes, small but definite scratches inside the lock," Holmes murmured. "This is where the thieves effected their entrance."

Just then a footman found us and stated that the carriage was ready. We followed him to the entry hall where Sir Forster was waiting.

"Ah, there you are," he said. "The carriage awaits, and I had Cook prepare you these two packets of sandwiches, as I thought you might not get another opportunity to eat until tonight."

"Thank you very much, Sir Forster, and for the use of your carriage," said Holmes. "One question – has it rained here since the night of the theft?"

"No, it has been fine but cool since Tuesday."

"Thank you. Scotland Yard will be in touch if we make any progress."

We went outside, and were just about to get in the carriage when a post office messenger arrived on horseback. He dismounted, strode over to us, and touched his cap respectfully.

"Telegram for Mr. Sherlock Holmes," he said, looking at each of us in turn.

"I am he," said Holmes, stepping forward, taking the wire and reading it.

"It's from Gregson. Another Alma-Tadema theft has been discovered. A Mr. Robert Eliott-St. John of Richmond has returned from a trip to discover his painting titled *Between Hope and Fear* has been stolen. Bad luck for the owner of course, but good for us in that we now have another set of clues to look at. The more thefts there are, the more chance there is that someone will make a mistake that will help us. However, we have this murder to investigate first, to see if it bears any relation to the theft here. Good day, Sir Forster."

We stepped into the carriage and set off for the village of Upper Poppleton.

\*\*\*\*\*\*\*\*\*\*

After a drive of some forty minutes during which we consumed our sandwiches, we turned on to a side road and soon saw a signpost declaring we were about to enter Upper Poppleton. Holmes suddenly rapped on the roof of the carriage and called for the driver, whose name was Johnson, to stop. We alighted from the carriage to see the village about one hundred yards ahead. Holmes asked Johnson if he knew where in the village the smithy was located.

"Aye, sir, I do," he replied. "It's at the far end of the village, last house on the right."

"Very good. There is, I assume, a public house?" asked Holmes.

"Yes sir, The Crown."

"Excellent. Please wait there for us. Here is a shilling for you to make the time pass more amenably."

"Thank you, sir! Most kind."

He touched his cap and drove on. As we started to walk into the village, I asked Holmes why he had not driven right up to the smithy.

"I have a hypothesis, Watson, and I did not want our carriage tracks to interfere with any traces that may already be there. As Sir Forster said it has not rained since the night of the theft, we may be fortunate."

We passed through the village and came to the smithy, attached to the cottage of its owner. Holmes bade me to wait, and I watched as he carefully examined the ground. I could see nothing but some wheel tracks and hundreds of overlapping footprints, but I knew Holmes's sharp eyes would be able to distinguish the differences. He sidled around the area, occasionally lying on the ground and using his lens, and several times picking up something. After fifteen minutes he rejoined me, trying to brush the worst of the dirt from his clothing.

"There have been several visitors since the murder. Obviously there was whoever discovered the body, then the local constable, then probably an inspector from York with men to take away the body. The traces they all left have made my task more difficult, but I believe I have the general picture."

What do think happened then?"

"A small four-wheeled vehicle came here, pulled by a single horse. I believe it was the thieves making their way from Hammerton Hall early Wednesday morning. It is clear that this horse had a shoe missing from its off foreleg, which of course slowed them to a walk. This is why they came to the blacksmith, to have the horse reshod. Having awoken the blacksmith, they persuaded him to reshoe the horse, probably by promise of a larger fee than usual. While he was performing the task, three men stood in a group waiting, two smoking cigarettes and one a pipe. A fourth man, perhaps their leader, paced up and down in front of them, smoking a cigar."

He held out his hand, displaying several cigarette butts, a plug of pipe tobacco and a cigar stub.

"When the job was complete, for some reason the blacksmith was hit on the head, several times I think. You can see where the body lay, and the large quantity of blood still visible on the ground and its distribution indicate multiple wounds. Perhaps they always intended to kill him, seeing as he was a potential witness, or perhaps he voiced suspicions at the need for an urgent horseshoe in the dead of night. Whatever the reason, they added murder to their crime of theft, then drove off. Here you can plainly see the horse's tracks leaving, with the sharp outline of the new shoe compared to the duller impressions of the three older shoes."

"Yes, I see. What is your next move?"

"A wash, an ale and a pipe at The Crown. Then Johnson can drive us to York, where I will tell the police investigating the blacksmith's murder of my findings. We can then return to London tomorrow, see if anything is to be found at the scene of the Richmond theft, and learn what Gregson has discovered in our absence."

\*\*\*\*\*\*\*\*\*\*

After an uneventful journey, we returned to Baker Street mid-afternoon the following day. Holmes had wired Gregson from the station to say we had arrived, inviting him to come around that evening to discuss the case. He duly arrived just as Mrs. Hudson was clearing away our dinner dishes. I poured a brandy for each of us, and we made ourselves comfortable around the fire.

"Now Inspector, tell us what you have discovered at the

auction houses and galleries," Holmes asked.

"I have other news first. We have been notified by the French authorities of yet another theft. John Fristonby is a rich tea importer, and owns a villa in the south of France, not far from Nice. He arrived there yesterday for a holiday to discover his Alma-Tadema, a work called *Pleading*, has been stolen. The villa has been empty for some months, but I would wager the burglary occurred last Tuesday night like all the others. So that's seven missing paintings in total now. The local police believe a door lock was picked to gain access, but there are no other clues or indications."

"Interesting. Do you have anything further on the New York theft?"

"Very little. Like the Academy job, it appears to be a thoroughly professional business. The lock was expertly picked on a rear entrance door. The two paintings were taken, no footprints or any other clues were left, and nobody heard or saw anything. A beautiful, clean job."

Holmes drew thoughtfully at his pipe .

"As for the auctions and galleries, I haven't found out a great deal, I think, though you might see something I don't. New paintings by Alma-Tadema have been sold lately at several galleries, for sums upward of one thousand guineas. Older paintings have changed hands at auction for similar prices. In all cases, the buyers are whom you might expect; aristocrats usually, and other rich men without titles, some of whom believe collecting art is a way of achieving social status and respectability. Or so a manager at Sotheby's told me; he was rather sniffy about those who have earned their wealth through industrial or mercantile means. You can't buy class, he said, though I think one does not need to be in Debrett's to appreciate art.

"Anyway, I have a list of names of purchasers of Alma-

Tademas over the last two years, and the dozens of others who were unsuccessful bidders. However, nobody stands out as being always unsuccessful; the persons who buy an Alma-Tadema on one occasion miss out on the next. Lord Keyworth and Robert Eliott-St. John, two of the victims of the thefts, are on both lists, having bid several times for works before eventually buying the one that has been stolen from them."

"Quite so," said Holmes. "Now did you have any luck with the enquiries I asked you to make in Loughborough?"

"I did, I think," smiled Gregson. "I had an inspector there conduct an investigation along the lines you suggested in your wire. Loughborough is a small town, and he soon discovered that four strangers arrived there on the Tuesday of the theft at Keyworth Castle. They booked the night at a small boarding house, and were seen at the nearby public house drinking well into the night. Then as you know, early on Wednesday morning they went to the station, where the porter saw them boarding the train to Leicester. I have several good descriptions from the boarding house proprietor and the barman. They also agreed that the men had Midlands accents."

"Excellent, Inspector! As the men are highly likely to have criminal records, enquiries in the major cities and towns of the region concerning men with those descriptions should prove fruitful."

"Already under way, Mr. Holmes."

"Very well. Now, what of the burglary in Richmond? You have been there I assume?"

"Yes, immediately after I was notified by the Richmond police. Mr. Eliott-St. John returned home from a business trip to discover his loss. I examined the crime scene, discovering only that again a rear door lock had been picked to gain entry, the painting is missing and the servants heard nothing. No other clues could I see, but you are welcome to look yourself. Another very neat job I think. Now you can tell me of your trip to the country – what have you discovered?"

Holmes rapidly outlined what we had found at Keyworth Castle and Hammerton Hall, and how he thought the murder of the Upper Poppleton blacksmith fitted in.

"So where does that leave us? We may find the men who did the Keyworth job, but are we any closer to solving the entire series of burglaries, and finding out who is behind them?" queried Gregson.

Holmes sat back in his chair and took several puffs of his pipe before answering.

"I believe so, though you may not like what I am about to suggest. I think it represents a serious threat to law and order in this country."

"Go on, I'm listening," said Gregson expectantly.

"Let us consider what has happened. There have been seven valuable paintings stolen in six separate burglaries. The total worth of these painting must be something close to £20,000, perhaps more. Artworks of that kind of value are not the province of your average thief. The thefts were all carried out on the same night, in three countries, probably by teams of four men. That implies someone with a large force of criminals at his disposal, and the brains to organise them. The conclusion is that there exists a large criminal organisation with international reach, as they can apparently plan and execute crimes in the USA and France; this is something that poses a serious threat as I said."

Gregson looked dubious for a moment, but then then nodded.

"What you say makes sense, but how do we then tackle this organisation?"

"I'm not sure, it requires more investigation and thought. But I believe that if we can at least solve these art thefts, perhaps the solution will give us a clue to the extent of this organisation, and perhaps to some of its members."

"You sound like you have a theory," I remarked.

"More a suspicion, Watson" Holmes replied. "I will tell you what it is, but I don't yet know what it means. Have either of you realised that one of the six thefts bears notably different characteristics from the other five?"

"No," said Gregson, and I shook my head.

"In five cases," Holmes continued, "entry was gained by the expert picking of a lock. In five cases there were virtually no clues left at the scene, save the blanket fibre at the Royal Academy. In five cases no footprints were found, and nobody saw or heard anything. In five cases, a thoroughly professional undertaking was carried out."

"The Keyworth Castle theft was different," I exclaimed.

"Indeed, Watson. Entry was gained by the use of a crowbar on a window. There were footprints in the soil outside the window, and a clod of the same soil on the floor in front of where the stolen painting had hung. The thieves spent the night of the theft drinking in a local tavern before apparently embarking on the job, which is surely inadvisable. They then allowed themselves to be seen boarding a train while carrying a package of the dimensions of the stolen painting. And I am still curious as to why they chose Loughborough to catch their train. Not as proficient or adept as the other jobs, do you not think?"

"I agree, but what about the Hammerton Hall thieves? They murdered the blacksmith, which they must have known would attract attention," I said.

"Yes, but that was forced upon them. Their horse threw a shoe whilst making their escape, and they would not have reached York with a lame horse. So they adapted to the situation, but ensured the blacksmith could not give a description of them by murdering him."

"So do you think that the Keyworth theft was undertaken by a different group of thieves, unconnected with this criminal organisation?' I questioned.

"It would be far too great a coincidence to think that a separate gang of thieves stole an Alma-Tadema on the same night six others were stolen. No, it must be connected, and we have to find the connection. My intuition tells me that the reason for the comparative sloppiness of the Keyworth Castle burglary is the key to this mystery. I will smoke several ounces of shag over this matter tonight, Inspector, and see if anything occurs to me. Just jot down the address of the last theft in Richmond, please; I will probably take a look tomorrow, but I am not sanguine it will give us anything new."

Inspector Gregson made his way down the stairs, and I bade Holmes good night, leaving him staring into the fire, wreaths of pipe smoke drifting to the ceiling. I knew he would be constructing hypotheses and theories in his head for hours, testing them against the evidence, discarding them or adapting them as necessary. Tobacco was the fuel for this concentrated mental activity, and he would go through several pipefuls when considering a difficult problem. I left him to it and went to my bed.

**********

I arose a little earlier than usual the next morning to find Holmes had already gone out. He had not breakfasted, as Mrs. Hudson told me when delivering my sausages and eggs, so I waited for him to return, reading the papers, all of which made mention of the stolen paintings. There was an interview with Lawrence Alma-Tadema himself, who, while flattered that somebody apparently had a great liking for his works, deplored their method of acquiring them.

Holmes returned just after eleven, looking rather pensive as he lowered himself into his favourite chair. He filled and lit his pipe, then turned to me.

"I believe Watson, that I have solved the case of these stolen paintings; at least, I know the who and the why."

"Indeed! May I know the answer?" I replied.

"I'll tell you my reasoning, and then I will reveal what I have discovered this morning."

"You have been to the scene of the crime in Richmond then?" I asked.

"No, I have been conversing with several people I know in the banking industry, who are not averse to providing me with information if it means bringing a criminal to justice. Normally, of course they are discreet about the state of their clients' finances, but they trust me as I have helped them out on occasion, avoiding scandals and the like.

Last night after several hours cogitation I was well into my third pipe, when I realized why the Keyworth Castle theft was different. It was obviously not carried out by the same organisation which executed the other five thefts, but equally obviously it was connected, being a theft of a painting by the same artist, and on the same night. The only explanation is that the theft of Lord Keyworth's Alma-Tadema was a blind, designed to show that His Lordship was not involved in the thefts, as he himself had apparently suffered a loss."

"So you're saying Lord Keyworth is behind all the other thefts!" I exclaimed.

"Yes, but only insofar as he is the instigator of the crimes. His is the desire to own Alma-Tademas, but the entire series of thefts was planned by a master criminal, in charge of a highly professional body of expert criminals. Each theft was accomplished by a team of four competent housebreakers, including a lockpicker. Lord Keyworth employed this organisation to fulfil his dreams of owning the paintings, but in order to deflect any suspicion falling on himself, he arranged the fake theft of his own picture. He used the crowbar to open the window, made the footprints, and dropped the soil in the room. He also paid four men to stay the night of the theft at a Loughborough boarding house, and then be seen boarding a train the next morning, with a package the size of the painting. And why Loughborough? That puzzled me, you recall. It is a smaller and much quieter station than Nottingham, which was closer to Keyworth Castle, but that was exactly the point. It was so quiet at that time of the morning, there was an almost certain chance of one or more witnesses to their departure. Lord Keyworth wanted them to be seen, to provide even more evidence that his painting had been stolen. But it was gilding the lily, as he did not realize that the other thefts would be so clean and professional. His efforts made his crime scene unusual compared to the others, and have led to my discovery of the plot."

"Do you have a theory about why he has this mania to own works by Alma-Tadema?"

"No, but it is now clear to me that he favoured his picture over all the others in the library. I did not attach enough importance to it at the time, but I did notice that his Alma-Tadema was positioned between the windows, so that no direct sunlight would fall upon it and perhaps over time fade the colours and yellow the varnish. He could also then see it while working at the desk. He had other artworks by important contemporary artists such as Watts, Leighton and Sargent, but the Alma-Tadema hung in pride of place."

"And have you any idea as yet to the identity of this master criminal he employed?"

"None whatsoever."

"Your sources in the banking industry – what did they tell you?"

"They provided the reason for the thefts. It is simple, Watson. Lord Keyworth is in debt over his head, and cannot afford to buy the paintings he wants, so perforce has had to resort to stealing them."

"If he has no money, Holmes, how then can he afford to pay someone to steal the pictures for him? That would not be cheap, I imagine."

"That I don't know, Watson. Perhaps he borrowed the money, or came to some arrangement with the head of the organisation. We might find out when we go with Gregson to arrest him tomorrow. I wired him to be here this afternoon to enable us to coordinate our strategy, so I expect he'll be along presently."

\*\*\*\*\*\*\*\*\*\*

The next morning found Holmes, Inspector Gregson, a sergeant, six constables and myself on the train to Nottingham. Gregson and Holmes had devised a plan the afternoon before, and thought the additional police presence might be required in case some of Lord Keyworth's staff were party to his thievery, or a search of the house and grounds became necessary.

We arrived just after 10:30, and were met on the platform by an Inspector Craig of the Nottinghamshire Constabulary. Gregson had arranged that he should accompany us and provide the transport with drivers, so after a brief delay for tea and biscuits, we set off for Keyworth Castle. The sergeant and constables divided themselves between two Black Marias, while Holmes, myself, and the two Inspectors travelled in a regulation police carriage. After an hour's drive, we pulled up as arranged a hundred yards short of the entrance to the Keyworth Castle estate.

Gregson then ordered his seven officers to various points around the house, effectively surrounding it. They did not need to use the entrance gates, as the estate was surrounded only by a low wall at this point. After giving them ten minutes to reach their assigned positions, we scrambled over the wall ourselves and approached the main entrance on foot. Gregson marched up to the door and rang the bell. The butler answered, looking a little surprised at our deputation. Gregson strode in, the butler backing away before him.

"We are here on official police business," he said authoritatively. "Where is Lord Keyworth?"

"His Lordship is in his study, sir. I'll show –"

"No thank you, please remain here in the hall. Direct us to the study."

"Down that corridor, sir, second door on the left," said the obviously put out butler.

We trooped down the corridor indicated and Gregson rapped on the study door, then pushed it open and we all entered. Lord Keyworth rose from behind the desk.

"What the! – Mr. Holmes, who are these men?"

"Your Lordship, this is Inspector Gregson of Scotland Yard, and Inspector Craig of the Nottinghamshire Constabulary."

Gregson stepped forward and spoke up.

"Lord Keyworth, I am arresting you for being involved in the theft of several paintings by Lawrence Alma-Tadema from different locations on Tuesday night last."

Lord Keyworth blanched, then sat back down in his chair. His right hand reached for a drawer, but Holmes leapt forward and grabbed his arm. Gregson then produced his handcuffs, and with Holmes's help manacled the peer, who then sat with a morose expression on his face. Holmes opened the drawer and removed a revolver.

"We cannot allow you to evade justice, Your Lordship," said Holmes. "Besides there are some questions I would like to put to you. Firstly, have any of the paintings you arranged to be stolen been delivered to you?"

Lord Keyworth shrugged.

"I suppose you will find them anyway, whether I speak or not. The two from New York are on their way here by steamer. The ones from the English thefts arrived the following day, and the one stolen in France was delivered yesterday."

"And where are they now?"

"In a specially fitted out cellar, with all my other favourite pieces. The key is in my pocket. Or Olverton, the butler, can show you. He also has a key."

"Are Olverton, or any of your servants, involved in the thefts?"

"No, they think I buy them through auctions or from galleries."

"Last question, your Lordship. Whom did you employ to steal them for you?"

"I can't tell you that, I don't know his name."

"How then did you find out about him?"

"One night I was at my club in London talking with some fellow members. I mentioned in passing that I loved the work of Alma-Tadema, but that his fame and popularity were such that his paintings were now out of my reach. I said in jest that the only way I could own one was by stealing them. Afterwards, one of the members who had heard me told me that if I seriously wanted to have something stolen, he could put me in touch with someone professional and discreet who could make it possible. Turns out his daughter had fallen in love with a most unsuitable person with neither title nor money, and he had eventually paid to have this person 'removed,' as he put it. I was shocked at first, but the idea grew on me. He gave me an address to which to write, and I did. The letters are in the desk in the cellar."

"What was the address given to you?"

"It was the Carlton Hotel, to be kept until called for."

Holmes looked at Gregson.

"I think we should have a look in this cellar, Inspector," he said.

"Indeed. Craig, would you mind the prisoner while we do so?"

"Please – please," blurted Lord Keyworth. "May I come with you? It will be the last time I will get to see my paintings. Please?"

"Very well. But you behave, mind," said Gregson. "Craig, would you go tell my sergeant to collect his men and wait in the hall? Thank you."

Gregson held His Lordship by the arms as he led us to the cellar. Gregson found the key in His Lordship's pocket and opened the door. There was an oil lamp hanging just inside, and Holmes lit it and went down the stairs.

"Just wait a minute, Inspector, I will light the other lamps in here," he said.

As lamp after lamp illuminated the room, we saw a large oak-panelled space, with a thick carpet. Armchairs were scattered about, there was a side table with decanters and glasses, and a desk in the corner. The walls were hung with artworks of every description; oils, watercolours, pastels, etchings, and pencil sketches. Gregson led his prisoner into the room and sat him in one of the armchairs. Holmes was already going through the desk drawers and reading the various papers within them. He turned and handed Gregson a letter.

"Here it is, Inspector. This is the first letter from our unknown opponent."

Looking over Gregson's shoulder, I read:

*Dear sir,*

*I refer to your letter of the 6th inst. The undertaking you describe requires much planning and manpower, and this is reflected in the cost. The three operations located in England will be £500 each, the one in France £600, and the one in the USA will be £750, a total of £2,850. The terms are 50% in advance, and the remainder payable upon delivery. Cash only, gold or notes.*

*Please reply if this is acceptable, and I will then move forward with this project.*

*M*

"The other letters contain details of the plan and arrangement for payments, etc," Holmes continued. "It was your idea to fake the robbery of your own painting, was it not, to divert suspicion?"

"Yes. Your presence here indicates it didn't work, I take it?"

"No," replied Holmes. "It was unnecessary, and its nature drew attention to yourself. How did you manage to pay for these thefts, Lord Keyworth? My researches indicate you are in a great deal of debt."

"Yes, that's true. But don't you see, even if the paintings I wanted were for sale, I would have to pay thousands of guineas each for them. To obtain six for only £2,850 was too good an opportunity to miss. I therefore went to my younger brother, who has been far more prudent with his investments and his spending than I have."

"And he lent you the money?" asked Gregson.

"No, I – I didn't ask him. I stole the money from his safe, as I knew where he kept the combination written," said Lord Keyworth, hanging his head. "He knows it was me, but has not called the police so as not to bring shame upon our family name."

"I see," said Gregson in a censorious tone. "You robbed your own brother, then robbed other people of their valuable artworks, just so you could have them all to yourself. An innocent man was killed by the thieves you employed for the Yorkshire job, so that is on your head as well. And you have no idea who this 'M' is you say?"

"None. If I knew I would tell you."

"Very well. Which of these pictures are the Alma-Tademas?"

Lord Keyworth stood up, walked over to a section of the wall and indicated four paintings with his manacled hands.

"These, Inspector," he said gazing at them while a tear crept down his cheek.

**********

An hour later, the constables had boxed up the stolen paintings and placed them in one of the Black Marias, Lord Keyworth had been placed in the second with three constables and Holmes had collected all the letters he thought might be useful in tracking down the mysterious "M."

We were in the hall, ready to leave. Holmes was talking to Olverton, and I asked Inspector Gregson about the two paintings still on their way from New York.

"We shall have police waiting when that ship docks, and we shall arrest whoever collects them," he remarked. Which I may say here he did, but the two men he arrested protested their innocence; they had just been told to collect the packages, and had no idea they contained stolen art. Gregson was compelled to release them.

Holmes walked over and joined us.

"Ready to leave then?" asked Gregson.

"Indeed. But Olverton has just given me a perhaps useful

snippet of information."

"Which is?" I asked.

"He states that yesterday the painting was delivered from France by two men. They saw His Lordship who must have paid them as per the agreement. He, Olverton, was then showing them out, when he overheard one of them ask the other if they had time for a drink in Keyworth before heading back. The other man replied in the negative, saying that there was another job waiting for them, and they had to see the Professor for instructions."

"The Professor?" Is that the head of the criminal organisation? Is it only a nickname, or a real professor do you think?"

Holmes paused, looking out the open front door, over the greensward and beyond to the forest, a faraway look in his grey eyes.

"I don't know, Watson, but I intend to find out."